Mr. Sportsball

by

K.P. HAIGH

Cover by Najla Qamber Designs
Cover photo by Lindee Robinson Photography
Cover models are Andrew Kruczyriski and Alyse Madej
Developmental editing by Judy, Write Techniques
Copy editing by Caitlin, Editing by C. Marie
Proofreading by Wendy, The Passionate Proofreader

ISBN: 978-0-9977895-1-5

Dedication

To every girl who has ever watched a football game and thought, "Damn, I wish I was reading."

Prologue

Nine Years Ago

The faster you want time to move, the slower it goes.

Sitting in seventh period English Lit was the epitome of time crawling. Why did we have to study all the depressing books? *Of Mice and Men. Death of a Salesman.* Ugh, *The Grapes of Wrath.* Seriously, where were my happy endings? Where was my unruly adventure that would take me to faraway exciting places? Clearly it wasn't sitting at the end of a book that was listed as required reading for this class.

At least I had my best friend. Our last names put us next to each other in class: Montgomery Bell and Andie Bertelli. Andie and I had been sitting together in every single class we'd ever had since she'd moved to town from New York in sixth grade.

At first glance, our similarities stopped at our long brown hair and green eyes. I was already almost a foot taller than her; my growth spurt had shot me close to six feet, and Andie was left waiting for hers to kick in.

But at the core, we were like sisters. She was the strong to my silent and the nerdy to my bookworm.

We'd both already finished the assigned reading for class and had moved on to a rousing game of Kill, Marry, Screw. Andie had just passed back a note with her latest choices: Jesse McCartney, Jason Segel, and Ryan Reynolds.

I nearly snorted while reading her list. She was ready to destroy all the radios on the face of the earth; that Jesse McCartney song was driving her crazy. She had me at Jason Segel—that dude was funny, and that was always Andie's style. She'd take the hilarious over the blatantly hot any day of the week. As if she was reading my mind, she turned around and waggled her eyebrows dramatically. I loved my best friend and her ridiculous sense of humor—something that was hard to come by in high school. Hormones and social anxiety trumped being funny.

I tapped my pencil against my lower lip. I knew who mine were, but I was nervous to put it down on paper. I hadn't even told Andie about him yet; I was too embarrassed to say it out loud.

Cody Maxwell.

I had been developing a slow burn crush for the past few months, ever since he had said *hi* with a slow, easy smile when I'd accidentally bumped into him in the hallway during a rushed passing period.

I should have known better than to form a crush on a guy with two first names—let alone the star quarterback of our mediocre but much admired varsity football team.

But, my teenage brain had found a target and latched on and wouldn't let go until you pried it from its cold, dead hands.

I idolized a boy I had only mumbled a tangled apology to. He didn't even know my name. He was two grades above me, and I was sure he had smiled because I was a fumbling idiot, not actual dating material.

No one knew about my infatuation. That was the great part

about being invisible in high school: no one paid attention to who you were staring at, even if it was them.

I blushed just thinking about drawing the first letter of his name. I tapped my pencil against my lip again, gathering up my courage.

Andie jabbed the heel of her black boot into my outstretched toes, and I cringed at the sharp sting where her sole connected with my big toe.

Fine. I scribbled down my answers and refolded the creased paper, passing it up around the side of the desk to the top of Andie's backpack. She quickly snatched it up and spread out the lined paper underneath her open book decoy.

She giggled under her breath. My stomach did a somersault. I knew this meant I would be explaining my secret crush in piercing detail on the phone with her later that night, but the ache of telling the secret was washed away by the overwhelming relief of letting my best friend help bear its weight.

Ms. Phillips turned her hawk eyes on us. "Girls, this is reading time. It is not do-whatever-you-please time."

"Yes, Ms. Phillips." I would have done anything to get the spotlight off of me right then.

Andie crinkled our note up and reached down for her backpack.

I shoved my foot out in front of me to kick her, but my toe connected with the hard metal of the chair post instead. I bit back a scream.

Ms. Phillips was not impressed with what was going on in our little corner. She stood up from her desk and started to walk over to us. "And what is it that's so funny over here?"

Ohmygod, please hide that note. Please hide that note. Andie's left hand connected with the zipper of her bag, but without leaning over to use her other hand to give it resistance, she couldn't slide the zipper back to open the top.

I stopped breathing, my eyes stuck on our teacher, who was rapidly approaching. *Come on, passing period bell, please ring.*

Ms. Phillips's eyes narrowed on the piece of paper Andie was desperately trying to stuff into the tiny opening of her bag. She walked over, reached down, and plucked it right out of Andie's fingers.

I tried to sink as low as I could in my chair, but my 5'11" body didn't exactly give me many options outside of sinkholes randomly appearing and devouring me and my desk whole.

Ms. Phillips's red talons peeled the note open. She studied it for a moment, and I silently prayed to every god I'd ever heard of that she would read it and then drop it in the trash. *Athena, do me a solid on this one, pretty please?*

"Miss Bell, would you do me the honor of explaining why you have listed Sabrina Lang, Cody Maxwell, and Cody Maxwell under the labels kill, marry, and screw?"

I would have dug my own sinkhole with a spork to escape the situation with any trace of social dignity intact, but apparently Ms. Phillips was unaware of how much it sucked to be a teenager.

I swore I could see a smile tucked behind the thick lines that bracketed her pursed lips. I wanted to tell her where she could shove her authority, but I was too scared of expulsion, the threat every teacher hung over our heads like a rusty old guillotine.

Andie spoke up for me. "It's just a game."

I appreciated her words, since mine were stuck somewhere between my stomach and the ball in my throat.

"Well, these are not the words you should be studying during class, and I certainly do not like the implication of killing anyone, game or not. Miss Sabrina Lang is a very fine young lady."

Fuck Sabrina Lang. Fuck her and her perfectly blow-dried, honey blonde hair. I couldn't have managed a round brush and a hair dryer if I'd had four hands and eyes on the back of my head, but Sabrina walked in every day like she was starring in a goddamn hair commercial. Everyone ate it up—including Cody.

They were the quarterback and star cheerleader, the top of the high school social food chain. So, no matter how many times the rumor mill spun with the news that their relationship was on the rocks, they always ended up back together, the king and queen of our high school.

I could hear the whispers in the class as everyone pieced my list together: kill Sabrina Lang, marry and screw Cody Maxwell.

Awesome. I figured I should just head home on the bus, climb into bed, and die under the covers.

The bell rang, and everyone scrambled up and out, anxious to get to the last period of the day. I stood up, my head bowed down, as if not seeing my classmates would mean they hadn't just heard the most embarrassing unintentional confession of my life.

Ms. Phillips retreated back to her desk, dropping the note in the trash on her way there. I vowed to look up voodoo doll torture when I got home.

Andie fell in step with me as we walked out the classroom door into the crowded hallway. "Ms. Phillips is an evil hag."

I pinched my eyes closed to hold back the overwhelming despair that threatened to break free. I could hate my English teacher all I wanted; it wouldn't stop my secret from spreading person to person like a line of ants marching back to the hill with a trail of breadcrumbs.

Andie's next class was at the opposite end of the school. She reached out and squeezed my hand.

"It's gonna be okay. No one is going to remember this tomorrow. Hell, if you need me to go flash everybody before school ends today, just say the words."

I smiled at the thought. I knew she would if I asked her to; that's what best friends do for each other.

"It's okay. This is going to blow over." I didn't believe it for a second, but I thought maybe if I said the words out loud, it would make them true.

I tried to pretend I was invisible all the way through my next class, even though it felt as if there was a magnifying glass held right above my head, directing the brutal force of a spotlight straight on me.

When the final bell rang at the end of the period, I raced out to my locker, anxious to get on the bus. I grabbed my coat and shut my locker. When I turned around, my body slammed into a tiny rock of muscle behind me.

I looked down to see one of the younger members of the cheerleading team looking up at me. I couldn't remember her name, but I knew she was in my grade. We'd had second period geometry together the year before.

"Um, hi," she chirped. "I heard about the whole Cody Maxwell thing, and I wanted to come talk to you."

I closed my eyes in defeat. Why did time have to move so slow but information traveled at the speed of light? I started walking toward the line of buses outside to escape, but the little cheerleader followed me.

"I just wanted to let you know that Sabrina and Cody broke up. It was, like, kind of under the radar. But, he heard about whole note thing, and he's interested."

What. The. Hell. My universe felt like a piñata of confetti had just burst open, covering the whole thing in tiny flecks of bright color.

Little cheerleader didn't seem the least bit phased by my open-mouthed, stunned expression. "So yeah, you should come to the game this Friday. I think he'd really like it."

I nodded.

"Um, thanks."

Part of me wanted to hug this tiny messenger, but I was too discombobulated to do anything else besides put one foot in front of the other.

I might not have known how to blow dry my long, wavy auburn hair, but I was pretty sure that was my homework assignment for the next three days—that, and learning how to apply something more than mascara and lip gloss.

When I got home, I thanked my lucky stars Mom was stuck in a work meeting until the early evening. I had the house to myself, but I raced up to my bedroom and locked the door anyway. I didn't want to tempt fate into sending any more embarrassment my way.

It only took two rings for Andie to pick up.

"Okay. Start at the beginning and tell me everything."

Like any good teenager would, I went through every painstaking detail: Cody's first smile at me, every single nanosecond of the encounter thereafter, my thoughts on how he seemed really nice because I had seen him help unjam a freshman's locker door one time, and so on.

Even hashing out all of those details, I only managed to fill up fifteen minutes worth of conversation. It was a teenage-sized crush; the sugar content was high, but the nutritional content was shamefully low.

But I wasn't even at the good part yet.

"Remember that cheerleader who was in our geometry class last year? The really short one with blonde hair."

"Yeah, Gwen, right?"

"I think so?" The name still didn't ring any bells, but our conversation was on a constant loop in my brain. "Anyway, she found me at the end of the day and told me Sabrina and Cody are on a break."

"They take more breaks than a Kit-Kat bar." I could hear the smirk in Andie's voice.

My palms started to sweat, and I rubbed them back and forth against my jeans while I held the phone wedged between my ear and my shoulder. "Gwen said he heard about our note and wants me to come to Friday's game."

"Are you serious?"

"Yeah. Dead serious."

"What are you going to do?"

I paused and took a deep breath. "I have no freaking clue."

The line went silent for a moment, and I couldn't decide if I wanted Andie to tell me to go or to forget the whole thing ever happened. The idea of showing up to the game was terrifying, but I also knew I wanted my Rachel Lee Cook moment where I turned from underwhelming nerd in an art smock into oh-my-gosh-she's-a-knockout-in-that-red-dress. I didn't know where to get a red dress that would actually go more than two inches below my butt—thank you, absurdly long waist—but that didn't mean I wasn't holding out for my fairy godmother to show up, Freddie Prince Jr. or otherwise.

"I think you should go," Andie finally replied.

"Really?" I had my reservations. It seemed too easy—a major embarrassment turned into a social triumph.

"Yeah. I mean, Gwen's really nice, and Sabrina and Cody are *always* taking breaks."

"She wasn't just messing with me?"

"There's only one way to find out."

I figured she was right, and I mean, I would have always wondered.

"You'll go with me right?"

"I'll be the Clyde to your Bonnie, and we'll go steal some hearts." I heard her wide grin through the phone.

At least I had my best friend, even though I couldn't shake the idea that we were better off staying in with *Friday Night Lights* than we were trying to chase them in real life.

Friday night arrived. I begged my parents to drive me to the school stadium, and even though they gave me serious side eye, they didn't question me—their book-loving child who only knew the rules to a fictional sport that used brooms and wands.

I sat through the entire game, too nervous to focus on anything except the brightly lit countdown clock on the board. I couldn't figure out why it kept stopping, and whether it was just time being a bitch or if the rules of the game meant sometimes the timer ran and sometimes it didn't.

I nearly cut off all circulation to Andie's hand from squeezing it like it was my life raft in the middle of a freaking hurricane, but she didn't complain for a second.

Five minutes before the end of the game, her cell phone rang.

She pushed it to her ear and cupped her hand around her mouth and the bottom of the phone. "Yeah…um, can't I stay for another half hour? … Well, can I get a ride home with… Seriously? … That's so lame. Fine…okay, yeah, fine. Bye."

I already knew what she was going to say. Andie had four siblings and parents that worked 24/7. They weren't always around, but when they were, they always seemed to try to make up for it with extra parenting. I guessed on this night that meant Andie going home early.

"You gotta go?" I tried to keep the disappointment from coloring my voice; there wasn't any use making Andie feel bad about a situation she couldn't change.

"Yeah. My brother has the car and he's on his way home from some band thing. He's going to be here any minute." Her shoulders slumped forward.

I pulled her in for a hug.

"It's okay. I'm just going to go get my heart crushed." I was trying to defuse her frustration, but the words hit a little too close to home. My nerves started to shake like a warning of impending seismic activity.

"You're going to be great. Call me when you get home and tell me everything, okay?"

I gave her a weak smile. *Why did I decide to do this again?*

We snuck out of our spot on the bleachers, and Andie walked with me to the back exit of the field house.

"Maybe I should just go home with you," I whispered.

Andie stopped and turned to face me. She grabbed my shoulders and squeezed.

"Love is worth the risk."

Her words were so sincere, even though it sounded like something they would say in a made-for-TV movie.

I closed my eyes. *I can do this. Gwen is really nice, and Cody totally likes me.*

Andie's phone started to ring again, and she gave me one last hug before she raced toward the parking lot. I turned back to the field house. I swore I stood there for an hour. It was probably more like twenty minutes, but each and every second was like a shot of adrenaline to my soul. I was jittery and excited and one hundred percent terrified.

But, I was being brave, and the feeling was intoxicating.

I heard the trail of voices headed toward me before I saw the bodies that belonged to them. I immediately regretted my plan. I should have gone with creepy stalker hanging out by Cody's red car versus weird loner hanging out by herself outside the locker room, but as the first player rounded the corner, I knew it was too late.

A crowd of boys stopped in front of me, and there was Cody, right in the center.

"Uh, hi?" He looked straight at me, and I knew instantly that I had made a terrible mistake.

He had absolutely no fucking clue who I was.

My brain scrambled to figure out an exit strategy. *Do I know another player on the team? Could I say I was lost?*

I didn't register the extra set of voices until they were right behind me.

"Montgomery Bell."

I hated hearing my full name almost as much as I hated the voice that said it. I turned around and saw Sabrina Lang, flanked by her crew of cheerleaders, including Little Miss Hallway Helpful, Gwen.

"Um, hi." I blinked frantically, as if pulling the picture into focus would have helped my understanding of the situation. This wasn't a 3D optical illusion. I wasn't going to find a hidden picture of myself in Cody's arms.

I should have known when I heard Sabrina's cackle. I should have known when I saw Gwen's smile flinch when she saw that I still hadn't quite turned the puzzle piece to the right alignment.

Sabrina twirled a strand of her thick blonde hair between her fingers. "You're a piece of work, Montgomery. I can't believe you even had the balls to show up."

The words almost twisted themselves into a compliment around me, but there were too many barbs to tie it into a perfect knot.

Cody walked over to her and wrapped his arm around her shoulders. Those barbed compliments finished twisting around me and someone yanked at both ends, digging their meaning into my flesh. I was a piece of work to think for a second that someone like him could like someone like me.

Sabrina pulled Cody in for an exaggerated kiss, all the while keeping one eye open to make sure I was taking in all of her theatrics.

How could I not? I couldn't have moved a muscle even if my flight mode had finally kicked in.

Cody pulled away, looking drugged with lust. I wondered if she liked him as much as she liked the power of being with him. Was she ever drunk on *him*, or was it just the idea of him?

He looked at me and, for a second, he seemed to remember I existed. "Were you waiting for somebody?"

God, he was even stupider than me.

Sabrina laughed and clutched her arms around him in a possessive cuddle.

"She came to see you. She has a stalker crush on you and thought we had broken up."

He looked straight at me, taking in that idea, and then he nodded his head as if teenage girls followed him around, declaring their love for him on a regular basis. *Oh, another one? Sure, why not?*

I wanted to vomit—preferably all over Sabrina's perfect white tennis shoes.

She smiled back at me like she knew what I wanted to do, and that I wouldn't dare try it.

"Let's get out of here. We've taught this loser her lesson. Kingsley!" she shouted back at one of the players behind me. "Aren't your parents gone tonight? We need to get wasted—like ASAP."

Plans were decided and as quickly as I had been surrounded by the swarm, they left with their queen bee. Make that a capital B.

I had learned my lesson all right. Football players and their cheerleader girlfriends sucked, and I was going to take out a restraining order on their kind until the end of forever. *Sorry, you play sports? Please stay at least a hundred yards away from me at all times. Kthanksbye.*

Football and I were done, and there was no way I was going to make the mistake of trying to pretend I liked it ever again.

Chapter 1

Present Day

Click. Click. Click. There's a hum of background noises: laughter-peppered conversation, the gentle dings of crystal glasses, and the sweet strums of the classical guitar.

The only thing I actively hear is my breath. Out. In. Hold. Click. Out. One of my favorite photography instructors told me he held his breath every single time he pressed the shutter.

It's my own form of yoga, meditation behind the lens.

I move through the clusters of conversations, trying to catch wit and delight like they're two friends out at a bar for a drink. When I get it right, it's almost like you capture the words themselves in vivid color.

Set against the backdrop of the tall, arched ceiling and long-paned windows of the old university ballroom, this donor event makes me wish I had thousands of dollars to drop to show up at a party like this.

My black pants and white button down are more in line with the catering crew than the long fancy dresses and pristine tuxes of the guests, but I'm here for my job as a photographer for the Ann Arbor Daily. This is work, not play. I press my camera back up to my face and start to breathe.

"How long have you been back?" one of the men in front of me asks the woman to his right.

"Only a week. I would fly back in a heartbeat. It was so moving to see all our hard work actually making a difference in the field." I recognize the woman: it's Irene Collins, renowned philanthropist and one of the largest donors to our alma mater, Michigan University.

I've never actually seen her at one of these events before. She's nearly always abroad, but as a fellow alumni, I've spent years seeing her portrait. She's a legend, one of the first female computer science majors here, and then founder of one of the most influential tech companies in the world. She stepped down as CEO and started a nonprofit that has arms stretched out to help positively impact dozens of global issues.

I have to get her picture for the paper, but the stupid light is filtering in awkwardly, turning her face into a Phantom of the Opera mask of light and shadows. I still have a handful of shots to get left on my list, and there are only thirty scheduled minutes left of this fundraiser.

Ugh, I hate this part. "Excuse me, Ms. Collins, would you mind stepping to the left? I'd love to get a photo of you two in better light."

"Of course." She smiles gracefully and takes a step over, continuing as if the conversation was never interrupted.

Click. Click. Perfect. I'm always nervous to remind guests at these sorts of functions that I exist. They always want to turn and wrap their arms around each other as if I'm taking a family portrait at a wedding. I hate using posed photos, though my boss couldn't care less—she just needs something to print in the society section of the newspaper and its online counterpart.

I snap a few more pictures of Ms. Collins, and I turn to search out the last few shots on my list. Just as I'm about to walk away, I hear her voice. "Pardon me?"

I turn back to see Ms. Collins looking straight at me.

I look around. Is she talking to me? There's no one in our vicinity; the man who had been talking to her must have excused himself.

"Yes?" I finally answer, still unsure if I'm the intended recipient.

She gives me a kind smile, reminding me of Helen Mirren. I bet she gave the boys a run for their money when she was a student here. She's very proper, but there's something hiding in her eyes that makes me think she's a reformed firecracker.

"Are you a student here?"

I let go of my camera, letting it hang from the brown leather strap around my neck. "I was. I graduated two years ago. I do freelance work now, mostly for the Ann Arbor Daily."

"Do you enjoy your job?" she asks with a curiosity that should be reserved for talking to doctors who research cures for life-threatening illnesses, or engineers who are trying to figure out how to send humans to the next solar system.

"Umm, it's been an amazing learning experience." Ugh, I think that answer came with a side of vomit. Try again. "I admire what you do—impacting the global community."

"It's very fulfilling work. We're certainly in need of good photographers. There's nothing quite like perfectly captured images to highlight the causes we champion."

My mouth goes completely dry. Working for her nonprofit is pretty much the poster I have in my head for 'dream job.'

Ms. Collins laughs softly, and I realize my mouth is wide open. I can't seem to find any words that aren't *Ohmygod, are you serious?* So, I clamp it shut.

She reaches into her purse and pulls out a card. "Send me an email next week with your portfolio. I'll forward it on to my HR director."

I nod my head—that's about all I'm capable of right now—and take the card.

"Good. I selfishly try to recruit Michigan grads any chance I get," she says with a twinkle in her eye.

I don't know how or why I became a worthwhile recruit of one of the wealthiest female philanthropists in the world—I'm just a twenty-three-year-old who takes pictures for a local paper, as easy to forget as what you ate for breakfast yesterday—but I'm not going to ask questions. I'm going to go home and spend the next forty-eight hours crafting the perfect email.

"I need to catch Steven before he sneaks out. It was nice to meet you…"

"Montgomery," I offer back when she pauses.

"Montgomery, it was a pleasure. I look forward to seeing your portfolio." She turns and waves at the university president.

My head spins as if I stood up too fast. I can't believe that just happened. I take a deep breath and let the awe sink into my bones before reaching back for my camera and scanning the room, trying to catch the last few shots I need.

I finally make it back to my apartment, and the sun has softened into a rosy gold hue near the horizon. I have about seven hundred images to go through tonight, but I think I need to grab a beer, go sit out on my roof, and decompress first.

I have an excitement hangover, and there's no way I'm going to be able to focus for long enough to pick out the best images or do any of the necessary lighting touch-ups.

No. I need to pour some liquid straight onto this electrical wire of mine and let it crackle and smoke its way down to silence.

I set my bag down on my bed and take three steps over to my kitchen. My apartment isn't very big, barely 400 square feet, but it's cozy and relaxing, two things I desperately need after being around people for work. I'm a classic introvert; I would go crazy if I had to come home to more required conversation and haggling for music playlist airtime.

No, thank you. I'll take my petite studio decked out in bright prints from World Market, faded leather seats from Goodwill, and faux sheepskin rugs. It's a luxury on a freelancer's budget, but I saved every penny I earned working summers growing up. Then, I doubled it when I put up a flyer at the drama school a few years ago to take half-price headshots. It's enough of a buffer to be adventurous, which makes it even more embarrassing that my current definition of adventure is a studio twenty minutes from my childhood home.

I open up my fridge and grab a can of cheap beer. My phone chimes from my bag, and I quickly grab it on my way over to the large window that opens to a relatively modest slope of the house roof. My studio takes up half of the top floor of a house that's been converted into apartments. My half faces west, which is perfect for long spring nights like tonight.

I sit down on the shingles, pull out my phone to check my messages, and see Andie's text.

Are we still on for tomorrow?

I thumb a quick yes, and her response is almost immediate.

Good. I'm craving beer and wings. Can we go to Halftime? Plz?

Ugh. I hate that place. There are a million televisions going at the same time, and the servers all have to wear these cheesy referee costumes—surprise, surprise, they're pretty much all female. It's like a costume you'd wear to a bad college Halloween party. I want to take a hoodie every time I go—not for me, for them.

But Halftime's wings are like crack, and Andie is rarely ever free these days. She's in the last couple weeks of her second year of medical school. I don't understand why they bother to distinguish years—she barely gets a sneeze of a break and then she has to start her third year this summer. I'm pretty sure admission into the program required signing over a kidney, enough money to bankroll a small country, and all of her free time. I'm not going to turn her down.

I quickly reply and then turn my phone on silent so I can get back to my beer and sunset relaxation.

It lasts for about five seconds before I realize I'm going to need to get a passport.

I try taking a few more sips of beer. *Be in the moment. Enjoy the sunset.*

My brain races through a list of questions. *How much does a passport cost? How long does it take to get one?* I crawl back inside and open up my laptop.

I know I'm being silly. I don't even have the job yet. Geez, I don't even know if there is a job. Ms. Collins implied there was an opening, but I doubt the head of a large nonprofit keeps detailed tabs on current openings. She simply said she would pass my portfolio along. I could be excited over nothing.

If I got the job though, I would finally get to travel. I would finally step foot outside the States.

I guess technically I already have. I went to Canada when it was still cool to use a license to cross the border between the two countries, but that's like saying a kiss on the cheek counts as the real deal. It's close, but you're not quite there yet.

Maybe I'll finally change that. I think about the business card sitting at the bottom of my bag. Maybe the universe is giving me a kick in the butt down the right path.

It's too good an opportunity to pass up. I've been comfortable in my own little bubble for long enough.

When Irene Collins hands you a business card, you take it, and you better use the damn thing, whether it scares you or not.

I tap the spacebar on my laptop so I can get to work. I have a job to do and a job to chase. I feel like I just pounded a double shot of excitement espresso, and I'm sure as hell going to put it to good use.

Chapter 2

I almost groan out loud when the hostess at Halftime leads me over to one of the bar tables in the center of the room.

She smiles blankly. "Your server will be over in a second."

Before I can ask to switch to a booth in the corner, she walks away. Okay fine, I wouldn't have actually asked anyway; I suck at that kind of stuff.

I feel as if I'm standing front and center at a rock concert where ten different bands are playing all at once. Realistically, I know there are only a couple TVs that have their sound on, but the volume combined with twenty LED TVs flashing different sports makes it seem worse than it is.

I kick myself for forgetting earplugs. At least I have my Kindle, which is a core member of my squad. I never go anywhere without my digital bestie.

Just as I sit down, Andie texts that her study session is running over. Of course it is, and I immediately regret my decision to grab a table early instead of popping down the block to wait at the coffee shop until she's ready.

At least they have beer here. I order a summer lager, the one with an orange slice hooked onto the rim of the glass, and try to forget where I am.

I'm a beer and a half into my book when I see someone walk up to the seat across from me. *Ah, finally.* I look up with a grin stretching wide across my face, expecting to see Andie.

Instead, I'm looking at the broad chest of a giant, and I don't say that lightly. I am only an inch short of six feet, and I'm well aware of being on the tail end of the average height bell curve. It's not often that I feel small.

I look up to see the face of a man who looks perfectly content to be hanging out in a sports bar. He's wearing a baseball cap that says *Aloha.* If I had seen him from the back first, I would have guessed his hat would be for some sports team. Granted, I'm not exactly up to date on my sports references; maybe the Alohas are a new team.

"Sorry to interrupt, but I had to stop by and say hello before I left." His voice is deep and smooth, like slowly rocking back and forth on a porch swing at dusk.

I scan his face again. Even hiding under a hat, I can tell it's not a face you forget. It's all lines and angles, like a statue you would spend hours studying in an art history class. I would remember a face like that. Hell, I'd photograph it from every angle if I could.

"Um, have we met before?"

He tilts his head to the side as if I said something funny. His blue eyes are piercing, but the soft lines that frame them when he smiles make them kind. "I don't think so. I'm Baron, and you are...?"

This is the part where I usually give a fake name, something popular like Michelle or Monica, but his eyes...I can't stop staring at them long enough to form coherent thoughts. Well there's that, and the fact that I'm drinking on an empty stomach.

"Montgomery, but everyone calls me Monty."

Baron motions to the barstool across from me. "Would you mind?"

I should say I have a friend who could be here any minute, but for all I know, she could be another hour.

I find myself saying "Sure." This is twice in twenty-four hours I've been approached by someone who intrigues me; I'm curious what fate is dishing out this time.

"What are you reading?" It's a casual question, and his tone sounds as if we're old friends catching up rather than complete strangers.

"It's a romantic suspense novel." I'm usually grumpy when someone stops me in the middle of reading to ask me about the book. I mean, *dude, I'm reading.* Instead, my body is leaning toward him, as if I can't get close enough to this conversation.

"Hmm, I had you pegged for a nonfiction type." He taps his fingers along the soft dip beneath his lower lip, and I am acutely aware of our knees touching under the table.

"How's that?" I ask.

"Well, you're sitting in the middle of a sports bar, reading. Intently," he adds. "I just imagined it was something serious."

I don't mention that I just finished a book of essays by women who grew up in the Middle East. I focus on the heart of the matter. "Eh, I just don't really like sports that much."

Baron laughs. It's a deep, warm sound, and my heart does a little somersault in place. "Yeah, I figured."

And I'm guessing he's someone who does like sports. Judging by the way his shoulders taper down to his waist, I get the sense that he's on first-name terms with his local gym.

I lift my shoulders and scrunch my nose as if to say *What are ya gonna do?* I have no idea why I'm being so honest with a stranger in a sports bar. If I repeated what I just said loud enough, they might drag me to the back and shoot me. We are in one of the most fiercely loyal college towns in the Midwest—sports are life.

"I had to know…what is a girl who doesn't like sports doing in the middle of a sports bar?"

It finally registers. Ah, he came over to inspect the freak of nature. A tiny part of me is disappointed; he wasn't coming over to hit on me. "That's why you came over?"

He nods.

My openness shuts like a thickly bound book. "Well, I'm waiting for a friend who loves the wings here." I wonder if he'll walk away now that the case is closed. Something bristles in me. Silly me for thinking he came over for anything other than solving the mystery of the preoccupied nerd.

Baron leans his bare forearms on the table, and I try not to stare. I can be uninterested in more than just this bar.

"So, are you not into any sports, or just the ones that get a lot of airtime? Do you root for the underdog, like curling or archery or something?"

Why is he still here? I don't really want to be the guppy in the fishbowl anymore. My tone takes on a sour bite. "Nope. I'm not really a fan of anything with points and a scoreboard."

"Hmm." He smirks, and one of his eyes closes more than the other, as if he's slowly winking at me.

It only makes me prickle more.

"What don't you like about them?" Baron's poking a sleeping dragon.

I've never been a fan of the world that pretty much everyone else goes stark-raving mad over. Something in me snaps. *You want to understand the freak of nature? Fine.* "What's your favorite sport?" I ask.

"I have to pick one?"

God, I bet this guy played all the sports in high school, was one of those who had a different set of teams every season. I bet his mom spent half her life in a minivan. Poor woman.

"Yes, just one."

"Okay. Football."

I'm secretly pleased with his choice. I can rail on soccer players

23

for their no-hands-but-heads-are-cool rule for a little while, but football? Football has a special place in the dark crevice of my disdain.

"Football is a bunch of stupid, oversized beasts who just want to get their aggression out while being strapped down with enough protection to make it seem like running at each other at full force is a good idea."

Baron chuckles softly, like he's heard that one before. I'm surprised he doesn't immediately try to refute my hatred with a long list of the wonderful things about the sport. His silence just eggs me on.

"The whole system is rigged to make a bunch of money for universities by exploiting the physical talents of kids while pushing them so hard they can't actually focus on getting a decent education."

That really gets me. I watched my own university make buckets of cash from its players, and I met a couple of them along the way. They could barely keep up with their coursework. It makes my blood boil.

"There's no guarantee they'll be able to play after college, and if they do, they'll get so many concussions, their brain will be useless after they're retired."

Baron's smile fades and his eyebrows are heavy in thought. He lets me continue, and now that I've started, my words are a runaway train.

"And the fans? Ohmygod, if your team doesn't win—which, *spoiler alert*, you only have a fifty percent shot that they will—your whole day is ruined after you already wasted four hours watching big brutes chase after each other and a stupid ball that isn't even round. Come on, do something productive. Go outside for a hike instead of sitting inside and eating a plate of nachos."

I stop, satisfied that I've played the freak show part, and I take a drink from my almost empty beer.

Baron watches me closely, but he stays at the table.

"Don't you want to leave now?" I ask. "I'm sure I've offended you."

Baron's face lights up with a smile that could power a small city as he starts to laugh. "No—if anything, I really want to stay. Not many women are that honest. You're fascinating and sexy as hell when you get feisty."

Oh.

I don't see Andie walk up until she reaches the side of the table between Baron and me. She's staring at Baron like he's Tarzan plucked directly out of the jungle, a mixture of disbelief and holy-shit-he's-hot playing on her face.

Baron finally breaks his eye contact with me, and I realize I haven't taken a full, deep breath since he sat down. My heart is working like I just ran a seven-minute mile.

"This must be your friend." He gives Andie an appreciative smile. "Thanks for letting me borrow your seat."

Andie just stands there, her eyes wide. I don't remember the last time I've seen her shell-shocked.

Baron's attractive, but we live in a college town. It's not like we're at a loss for attractive young guys around here. A new batch gets delivered every fall.

Baron stands up and takes a step toward me. He reaches into his back pocket and presses a napkin in front of me on the table. "I really hope you'll use this. I'd love to see you again."

I look down and see ten numbers scrawled across the white, Halftime-branded napkin. When I look back up, Baron is two steps away from the front door. I almost chase after him to clarify. *Is this your phone number? Did you just ask me out?*

Andie sits down across from me and starts hyperventilating. "What. Just. Happened?"

"What?" That's twice now in a matter of seconds that I feel like I'm missing something.

"Don't you know who that was?"

"Some guy at a bar? He said his name was Baron."

"Monty. That was Bear Richards." Andie's eyes are serious, but I swear she said the word "bear"—she can't be serious.

"What are you talking about? Who's *Bear* Richards? He said his name was Baron."

Andie sighs like she has to re-explain the quadratic equation to me.

"Baron 'Bear' Richards is one of the star players on Detroit's football team. He's a beast on the field and sex-on-a-friggin-goalpost off it, and he just gave you his number."

It takes me a few seconds to process this new information, probably because I'm scrambling to replay the conversation I just had with Baron while my brain is in a beer haze.

My face runs the whole gamut of the Valentine's Day color spectrum. I just told a professional football player he was a big doofus who was likely to end his career with a horrific injury and no education to actually make anything of himself afterward.

Lovely.

The way I see it, I have two options: massive embarrassment or blind denial.

"Um, can we just forget about this for now?" Yup, I'm taking the blissfully ignorant route.

I can tell Andie wants to get the very detailed play-by-play of this encounter, but there's a reason why we're best friends; she knows when I get backed into an emotional corner, I curl up and try to pretend I don't exist. So, she nods and picks up a menu.

I slip the napkin into my purse and chug the last three gulps of beer from my glass.

I have no idea what I'm going to do with the number, but I do know I'm going to try to forget about it for now.

For the first time in my life, I'm grateful for the two dozen television screens lining the walls of Halftime. I'll take any distraction I can get.

Chapter 3

Andie comes back to my apartment after we eat a bucket of wings and down three more beers—*each*. I'm toeing the line between blissfully tipsy and haphazardly drunk. Okay, maybe I am violently swaying, but still.

At least drinking has dulled my senses enough that I don't implode from lust every time I think about Baron. Although…it has lowered my inhibitions, so I might just start humping a pillow like a puppy.

You win some, you lose some.

When I throw my purse onto the bed, it hits the edge and tumbles to the ground, dumping all the contents out on the floor. Andie and I both bend down to pick up the various vital accouterments—lip balm, wallet, keys…professional football player's cell number.

Andie picks up the napkin and stares at it. "You really didn't know who he was?"

"Nope," I say, followed by a hiccup. *Hmm.* I think I'm veering onto the wrong side of the inebriation line.

"You didn't recognize his face?"

"Why would I recognize his face if I don't follow football?"

"I don't know. He's had like a million sponsorship deals, and he's only like twenty-seven or something. He was good enough to stand out in college, and when he got drafted by Detroit, he took it to a whole new level. It helps that he looks like a freaking Adonis. He shows up everywhere now. I wouldn't be surprised if he was on one of those cereal boxes."

"I'm more of an oatmeal fan, myself. Besides, I've never idolized the .001 percent of people who are genetically gifted enough to play professional sports."

"You don't have to watch the sport to appreciate the physique."

She's had a front row seat for my disdain for sports—particularly football—for years, yet it still throws her that I wouldn't at least keep up on the eligible players.

"I saw the way you looked at Baron. You'd let him lift you up and press you up against a wall any day of the week."

I don't care about eligibility or body fat percentage; the main point is still the same. "But he *is* a football player. You know how well that worked out for me last time."

Andie rolls her eyes. "Yeah, but we're not in high school any more. Bear seemed really nice."

"Hey, you were wrong last time, and I have the emotionally scarring humiliation to prove it." I swear if you lifted up my shirt, you'd see the embarrassment tattooed somewhere on my body.

"I'm sorry I told you that cheerleader girl was nice. To be fair, I was thinking of the wrong cheerleader. Besides, I was drunk on a diet of Top 40 radio, *Friday Night Lights*, and teenage hormones. Everything was the beginning of an epic love story," she reasoned with a casual shrug.

"And now you're just drunk."

Andie looks at me with a sneaky little grin. "Then you won't mind if I call him."

She's trying to call my bluff, but I'm not going to take the bait.

29

"Nope."

Her grin only grows wider. She swipes her thumb across the phone in her hand and starts pressing the numbers written on the napkin into the keypad.

Wait. The case on her phone looks different. She presses the last button and moves it up to her ear. *Ohmygod, that's my phone.* I reach out for it, but considering Andie is two beers shy of my five, she dodges my advance easily.

I hear the line ringing. *Please don't pick up.* I take another step toward Andie and reach for her shirt. I catch the edge of the hem and tug. She trips and I lose my grip, sending us both down to the floor. My phone flies out of her hand and lands two inches in front of me.

Aha! I grab it, scrambling to hit the red 'end' button. It takes about four flailing jabs, but it finally stops ringing.

"What were you thinking?" I'm livid.

Andie is unfazed. "I was thinking that a hot guy gave you his number and you should go out with him."

"You're a psycho."

"I'm a psycho who loves you."

I take a deep breath. Andie and I are wildly different people, but she's my people. Even though she drives me crazy sometimes, I love her too.

At least the call didn't connect.

I take a deep breath, and my world starts to spin with a beer-bubbled hue. I decide to drop it and get ready for bed instead.

I walk over to the bathroom to brush my teeth. "You're crashing here tonight, right?"

"Yup. I'm not walking all the way back to my apartment now. I need to wake up early and get more work done, so I'll be out before you wake up."

I look back and see Andie pulling some sweatpants off the chair by my desk. Yup, she loves me. She knows the pile of clothes by my desk is always the clean pile. She's going to have to roll them up about ten times in order for them to fit.

It reminds me of what it was like sitting across from Baron. I felt tiny compared to him, which doesn't happen very often.

I need to snap out of it. He's not a date, he's just someone who gave me his number…which I'm not going to use…ever.

I start to brush my teeth and try to piece together how two very different people could be best friends. A little neon Baron sign lights up in my brain, but I'm not with it enough to process the thought.

Maybe I'll wake up tomorrow and this will all seem like a funny story I'll talk about when I'm old and senile. *When I was younger, this big-shot Mr. Sportsball gave me his number.*

They'll never believe me.

Ohmygod, make those bells stop. Somebody, please.

It's as if they're clanging together an inch away from my ear. I lift my hand and try to swat whatever stupid thing is making that sound.

I hit my bedside table with a loud and painful thump, and something falls to the floor.

The bells stop. Finally.

I hear a muffled "Hello?" coming from the floor.

Oh shit. I jolt up, and it feels like I just stepped off a moving walkway. Even though I've stopped, my body feels as if it's still moving right along.

"Hello…Monty?"

Ohmygod. My brain feels like it got dunked in a bucket of thick sap. All my thoughts are sticking together.

I reach down, grab my phone off the floor, and press the screen

31

to the side of my face.

"Hi." My voice sounds as if it's being pulled against sandpaper.

"Rough night?" The voice on the other end sounds like the strings of a bass guitar being pulled back and released, filling the room with warm, rich vibration. It hits me—I know that voice.

I'm going to kill Andie.

"Baron?"

"Yeah. You called me last night…?"

Oh Andie, when my brain stops sticking to itself, I'm going to figure out an elaborate plan of revenge.

Right now, I don't think I can put multiple sentences together. I can't explain that it was my phone but not me that called. I keep it simple. "Yup."

"I'm glad you did. I thought I had a fifty-fifty shot."

He thought he had a fifty-fifty shot? I'm pretty sure if I Google his exes, it's going to give me a composite image result of some of the most eligible ladies in America—hell, in the world.

I don't know how to form a coherent reply.

"So…" Baron presses the conversation along. "Can I take you out on a date? Maybe this Friday?"

I don't need to pull up my calendar to know my schedule is wide open. The problem is, I don't know how to say no. My brain isn't firing fast enough to come up with an excuse that won't have him just offering up another day instead.

I'm awful at saying no even in the best of circumstances, and this is the worst-case scenario.

My only option is a yes that I can beg off of later. "That sounds good."

I'll come up with my way out when I'm not hungover. Better yet, I'll make Andie figure it out.

"Cool." His word choice is casual, but even on the phone, I can tell he's smiling. "Want to meet downtown at Halftime at 8? I promise I won't actually make you go in."

I appreciate that he's not trying to pick me up at my place. Halftime is common ground.

"Sure."

"Okay, I'll let you get back to it. I'm excited for Friday."

"Me too." It comes out flat, but saying *Good for you* doesn't really have the same effect when you're both theoretically supposed to be excited.

The call ends, and I immediately open my calendar app and set an event for Friday at 8: *Date I need to cancel.*

I turn my phone on silent and drop my head back onto the pillow. I don't care if the president calls asking for my advice about how to stop global warming; my brainpower is maxed out, and I think I need about a Sleeping Beauty's curse worth of rest to recuperate.

I walk into work on Monday with jittery nerves and a flash drive of my best photos from Friday's donor event. I updated my portfolio and sent it to Irene Collins first thing this morning, and I think I've pressed refresh on my inbox about two thousand times already.

How long does it take for one of the richest women in the world to pass along a resume?

I wish there was email tracking so I could see that I sent the package, it was picked up by the carrier, it arrived at its final destination, and the recipient signed for it.

Instead, I just have to wait. And wait. And wait.

At least I have work to distract me.

The Ann Arbor Daily office looks impressive from the outside —all columns, arches, and big windows—but inside, it's one wood-paneled wall away from being a 1970s time capsule. Even the air smells like it's just been recycled over and over for the last forty-plus years.

I have a weekly meeting with my boss, Olive, at 9:30AM to go over what she needs for the week. It's only a ten-minute appointment sandwiched between dozens of other meetings with the writers, photographers, and editors she manages. I'm a cog in the wheel. I think if she could cut our time down to five minutes, she would.

I walk up to Olive's office door and look through the window next to it to see her leaning back in her chair, looking at something on her computer. Her face is unreadable, but if I'm waiting for Olive to look blatantly happy, I'll be waiting for a really, really long time.

This is my job—hopefully not forever, but it is right now.

I rap my knuckles lightly on the door frame, and Olive looks up and lifts her hand to wave me in.

We start with the obvious business: how Friday went, where she needs me this week, what freelancers are going on vacation that I need to cover for.

She stops after the last event request on her list and takes off her black-rimmed glasses. She closes her eyes for longer than a blink. She opens them, but she doesn't look straight at me. It's as if there's a poster of diminishing letters behind me and she's trying to test how far down she can read.

"Later this month, we'd like you to take a long vacation."

My heart stops. Is that like suspension for grownups? Did Donna in accounting report me when I accidentally ran into her and grabbed her boob? I swear it wasn't on purpose. I lost my balance and reached out without looking where my arms were headed.

"Did I do something wrong?" I ask. My throat is dry, but swallowing doesn't seem to help.

Olive leans her cheek on her fist, as if her head has suddenly gotten too heavy to keep carrying around. "No, nothing like that. We're just trying to trim the budget, so we need our freelancers to take a week off sometime over the next couple months. You're one of the, um, few who doesn't have vacation on the books."

Her words hit me like a sucker punch to the gut. I kind of wished Donna had reported me and I was getting in trouble. This somehow feels worse. I don't have any travel plans, and I'm one of the only ones who doesn't, but here I am daydreaming about taking my photography act on the road and living out of a suitcase.

I keep talking up a big game, but outside of sending one email to what could very well be a total long shot, I haven't taken a single step toward making my dreams happen.

I look up and realize Olive is still talking. "…some big changes coming. I would strongly advise you, as a freelancer, to pursue whatever other routes you can."

"Big changes?" I repeat the words while my brain spins through conclusions. *My job's on the line? Is that what she's telling me?*

"I can't say a lot right now, but I'm happy to be a reference."

Okay, I guess that's it. I get to sit on a ticking time bomb and hope Collins Aid United plucks me off my perch in time.

Or I could come up with plan B.

Olive's phone rings, and I take that as my cue. I have my marching orders: go to these events, find a new job.

No pressure.

Chapter 4

By the end of the week, I am sick of being in my own head. It's an endless loop of *oh-my-god-I'm-going-to-lose-my-job* and *please-let-me-get-this-new-job*. The universe is conspiring to keep the employment issue front and center; every time I try watching a show or movie on Netflix, I get five minutes in and realize one of the characters has their own work-life drama.

I can't handle it. I did my part. I sent an email to Irene, and after my meeting with Olive, I finally received a reply from her assistant. Irene is out of the country this week but will pass along my email at her earliest convenience.

What do I do with that? I can't exactly say *Hey, I know you're busy saving lives and helping eradicate massive global issues, but my job might be disappearing, so can you make your 'earliest convenience' happen sooner versus later?*

I don't even know for sure if my job is going away, let alone when. It could be tomorrow. It could be a year from now. Olive's warning wasn't very specific.

My head is buzzing with questions. Do I look for other jobs? How long do I wait to hear from Irene? If I take another job, what happens if I get a call from Collins Aid United?

Fortunately, it's the summer. I don't want to sit still in my apartment anyway. The lack of A/C turns my top floor into a glorified sauna. I could charge people for a hot yoga class if I actually knew any other poses besides downward-facing dog.

But, I'm a runner. Give me earbuds and a pair of sneakers, and I'm all set. It's exactly what I need right now—some Beyoncé and a sidewalk.

I need to get lost in my breath and step off this well-worn path of thoughts. I'd rather get lost in the wilderness of my subconscious than keep circling the same familiar terrain over and over.

I head out the front door of my building and head in the direction of the arboretum. I warm up with a little "XO," then catch my stride with "Run the World."

I'm just past the entrance to the park when the music fades temporarily for a little ding—my calendar notification. I slow to a stop, unable to recall what I'm missing. I have something booked tonight? There weren't any events I needed to photograph until Sunday afternoon. Andie is busy as usual, and I'm going home to visit my parents tomorrow.

So, what's tonight? It feels as if I'm fumbling around in a dark room to find the light switch.

And then something in my brain flips the switch on and my eyes go wide. I fumble quickly to get my phone out from my armband, and I nearly drop it.

I press the home button, even though I already know what I'm going to see.

When it lights up, I feel nauseous. There it is. *Date I need to cancel.* In one hour.

I don't know why it didn't remind me earlier—although I barely remember setting it, so it shouldn't really be a surprise I screwed it up.

I contemplate pretending I never got the reminder and just

continuing my run with Queen B on full blast to avoid my inner cricket shouting, *I am a horrible person.*

But I can't ignore the problem forever. I have a feeling Baron isn't the type of guy who doesn't follow up when he gets blown off. It takes a certain kind of person to approach a woman in a bar and start a conversation. It also takes a certain kind of person to willingly run out on a field knowing he's going to get tackled to the ground by some of the largest men in the American population.

Yeah, I'm pretty sure Baron would call me. Repeatedly.

Ugh. I need to go get my own game face on and handle this. I need to meet up with him and then explain that we're really not a good match for each other.

Even though I know what I need to do, I have a hard time moving my feet in the direction they need to go.

Deep breath. *We got this, feet.* I mean, hey, I've got Beyoncé to pump me up all the way home.

I know if I ask WWBD, the answer is getting my butt over to Halftime and putting my sexy stilettoed foot down.

Maybe I'll save the stilettos for Beyoncé. I'm more of a Converse girl myself.

By the time I get home, I don't have time to look Beyoncé levels of sexy. All I have time for is a quick shower and a half-wet side braid.

I open up my bathroom drawer and laugh. There's a tube of mascara, a few lipsticks in varying states of dried out, and some eyeliner. I'm not exactly stocked for looking like sex on wheels. I have a camera up to my face half the time, so any makeup I put on just gets smudged on the black plastic anyway.

YouTube tutorials may have taken the world by storm since I

was a hopeless high schooler, but my makeup drawer doesn't look any more grown up. I guess some things never change.

I've always been more of an awkward "Shake It Off" than a red-lipped "Wildest Dreams" Taylor Swift.

I quickly slip on my sneakers, shorts, and a tank then race out the door.

I make it to Halftime a minute past eight, and I see Baron sitting at one of the patio tables in a short-sleeved t-shirt and dark jeans. Just looking at his tanned arms flexing while he leans on the table sends shivers down my spine, and I secretly wish I could stop time to trace the lines with my fingers. *Whoa, come on, I'm here to let the guy down gently, not molest him. Geez.*

He sees me and smiles. You'd think for a professional sportsballer, his smile wouldn't be so goddamned perfect. *Wait, is it football players that lose their teeth or hockey players?* Whatever, either he won the genetic lottery or he has a really good dentist.

I give him a close-lipped smile back and make my way over to the patio. My hands are clammy. I try rubbing them off on the back pockets of my denim cutoffs, which takes away some of the moisture but none of the stickiness. Eww.

I'm regretting my decision to do this in person. Staring at the stubble that grazes the strong angles of Baron's jaw all the way up to his cheekbones makes me whimper. I'm turning down a man that hits a ten out of ten on my I'd-stare-at-that-all-day scale.

We're just not compatible, I remind myself.

Baron throws down a twenty and then steps over the railing that encloses the outdoor seating area.

"Hi." His smile is warm and inviting, and I almost forget I'm here to say kthanksbye. He walks up next to me with his hands stuck into his front pockets. He looks more like a nervous freshman than a professional beast. "I thought we could walk to Pinball Dave's."

I hear the words "Yeah sure" come out of my mouth. *Did I*

really just say yes when I came here to say no?

I don't know why I'm prolonging this. I want to say I'm walking to the arcade just a few blocks down the street because the patio at Halftime is fairly crowded and I'd rather not have an audience, but I know there's more to it than that. I'm intrigued by the man who spotted the nerd in the sports bar and thought, *I have to talk to her.*

I'll get to the letdown, but maybe a little teaser of the ride up wouldn't be so bad.

We walk along, and I find my steps matching Baron's almost exactly. His legs are long and pushed to their athletic max. His jeans strain against the muscles of his quads as we make our way down the street.

We hit the end of the block, and the crossing sign is a steady red hand. We're still silent, and I realize I have no idea what to talk about. Do I tell Baron I know he's a professional football player? Do I apologize for my rant the other night? Even if the man is intriguing, I'm not going to suddenly change my mind about the sport.

The crossing sign changes, and I swear I hear Baron let out a sigh of relief. I try to covertly steal a glance over at him, and I see him biting the corner of his bottom lip, his eyebrows pulled together in concentration.

I can't take it anymore. "So, how about that weather?" I joke.

Baron releases his lip and looks down at me—*down*...I still can't get over that—and laughs under his breath. "I'm sorry. I'm really nervous, and I don't remember the last time that's happened on a date."

I don't know what I was expecting him to say, but his honesty chips away at my resolve. He may be a bona fide celebrity, but he's still a human on a first date.

"Well, I'm not exactly Miss Confidence over here." *Clearly.* I haven't worked up the nerve to explain that I came here to let him down, but I feel an overwhelming desire to put him at ease. "When was the last time you were really nervous?"

Baron thinks for a second and then gets a big, lopsided grin on his face. "When my brother handed me my nephew for the very first time. He was only a couple days old at the time, and all I could think was 'don't drop him.'"

"Older brother?"

"Yeah. There are four of us, two older brothers and one younger sister." Baron's shoulders roll back down, but his hands are still wedged into his pockets.

"Are you from the Midwest?" I feel like I should have Googled him before meeting up with him tonight, but I already know that the millions of search results hold information I don't want to see. Considering I forgot this date was even on the calendar, my decision was made for me. I'm flying blind here, and I'm kind of okay with that.

"I'm from just across the state line, the one we don't mention here in Michigan."

Ah, he's from Ohio. I don't follow sports, but even I know that our two states have major beef that spills over into life off the field. "I promise I won't hold it against you."

He slips his hands out of his pockets. They just barely brush mine as he drops them down by his sides, and my body goes completely still for a split second.

We keep walking side by side, and I am aware of every single inch of him.

"Where'd you grow up?" he asks.

"Not too far from here, actually. My parents live about twenty minutes away in a house that's been in my mom's family for generations. I went to school here, and I just sort of stuck around." I hate admitting that. I am my own worst enemy—I say I want to travel, to live abroad, to photograph places most people won't see in their lifetime, but here I am, one short car ride away from where I was born and raised.

41

"I envy you. I hate that my schedule makes it hard to see my family a lot. It's been that way for a while, but it never gets easier." He lifts his hand and rubs the center of his chest, as if he's trying to make sure his heart is still safely contained inside.

I want to put my hand over his. The desire feels foreign; I haven't felt this comfortable this early with a guy in a long time— maybe ever. I cross my arms over my chest and keep walking. "Did you move away for college?" I shouldn't want to get to know this man I'm just going to turn around and walk away from, but I do.

"Yeah, I got a scholarship to a school down south. I couldn't pass it up."

A scholarship for football—it's a giant bathtub filled with ice water, and neither one of us wants to be the first one to dunk our heads into the freezing water.

We walk up to the glowing neon sign for Pinball Dave's. Part of me wants to walk right in and pretend I'm just on a date with a guy that gave me his number.

But that's not reality. I'm standing next to Bear Richards, the football star. He's still just a guy who gave me his number, but I can't seem to separate the two.

Baron opens up the door for me, but as I open my mouth to speak, a group of teenage boys walk out the door. Their words overlap, but you don't have to hear the conversation to know they're enjoying a warm summer evening hanging out with each other. Life is simple: food, video games, friends.

I look at Baron and he smiles back at me, and my heart feels light. I could pretend life was simple. I could let it go for a night and just enjoy the time we have.

One of the boys stops and looks straight at Baron. "Wait— you're Bear Richards?!" All his friends stop and look back at Baron, and I swear I see a frown cross his face for a split second.

It's quickly replaced by a wide grin. "Sure am." I haven't known him for very long, but I can already tell it's the football player talking and not the man I was just walking with. Both are kind, but only one is real.

Damn, the water in that bathtub we were circling is cold.

Baron lets the door handle slip out of his fingers as the boys start to ask a dozen questions. Someone finds a pen, and he spends the next five minutes signing something for each of them.

He's made their night—probably their summer—but I can't help but feel disappointed. I can't pretend life is simple. It isn't just beer and wings and video games.

It's football too, and that makes all the difference.

"Sorry about that," Baron says. He's trying to apologize without making it seem like a big deal. The boys have finally gone off to the rest of their evening, and Baron opens up the door, hoping to start the rest of ours.

I shake my head. "I'm sorry."

He frowns, but he keeps holding the door open. "What are you sorry about?"

I'm sorry I can't walk through that door. I'm sorry I can't date a football player. I'm sorry I can't seem to get over that detail. "I can't go on a date with you."

"Tonight?" I can tell by the way he asks, he already knows the answer. I see his fingers loosening their grip on the door handle.

"Ever." The word feels like a heavy stone thrown to the bottom of my stomach. The weight is sudden and uncomfortable.

"Because I play football?" He says it like it's a hobby he picks up from time to time, like he knits scarves or paints watercolors of sunsets, as if it's something that can be taken out and then packed away when the hour is up and it's time to go back to normal life.

But, this is normal life.

People recognize him. He has the power to make or break someone's day, and all because he plays a sport I would rather pull off my own fingernails than sit down to watch. I look at him, and that stone in my stomach feels even heavier.

"We're just different people."

"Because I play football." He lets go of the door and walks over to a chair underneath the coffee shop awning next door. He's processing what I'm telling him, and I follow him and sit down too.

He's quiet for another moment, and then he turns to look at me. His blue eyes are so crisp, I bet if I looked close enough I could see his thoughts like an airplane spelling words across the sky.

He leans his elbow on the table and rests his chin on his fist. I have to use all my willpower not to stare at his tan forearm, but really, I don't know where to stare that doesn't make me want to throw my defensive stance out the window.

"So, you're telling me that if I had walked over to you and given you my number the other night, and I was a professor or a plumber or a bartender, you'd go out with me. But because I play football for a living, you're turning me down."

"Yes," I say quietly. The word feels hollow. It seems silly, but I know I'm right. Even if it is silly, I can't get past it, and I'm not going to lie and go on a date with him just to say I did.

"Hmm." Baron laughs to himself, like he finally gets the joke. "That's never happened before."

I can't help but laugh too. Women probably throw themselves at him on a regular basis because of his status, and here I am turning him down because of it.

"So, you didn't know who I was when I walked over to you?" I can see him trying to piece together the variables, as if understanding the order of events would help him figure out where this took a wrong turn. The problem is we were never on the same path to begin with.

"No. My friend Andie did though. She told me after you left."

"If you hadn't figured it out…" Baron's voice trails off at the end, but I can fill in the blank: I would have walked through the door to Pinball Dave's with him. It would be easy to say yes, but football is as much a part of his identity as photography is mine.

"I don't know." It's not a good answer, but it's the only one I have for him.

"And I can't change your mind? Maybe give you a list of references, my previous dates and girlfriends?" He smiles to himself, and I wish I could join him.

I stand up and tug at my shorts. "I'm sorry. I should have said no on the phone. I'm just really bad at this sort of thing." I can't look him in the eye, but I can feel him looking at me. My whole body feels it; every cell is on high alert.

"No, don't be sorry. I'm glad I got to see you again."

I look over and see that his eyes are kind, but his shoulders are heavy.

His lips curve up to the right. "There's something about being around you…I can't put my finger on it yet. But, it was better to get a no in person, no question."

My heart skips when I hear him say *yet*. It's as if he snuck a word in there to let me know this isn't final. I don't know how to tell him it is. Hell, I don't know how to get that message to the rest of my body. My heart has gotten more of a cardio workout in the past twenty minutes than it did on my run.

"It was nice to meet you." That's all I've got. I toss it out and hope it sticks.

He stands up from the table and slips his hands back into his pockets. "You too, Monty. You too."

I turn around and start walking back to my apartment. I should feel relieved. I did what I came there to do.

So why do I feel like that stone in my stomach has turned into a boulder?

45

"And you just walked away?" Andie asks. She's sitting in the middle of my bed with a bowl of ice cream. That's how you know it's true love: you'll even let them eat sticky, drippy food on your bed—not that I won't give her crap if she spills it.

"Yeah." I'm still sort of shocked I said no to Baron. If you had flipped a coin while we were walking to the arcade, it would have had just as much of a shot at predicting my decision as I did. Running into those kids put everything into perspective, and I didn't like what I saw in my viewfinder.

"But he's Baron Richards," Andie says with her mouth full and eyes wide.

"Exactly. He's a football player." I keep pacing back and forth, unable to sit still while we're dissecting my decision to turn down what might have been one of the best dates of my life.

"That's the point. He's paid buckets of cash to get ripped and increase his stamina—which part of that offends you, exactly?"

"He's a football player." I can't help but let a whine sneak into my tone.

Andie puts her spoon down, and I know I'm in for it. "I get that you want to avoid feeling the way you felt when we were in high school, but there comes a point when you have to stop avoiding the good things just because you're scared of the bad."

I walk over to the freezer and grab the rest of the half-empty quart of ice cream and a spoon. "Maybe I just think we're different people."

Andie looks at me as if she could smell my bullshit before it even left my mouth.

It only makes me want to double down. "Seriously, we're opposites, and I don't buy into that whole opposites attract business. That's for magnets and Paula Abdul."

"Whatever. I just think you're writing him off before you've even dug deeper than his chosen profession. I'm more than a doctor, and you're more than a photographer; why can't he be more than a football player?"

God, I hate when she's right. It still doesn't change the fact that I turned him down. As good as the date might have been, the decision has been made.

I have the sudden urge to eat the rest of this tub of ice cream.

"Besides," she says with a mischievous smile, "you're always talking about being more adventurous. I bet you'd gladly take a detour down his street."

I give her the stink eye.

"What? It's not like either of us are in the habit of getting numbers from extremely eligible men. Remember the last time someone hit on me and it turned out he was a freshman? In *undergrad*. That is not in my definition of eligible, even in a broad sense."

I can't hold back a snort. It happened on her way to class a couple weeks ago, and it still makes me laugh when I think about it. She swears up and down she didn't realize how young he was until she Facebooked him when she got home.

"Just because we're low on prospects doesn't mean I need to sell out when a hot one comes along."

"Oh come on, sell out for me. Give me a life full of wild sex and lavish dates to live vicariously through. It's your job as my best friend."

"Can we just trade? You go on the dates, and I'll sit at home on Friday nights and read books."

Andie shakes her head just as she finishes the last of her dessert. "You're such a weirdo."

"And you love me," I say with a smile.

She bounces off the bed and accidentally tips the bowl to the side, flinging the spoon onto the comforter before she pulls me into a hug. I just shake my head.

"I just want you to be happy." Her voice is full of truth.

"Me too."

I want happiness for the both of us. I don't know what that looks like in the long run, but I know we have each other to help figure it out.

Chapter 5

It's times like these that living a predictable life really sucks. Normally, I like ordinary, mundane life. Waking up and drinking coffee—not even particularly good coffee, just coffee with some cream. Going to work. Seeing my parents every week for Saturday dinner.

It's comfortable, familiar, like my old high school sweatshirt that's been washed and worn so many times there are holes in the armpits. It doesn't matter if the holes get so big you can stick your hand through them, you're never going to throw it away.

Craving adventure feels like lusting after the floral romper. You want to try it on. It looks exciting, and you know it has the possibility to rock your world. But, what if it just doesn't fit? I mean, rompers are kind of tricky that way. It might look good in the dressing room, but take it for a spin and you find out it gives you a nonstop wedgie and you can never go to the bathroom—ever.

Right now, I'd take the risk of the most epic wedgie in the history of ever over the comfort of the sweatshirt I keep reaching for again and again. My life feels stagnant, like everyone else is moving forward and I'm standing still.

There are whispers dancing around the halls of the newspaper. Everyone has a different theory, but they all seem to signal massive layoffs.

I still haven't heard from Irene Collins. I don't even want to think about that. It makes me sick to my stomach every time I do. I want it so badly, and I have no idea what I can do to make it happen.

And then there's Baron. It's been a few weeks since I told him I couldn't date him, and I haven't heard from him since.

Which is exactly what I wanted. So, I have no idea why I've typed "Bear Richards" into the search box about ten dozen times and hovered over the *I'm Feeling Lucky* button. I don't want to see everything, just a glimpse...just a little piece to satisfy my need to know more about him.

I told him no, and like a decent human being, he respected that. And I hate it. I wish I could snap out of it and go back to enjoying my regularly scheduled life, but no; here I am wishing my life looked a little less ordinary.

Fortunately, it's the end of May, which means it's time to go be surrounded by ridiculously adorable fur-balls. At the end of every month, I go photograph the newest animals at the local shelter and post the images online. I've been doing it for a few years now after reading about a professional photographer in another state who tried it and saw a massive increase in adoption rates.

So, at least for the next few hours, I'll be distracted. I open the glass front door of the shelter and the little bell overhead dings.

One of the undergrads volunteering for the summer is sitting at the front desk with a huge smile on her face. I walk up and introduce myself, explaining that I'm the photographer coming in to take pictures of the new animals.

"Hi! I'm Ivy. Oh my goodness, are you just so excited?" She's beaming as if we're involved in a mission that's about to end the suffering of every animal everywhere. Granted, I support that cause, but this afternoon's photo session is not *that* exciting.

"Totally." I don't want to rain on her parade. Besides, we are talking about cats and dogs here; there aren't many things in the world that are better than being surrounded by dozens of them, playing for a few hours, and not having to clean up the poop.

Ivy gets up from her desk and walks over to the locked double doors that lead to the back hallway where there are kennels, play areas, and various rooms for exams.

She pauses just as she flips the bolt to the unlocked position. "I mean, we're going to get so many more adoptions this month. I can't believe some of Detroit's football team is going to be here today. I hope Bear Richards shows up. He's so hot."

I can feel all the blood rushing out of my face. I have no idea where it's running off to, but it's attempting to make an escape.

"Umm, are you OK?" Ivy asks.

I look over at her and nod. I have no idea if I will be, but it's not exactly like I can extract myself from this situation. *Or maybe...*

"Wait, are they going to have a photographer with them?" I ask. If there's someone else here taking photos, I could sneak out and come back later.

"No." Ivy looks confused, but something tells me I'm the one who's confused here. "You're the photographer."

"I'm the photographer?" *Wait, am I the one who's supposed to be taking pictures of the team? What is going on here?*

She points at my camera. "Yeah, that's your camera, right?"

I'm missing something here. I try going back to the basics. "Yeah, I come in to take pictures of the new pets up for adoption every month, but Kim didn't say anything about a special event today."

"Ohhhh," Ivy says slowly, recognition dawning on her face. She gets it. I still don't. "Kim must have forgotten to mention it. Apparently, someone from the team called this week and asked if they could come help with the photos. They figured more pets would get adopted if they posed with them. You know, it will generate more publicity, which will totally help, since we're almost full to capacity this month with new intakes."

Yeah, Kim must have forgotten to mention it. She's amazing with the animals, but as a manager of the shelter, some of her organizational skills are a little rough around the edges.

I guess I'll have some help wrangling the animals, and it will help adoption rates. No one can say no to a handsome football player holding an adorable animal.

"Okay, so when are the players showing up?" I ask.

Ivy glances at her watch. "Any minute!" This is probably the highlight of her summer.

I smile, trying to share her enthusiasm even though my nerves are fraying at the edges right now. Any minute, Baron could walk through that door, and I don't know whether I want to see him or run into a closet and hide.

I don't have any time to think about it before the main entrance bell jingles again. I turn around to see the familiar face of the football player I turned down, along with three of his teammates.

Baron stops and stares at me like a bear that just found honey after sleeping all winter long. "Hi, Monty."

My breath catches. "Hi."

I know every single person in the room is staring at the two of us, but all I see is Baron's face. I wonder why I ever said no in the first place.

The next hour is a flurry of activity. I don't know why I thought having four football players around would make my job easier: the end result is going to be amazing, but getting there is a tangle of trying to catch the right moments while there are fifty things happening at the same time all over the room.

If you ever want your ovaries to explode, just go watch some of the biggest men you've ever seen in your life cuddle with animals. It's like ultra-masculine sexiness doused in cuteness overload.

I can't even handle it.

I'm trying to focus on taking pictures of all four players, but I keep finding my lens drawn to one specific focal point.

Baron Richards.

I almost lose it when he picks up a young kitten and it curls into his neck, purring happily.

We're almost to the end. I've gotten pictures of all the new animals. Two of the guys are on their phones. One of them is flirting with Ivy, who is loving every single second of it.

And then there's Baron.

I don't think he's taken his eyes off of me for more than a minute. He's looking at me like I'm a ball he's determined to catch, and I can't figure out if I'm going to let him.

I do know that I am anxiously anticipating downloading these images later and having uninterrupted time to stare at his face—even though I know it'll never compare to the real thing.

"Okay, I think I've got everything I need," I say to no one in particular. I don't even think anyone besides Baron hears me.

He just nods, and I start to pack up my equipment. The other three players notice and slowly start to make their way back toward the door that separates the back hallway of rooms and front reception. Ivy opens the door, and everyone starts to file out... everyone except Baron.

He walks right next to me, his hands tucked in his pockets. We're two steps away from the door, and he stops. "Monty, I don't know about you, but I'm starving. Want to grab a quick bite? There's a great burrito place down the street."

I know exactly the hole in the wall he's talking about. It's walk-up counter style, and I wonder if he strategically suggested it because it's not a place you take a date.

I take a deep breath, and then my stomach lets out a rumble that rivals a summer thunderstorm. I can feel my face turning bright red; I guess my body is putting in its vote.

"Sure, I haven't eaten anything since breakfast." I turn to look straight up at Baron, and he stares down at me like I just told him there really would be snow on Christmas morning. He'd hoped for it, but he wasn't sure if it would actually happen.

"Okay, let's do it." He pulls off nonchalance, but just barely. I can see the bounce in his step that wasn't there when he first walked in.

Baron begs off from his teammates, saying we're going to go grab lunch. None of them seem too phased by the idea. We duck out of the shelter without any fanfare and walk the two blocks down to the restaurant.

We missed the lunch rush, so we walk straight up to the counter and order. I order a shredded chicken burrito and pull out my wallet, but Baron is quicker, pushing a twenty across the counter while ordering a beef deluxe. I almost change my order to match his. It sounds so good, but I wonder if that would be weird.

We step to the side, and I try to focus on anything besides how hungry I am. It makes me desperate…enough to unleash my curiosity.

"Did you know I would be there today?" I ask.

Baron clears his throat and swallows, but I see the hint of a smile in his cheeks. "Are you pulling together evidence for a restraining order?"

I laugh. "No, no restraining orders—not yet, at least."

"Okay, good."

I squint at him. "So how did you find me?"

He tilts his head to one side and then the other as if he's tossing around the idea of whether or not to fess up. "You're easy to find, but kind of hard to pin down. There aren't a lot of Montgomerys who live in Ann Arbor. There was an article about you taking photos of animals up for adoption. I called the center and asked a few questions. They said you'd be there. So, I made sure I was too." He stops suddenly and laughs self-consciously. "Wow, that sounds a lot creepier when I say it out loud."

It has the potential to be creepy. He's admitting to orchestrating a way to see me again, but when I look at the sincerity in his eyes, all I feel is flattered. He genuinely wanted to see me again.

"You dug deep into the Google dumpster of my Internet life." I find it fascinating that he looked me up—I'm sure I have about 100 results to his 100 million. I doubt I would have to dig very far to learn more about him than he could ever learn about me.

"I made my way through a few pages, yeah."

Our conversation is interrupted by our hot food. We grab the red plastic trays and take them over to the massive table that runs the length of the room and has benches on both sides. We sit down across from each other and unwrap the giant foil packages.

Oh man, I am going to look ridiculous trying to eat this, but I'm so hungry, I don't care.

Baron looks over at me and leans his massive burrito over the center of the table. "Cheers."

I tap my burrito against his and smile. This isn't what I expected.

He isn't what I expected.

I've been walking around with an image in my head of what football players are like, and it's starting to feel unfair to lump him into that pile. I've always assumed all sportsballers are cocky, arrogant pricks. Baron is the exact opposite.

Which means I am in serious trouble.

"So, you're in Ann Arbor a lot. Is this your normal stomping grounds?" I ask.

His mouth is full of burrito; I guess that makes two of us that look ridiculous eating these things. He shakes his head and swallows. "No, but my little sister goes to school here, so I try to stop by and see her...or really, I make up excuses to be in town so I can check in on her like the annoying big brother I am. She hates getting caught with me. I'm not exactly inconspicuous."

"Not when you show up at sports bars in the middle of a college town," I tease him with a wink. Something about being around Baron brings out a different side of me. I'm not as quiet or reserved. I thought when I met him it was the two beers talking, but I'm completely sober and am still saying things that are just a nudge further than I normally would. I kind of like it.

"You didn't recognize me when you first saw me." He responds as if I'm the only person who was sitting in Halftime that night.

"Yeah, I'm not exactly your target market."

"Oh, I think you're exactly my target market, to a T." The way he says it—leaning forward, looking straight at me with a smile sneaking up to one side—makes me blush.

Every single inch of me is turning bright red, and I think I might need a fire hydrant full of ice water to cool off.

I don't even know how to respond. The way he looks at me makes me feel alive and adventurous, two of the things I've been craving in my life—but they're also two of the things that scare me.

This man is nothing like what I expected, and that is both wonderful and terrifying.

When he was an undeveloped print, it would have been easy, but now that he's coming into focus...I like what I see, and I don't know if I can walk away so easily.

Even if this is a bad idea.

After lunch, we walk out and stand just outside the front door for a second. I went into this prepared to make a quick getaway after our meal was over, and yet here I am, both feet firmly planted right in front of Baron.

Baron stuffs his hands into his front pockets and rocks back onto his heels. Sometimes, I swear he's more like an overgrown kid than a full-blown adult. I guess the professional football league doesn't come with how-to-be-overly-suave-101 training, and I am perfectly okay with that.

My mind is running through every single option on the table here: goodbye hug, fist bump, taco emoji followed by heart eyes smiley face? Nothing feels quite right.

Maybe because I'm not quite ready for this to be over.

"Did you park close by?" I ask, trying to draw the encounter out.

"Yeah, just a few blocks down."

"I'll walk with you."

Baron smiles. "Okay."

We take a few steps back in the direction of the shelter, and I realize I don't have a game plan past asking to walk him back to his car. What was I planning to do with my extra three minutes of Baron Richards' time? Ask him about his plans for the night? Give him a goodbye kiss? Umm, no. I'm working on fanning the flame of my adventurous side, not setting it on fire.

"The weather's really nice out today." As soon as the words leave my mouth, I want to kick myself. *Really? You revert to talking about the weather?*

"Yeah, I was trying to convince my sister to play hooky with me and go out to Lake Michigan for a day, but she wasn't having it. I guess she actually likes her job." I love that Baron just took my awful start and actually went somewhere with it. I also love that he appreciates a good day off at the lake. Apparently he's been in Michigan long enough for us to wear off on him; any good

Michigander is always up for a day on the water.

"Hmm, what does your sister do?"

"She's working as an orientation leader this summer, something about introducing pre-freshmen to the campus."

Oh man, no wonder she loves her job. Leading orientation is one of the best college summer jobs on the planet. You get paid to live in the dorms with twenty other upperclassmen and show the incoming class how awesome it is to study here. I loved my orientation session. I even debated interviewing to be a leader myself one summer, but put me in front of a hundred people and I freeze. There's no way I could lead tours and make Michigan University seem appealing. I would have been one big sweatfest who could barely string two words together. There's a reason I hang out behind a lens, not in front of it.

"Yeah, I get it. It's a sweet job."

Baron laughs. "Well, that's good to hear. I thought maybe she was just blowing me off because I stick out like a sore thumb."

"Nope. Her job really is awesome. She's not lying."

Baron stops walking, and I look over at a blue Prius. Did he forget where he parked?

"This is me." He points at the Prius.

"Oh." *Huh.* For some reason I was imagining a tricked-out black SUV, something that cost twice what I make in a year. I have the strong urge to fist bump him right now. Environmentally responsible and budget friendly—Baron is full of surprises.

Baron chuckles to himself like I just handed him the punch line of a good inside joke. I wonder if I'm not the first one to be surprised.

He doesn't reach for his keys, and my mind wanders back to a goodbye kiss. I can't say I'm not curious. Every single square inch of my skin is curious. What would it feel like to have him wrapped around me, to have his fingers trace lines across my skin? Just the thought of it catches my heart mid-beat.

"Are you headed home?" I ask, scrambling for anything to get my mind off his lips and what they would feel like pressed against mine.

Baron shakes his head. "Umm, not yet. I was going to walk over to my sister's dorm and say hi."

"Oh. I just figured…"

"Yeah, you offered to walk me back to my car, and I wasn't going to say no to that." His smile is slightly self-conscious, but with an edge of charm to it. I feel a flicker of courage. Maybe I do want to kiss him.

No. I'm not there…not yet. "Is your sister in East Quad?" I vaguely remember that's where I stayed for my own orientation before I started school here.

"Yup."

Hmm, we're going in opposite directions. I'm still not entirely sure I want this to end, but I'm not ready to walk with him to see his sister. Plus, there's not even an offer to do so on the table.

Cause that's not awkward: I show up with him at his sister's dorm and say, *Hi! I just had a quasi-romantic meal with your brother. I'm Monty, want to be my new sister?*

"Umm, I guess I'll see you later?" I don't know if I'm posing the question to him or to myself.

Does he want to see me later? Do I want to see him later? Who's calling who in this situation? My brain is starting to short-circuit with questions I don't have the answers to.

And this is why I'm single.

"Yeah. It was really nice spending time with you today…" His sentence trails off at the end, and I wish he would keep going. It sounded like it was going somewhere good.

"Same here." We stand silent for a minute, and I realize I can't keep standing here waiting for him to say something. *Do something.* I lift up on my toes and give him the faintest whisper of a kiss on his cheek.

Okay, that was good. Sweet, but not too much. I pull back and see a smile bloom across his face. Really good.

"I need to get going, get these pictures uploaded." *And stare at your face for half the night.* I start to turn on my heels toward the direction of home, but just before I hit a full one eighty, I stop. "I'll see ya later."

It's a casual goodbye, but I mean every single word.

Chapter 6

Three hours and a nice cold beer later, I've gone through every single photo from the afternoon—twice. My laptop is overheating on my lap, but after staring at Baron's face for three hours, I think my whole body is running about five degrees hotter than normal.

I can confirm that staring at him on a screen is an extraordinarily close second to staring at him in person, except there's no time limit. He won't unfreeze and ask if he has something stuck in his teeth because I can't stop focusing on that gorgeous smile of his.

It's not because his smile is show-stopping, which it is—I mean, those teeth are a walking orthodontist advertisement. It's the way his smile pushes the corners of his lips up toward his cheeks, making these deep lines that frame it perfectly, like parentheses to happiness. I find myself smiling just looking at him, as if I can't help but join in because he's enjoying life so damn much. I want to enjoy it with him.

Mmm, and everything on him is proportional. His nose is strong but not overly dominant. His eyebrows are thick but not bushy. His jaw is chiseled but not so angular that you could cut a steak with it.

I see things through a lens, but I interpret them on a screen—and this interpretation? Yeah, it's saying this man makes my heart race a hundred and eighty beats per minute.

Staring at him is better than a damn workout, and that makes me want to sprint out of my comfort zone.

I'm twenty-three years old, and I've taken the safe route for every single one of those years. I went to college twenty minutes away from home. I took a job at the local newspaper and stuck around after graduation. The only remotely adventurous choice I've made was majoring in photojournalism instead of something more solid, like computer science or business. Granted, my performance in my freshman year calculus class pretty much took both of those options off the table.

Still, I crave adventure. I just haven't been choosing it. I pull my phone out of my bag and twirl it over and around in thought.

What if I called Baron? What would happen? We would spend time together, and I would get to know him. I would risk developing feelings for a man who is not at all the type of person I normally date. The last guy I dated was an English major trying to make his way writing satire, and he was the most miserable person I've ever chosen to spend time with. But, he was bookish and lanky, my version of a safe choice. He'd grown up in Michigan and had every intention of sticking around in his parents' basement for as long as possible.

What happens if I choose the unknown route? The route I can't see myself on?

I have no idea, and that's terrifying.

And kind of exciting. Kind of really exciting.

I stop twirling my phone and swipe it open. I press the last unknown number in my recent history and wade out into the unknown.

Baron picks up on the second ring. "Hey." He sounds surprised and pleased.

I have to admit I'm pretty surprised myself. I can't believe I'm doing this. "Hey, are you back home?"

"Nope, I was just heading back to my car. Why?" My pulse quickens at his answer.

I'm sick of playing it safe. "What are you doing tonight?"

"Whatever you want me to." His tone takes on a husky undertone, and I imagine a sneaky smile curving across his lips.

"Okay, I'll be at your car in fifteen minutes. Will you wait for me?" I close my eyes, squeezing them tight. I already know he's going to say yes, but this feels so much more daring than a simple request.

"Definitely."

My eyes spring open. I have five minutes to get out this door and ten more to walk the mile to the shelter. I quickly say goodbye then start to dart around my room. I don't have time to analyze clothing choices or think about where we're going or what we're doing.

I'm finally living in the moment, and if I had known it would feel this good, I would have started doing it a whole lot sooner.

I'm going to go hang out with Baron tonight.

Ohmygod. I'm going to go hang out with Baron. Tonight. I quickly pull on a pair of white skinny jeans and a sleeveless plaid shirt from the pile of clean clothes on my floor. As I'm zipping up my pants, I realize I'm wearing the comfiest pair of boy short underwear I own.

Yeah, that's not going to work. I hop over to my dresser, mid-wardrobe change, and grab a thong just in case living in the moment takes me places where clothing is optional.

By the time I check my hair and makeup and grab my purse, I'm already late.

I race out the door and run the whole way to Baron's parked Prius.

"I almost thought you'd leave without me." I stop running, but my momentum slings me forward and I barrel into him. He's like a wall of muscle. I guess it does make sense that they call him Bear. He catches me, and I suddenly want to thank my momentum for winning that round.

His hands linger on my arms for a second longer than normal. "Are you kidding? A girl calls you up and tells you to wait, you wait."

"Just any girl?"

"Only the really amazing ones." He opens up the passenger door for me. "Come on in."

I slip into the passenger seat and realize I told him we should hang out but have no idea where we're going or what we're doing, while Baron's acting like he does.

When he gets in the driver's side and turns on the ignition, I decide I'm too curious to wait to find out his plan. "So, where are we off to?"

"Well, you've showed me around some of your town, so I figured I would show you some of mine."

I smile to myself. He could take me anywhere right now and I'd go along with it. I don't know where this new adventurous Monty came from, but I'm sure as hell glad she decided to show up.

Baron maneuvers us out to the highway and merges on. He drives his little Prius more like a sports car than the moderately affordable fuel-efficient model that it is.

"So, is this really your car?"

"Why? What kind of car did you think I would have?"

"I don't know, an all-black tank with massive rims."

Baron loses it. Laughter tumbles out of him like champagne

from a shaken bottle. "Yeah, so I had one of those, but it got the worst gas mileage in the world. It was a hell of a ride, but when my lease ended, I switched it out for something more practical."

"You're full of surprises."

"So are you." The way he says it makes it seem like he thought I would call eventually.

I surprised myself tonight. "I've played it safe for a long time. Too long..."

"Well, I'm glad I was on the receiving end of that call."

"Me too." The words tumble out, but when I hear myself say them, I realize I truly mean it. I like Baron. He's the guy I met in the bar, and as I start to get to know him better, that side of him becomes the dominant vision in my head—not the other version of him that hulks up with chest pads and paint and goes out onto a field to play a sport I don't like or understand.

I'm going to let myself forget that part of him exists...for as long as I possibly can.

Baron exits the highway and weaves through the streets of downtown Detroit. We pull up to a massive old warehouse, and he presses a button that opens a thick metal gate, leading us down to a parking garage underneath the building.

We haven't even stepped out of the car, but I already know where we are. Baron brought me to his place. His place—where he eats, sleeps, and walks around butt naked.

I find myself really wanting to witness that last part. I'm sure football training does a body good.

We take the elevator up to the top floor of the eight-story building, and even though we're not touching, I am distinctly aware of Baron the entire ride up. I play with the strap of my cross-body bag just to keep my hands occupied. Otherwise, I have no idea if this new brave Monty would reach over and press them into Baron's chest, wedging us back into the corner of the tiny space.

It's a decent idea, but I'm not ready to hand over the reins to this new version of me quite yet.

The elevator dings. We step out and make our way to the only door on the floor. He slides his key into the lock and presses the door open, letting me in ahead of him.

A dim light in the entry switches on automatically, and my breath catches.

It's floor-to-ceiling windows, and it must be at least two stories high. It's got exposed beams and ductwork. Everything is leather, wood, concrete, or metal. It's as if I crawled into an *Architectural Digest* feature. I step toward the main open area, and I realize that the windows look out onto the river. The lights in the distance are from Canada.

It's a good thing Baron likes me, because I don't think I'm ever leaving. My apartment is cozy, but this place is magical.

"Welcome to Casa de Richards."

"Casa? More like penthouse dreamland."

I live smack dab in the middle of a college town. My definition of luxury is clean sheets that were purchased sometime after college graduation. My standards are not high, and I'm starting to think I've been doing it wrong. I thought it was a score to not have roommates. This is about two thousand square feet over that requirement.

"You like it?" he asks as he rubs the back of his neck.

I can tell I'm staring at something he created. It would be like handing him my favorite photos; they're pieces of me that exist outside my body.

"I love it." The space is huge, but all the furnishings are so warm and inviting. I feel like I'm walking into a Pinterest photo that gets re-shared millions of times. It's photo ready, and yet it still feels like you could curl up in your jammies and binge the day away with a pile of pizza.

"Come on, let me get you something to eat. That burrito was huge, but that was way too long ago."

I can't argue with him. I was wondering if there would be food in this plan. We walk into the open kitchen with its dark espresso cabinets and steel counters. I sit down on a barstool and watch him roll up his sleeves and start to work on an omelet.

"So you can cook too?" I ask.

He shrugs. "I have some of the basics down. My mom made sure all of us boys would survive in the wild. I do my own laundry too."

"Look at you, winning at adulthood," I say with a wide smile.

He looks up from across the counter, and our eyes connect. Even though he's not touching me, my skin tingles as if I'm saturated in him. He's set a filter over my life and brought out a completely different hue.

I like it. I like it a lot.

Chapter 7

I'm sitting at the counter with a clean plate in front of me. I demolished my omelet, but my appetite for Baron is anything but satiated.

Every moment makes me want ten more.

I keep forgetting we are anything but two people who are getting to know each other. The fact that he's a football player doesn't even factor in.

Instead I'm finding out what it was like growing up with three siblings. We both grew up on acres of land, but my childhood was spent on my own with my nose in a book while Baron was playing capture the flag with his older brothers and younger sister. Part of me envies the camaraderie. I wonder sometimes if I would be more outgoing if I had grown up trying to find my voice among the cacophony.

But my mom always likes to remind me that introversion is part of my neurological makeup. Thanks, Mom.

Baron is sitting on the stool right next to me, swiveling back and forth. I don't think the man ever really stops. There's always motion. I wonder if falling asleep against him would feel like being rocked to sleep by waves.

I wonder a lot of things about him. I feel like I could fill the space from now until tomorrow morning entirely with questions.

"So, where are your parents now?" I ask.

Baron's smile drops. "My mom is still in the house I grew up in, but my dad passed away a while ago from a heart attack."

"Baron..." My voice is unsteady. I don't know what to say. I never know what to say when grief shows up to the party. We both stand awkwardly in our own corners, waiting for the other one to make the first move.

Baron reaches out and wraps his hand around mine, and I swear I feel every single blood cell stop and flutter in place, trying to soak in the feeling of his warm skin on mine.

He looks over at me, and I know he's trying to tell me it's okay. It's okay to not know what to say. It's okay to not know how to comfort someone. Just be here; that's all he needs.

"Come on, I have something I want to show you." Baron slides off the stool and walks around to stand just in front of me, never letting go of my hand.

My lungs fail to move even a centimeter when I look him in the eye. I want to go everywhere with this man, and that feeling is exquisitely overwhelming. "Okay." It's all I can manage right now, but those two syllables are all Baron needs from me.

I slip off the stool, and he leads me over to a set of floating stairs tucked against the far edge of the room. I wonder if he's taking me to his bedroom. I wouldn't say no.

We make it to the landing and there is a set of sliding doors just to our left. Baron opens them, and for a split second, I'm disappointed. Then I see the view, and I know this is even better.

Every step draws us farther out onto the roof deck and into the inky darkness of the night. There's some traffic in the background, but it's a lovely hum. I've always been fascinated by cities; it's like their pulse lives outside their body, breathing for everyone to hear.

"This is amazing. That doesn't even… Can I just come live on this roof? I'll bring a hammock. It'll be like urban camping." I'm pretty sure I could spend ten thousand hours up here taking photos and never quite capture how amazing it really is.

Baron lets out a deep laugh, and I'm keenly aware that our hands are laced together. "It gets even better."

He pulls me around the corner, and there is a massive sectional couch that wraps around a table. Yeah, this is pretty nice.

He lets go of my hand, walks over to the table, leans down, and flips a switch. A bright blue flame erupts in the center of the table. *Oh. Yeah.* This really is better.

"Wine or beer?" he asks as he heads to the bar counter just behind us.

"Beer." I walk over to the couch and sit down. This rooftop deck puts my little crawl-out-the-window-and-sit-on-shingles view to shame, and I am one hundred percent completely okay with that.

"Here you go." Baron reaches over and hands me a can of wheat beer. I take a sip and close my eyes. I'm pretty happy with my life choices right now. I thought I would be going through photos and having a rousing evening of leftovers and Netflix.

Instead, I'm sitting on a rooftop in the middle of a big city, having beer with one of the most eligible men in the state—hell, probably the country. There are a lot of football-loving women out there. I bet they would stab my eyeballs out if they knew where I was, who I was with, and how much I don't love the sport he plays.

It's kind of like when the under-five-foot-tall girl ends up with the guy who's well over six feet—I mean, come on, couldn't you have fallen for one your own size?

He takes a long pull of beer, and I notice that his hands nearly cover the whole can. I'm sitting next to a giant with the largest hands I've ever seen. They could explore half of my body in the time it takes to unhook a bra.

"Whatcha thinkin' about?" Baron asks as he sits down next to me. There's a foot of space between us, but I feel magnetically drawn to him. I wouldn't be surprised if my body automatically closed the distance without even trying.

What am I thinking about? *Umm...*

"Just that you're the size of a Viking. I normally feel like a tree standing next to everyone else, but when I'm around you, I feel like a pixie."

"You *are* a pixie. I could lift you with one arm."

Why do I want to dare him to try?

A drum of thunder rolls in the distance, interrupting my thoughts. I take a deep breath. I love the smell in the air when it's going to rain. It's like sticking your head into a plate of moss, earthy and green and permanently damp.

"There's a storm coming..." My words trail off. There's more than one storm brewing here.

A second clap hits, followed by a shot of lightning. They're still really far out in the distance, but I am acutely aware of the fact that I didn't bring a second set of clothes. If these get soaking wet, they're coming off, and there is nothing to go back on in their place.

"Well..." Baron stands up, and I do the same. "I can, um, take you home now, if you want." The way he says it, I know he doesn't care to get back in his car any more than I care to step off of this rooftop deck. He's being a gentleman, and that makes me want to stay all the more.

I look up and catch his eyes with mine. "I don't really need to go home."

And I don't want to either.

I see him swallow. He reaches down and grabs my beer, setting both of our cans on the table. He straightens back up, and I think the earth has stopped moving. Everything is suspended in time, the moment happening while the rest of the world stands still.

"I need to kiss you, Montgomery Bell."

"You need to?"

"I don't think I'm going to be able to think straight until I do."

"Well, I'm not stopping you," I say with the hint of a smile.

"Not stopping and inviting are two very, very different things."

I take a step toward him and press my body to his. It feels like that gratifying snap of the cardboard when two puzzle pieces interlock.

"Okay, then kiss me." I breathe in the adventure and let it travel through my bloodstream.

Baron doesn't reply; he doesn't need to. He runs his palm along the curve of my cheek, sending each finger around the rim of my ear. My skin tingles at his touch, but it's the anticipation of what's to come that is sending my heartbeat into an upward spiral.

He leans down to me, stopping with just a whisper of space between our lips. I can feel his heart beating heavily against my palms, as if it's trying to break free of its cage.

And then he presses his lips to mine. The universe slams back into motion, swirling around us like a supernova. I feel like I'm being drawn into a black hole, as if I'm being pushed together and pulled apart at the same time.

I wonder if I'll make it out alive.

I reach my hands up toward the hair at the base of Baron's neck and pull myself even closer to him.

And then the rain starts. I feel a bead of water hit my arm, and then another.

Baron lifts his head up, but his eyes stay shut for an extra second, like he's savoring a sip of aged whiskey, drunk on its earthy flavor. They should put a warning label on kisses like that. *Caution: do not operate heavy machinery after consuming.* I'm wobbly, and I'm pretty sure I only drank a quarter of my beer.

The droplets continue to fall slowly, and a warm breeze is gently crawling along the rooftop.

"We should probably go in." Baron's voice is raspy.

"What if we didn't?" I don't want this to end, and I know walking back into the sharp light of the apartment will break the magic of the moment. Besides, a little rain never hurt anyone.

"We might get a little wet." There's a twinkle in Baron's eye. I know he's found the page I'm on, and he likes where the story is going.

I lift my shoulders and tilt my head as if to say *So what?* So what if we get a little wet? So what if I kiss the person I never thought I would spend more than five minutes with? So what if life isn't conforming to my exact expectations?

I like where it's headed, and isn't that what adventure is all about?

Baron leans forward and spreads his palms against my lower back as he lifts me up toward him. As soon as our bodies connect, my legs instinctively wrap around his torso. This man is more rock than bear. There's no outer fur hiding the pure muscle beneath. It's right there, ready to be studied, piece by glorious piece.

My head is level with his, and I take a second to look at him. When I look into his eyes, I see an honest man. There's a transparency there, like you're staring into the clearest ocean you've ever seen. There's nothing muddy or murky lingering anywhere close, and the realization hits me: he's not going to dick around with me like some asshole from high school.

I lean in and press my mouth to his, this time with a force that rivals the brewing storm. I want to taste him and experience him like he might not be here tomorrow.

Baron moves his hands up to wrap around my waist, and he walks us over to a wide lounger near the glass rail of the deck. I'm aware of the view on the edge of my periphery, just as I'm aware of the tiny drops of water that continue to bead against my skin. I'm aware of all that, but my focus is on the man in front of me as he lowers me and leans down on top of me.

He traces the edge of my top with such a light touch, I wouldn't know if it was him or a feather if I couldn't see him. My skin dances underneath the line he's drawing, and every other square inch is crying out to be next. His hand slips underneath my shirt and grazes up toward the outline of my bra. When he finds it, he follows the trail back toward the hooks, which he flicks open like the lock on his front door—it's so natural, he doesn't even need to think.

I try not to think about how he got so good at that. This is why I didn't Google him. My mind is blank, no images of ex-girlfriends for my brain to pull up.

I grab the collar of his shirt and draw him in close, trying to crush my thoughts with the pressure of his kiss. I have to discover every inch of this man. I reach for the hem of his shirt, taking a quick detour around the button of his shorts; I open my eyes just in time to see his roll back in pleasure.

I almost forget what I'm doing, but my fingers are on autopilot. They grab the bottom of his shirt and lift up. He sits up and helps me peel his shirt off.

My jaw drops. Baron must secretly be a Greek god. I mean, mere mortals are not allowed to have bodies that look like they're carved out of marble.

Or maybe he's a vampire. But he didn't sparkle in sunlight though or burst into flames. So, I think I'm just going to have to accept the fact that this pure marble rock kneeling in front of me is real life.

And real life is looking damn good.

"What?" Baron cocks his head to the side and squints at me.

"Oh, you know, just marveling at the statue in front of me. Shouldn't you be in a museum somewhere?"

"They let me out for special occasions."

And that is why I can't help myself around him.

My whole world is spinning, and the only thing that's keeping me from falling over is the touch of a man I didn't see coming.

A man who makes me laugh and whimper all at the same time.

"You know, it's a little chilly. I think I need some skin-to-skin contact in order to stay warm." His words are teasing, but his voice is pure appeal. I'd run around the rooftop naked if he asked me to right now.

I happily oblige him, grabbing the hem of my shirt and catching the band of my bra on the way up. In one satisfying swoop, we are both half naked. The rain is tiny little licks of cold against my skin. I pull Baron on top of me like a human shield, and by the smile on his face, I don't think he minds one bit.

He leans in to kiss me, and the lights and rain fade into the background again. My focus is centered in on the man I can't seem to get enough of.

As if on cue, lightning breaks the sky open and illuminates the night like a match ripped across sandpaper. Baron and I break apart just as a crash of thunder rattles the very furniture we're perched on.

Baron groans, and I know what's coming next. "We really should go in."

I let out a long sigh, but I quietly agree. This adventure is over, but now that I've gotten a taste, I'm only going to continue to crave it.

We untangle our limbs, and just as we're standing up, the bottoms fall out of the clouds. A sheet of water comes crashing down on us as we grab our clothes and run to the door.

Baron gets there first and opens it for me. I'm holding my shirt to my bare chest with an unrestrained grin stretching wide across my face. He closes the door, and I lose it.

Laughter pours out of me like the water that just drenched us.

He closes the door behind us. "I don't know if I should ask but…what's so funny?"

I start to hiccup, and it only fuels my laughter more. Baron laughs too, even though he has no idea if the joke is on him.

Finally regaining control of my lungs, I gasp. "That. Was. So. Much. Fun."

Baron shakes his head but continues to smile along with me.

I don't know exactly how to explain. "We barely know each other, and you're not my normal type, but tonight was the best night I've had in…I don't know…"

"Forever?" Baron asks, and the way his eyes narrow as they search mine, I know he feels the same way.

I'm not scared to admit it.

"Yeah."

This is the best night I've had, period.

"Me too."

He grabs my hand and presses his lips to my temple. I have no idea where this is going, but damn do I want to find out.

Chapter 8

I step out of the shower in the guest suite and pull one of the softest white towels I've ever seen outside a Crate and Barrel toward me.

I kept waiting for Baron to barge through the door butt naked and join me in the shower, but he was a no-show. I should be disappointed; instead, I'm kind of relieved.

I still can't believe we just made out on his rooftop in the middle of a thunderstorm. I feel like I need a moment and about ten thousand deep breaths to recover.

I said yes to adventure, and adventure gave me one hell of a fist bump in return. When I'm with him, I get swept up in it. He takes up the whole frame. When I step back and see the bigger picture, it startles me.

He's a football player, and I swore I would never make the same mistake again.

But here I am, and even though it's nothing like that night in high school when I stood outside the field house like a complete sucker, there's a part of me that worries we're two completely different people who just happened to show up at the same place at the same time.

I know timing is supposed to be everything, but how do you keep the good timing going when you're on two completely different trajectories?

The thing is, I don't even know what my path forward is. It could be staying in Ann Arbor at my job for another year. It could be quitting my job tomorrow and traveling the world with Collins Aid United. Or it could be one of the million other paths hiding in the shadows right now, just waiting for the sun to shine in their direction.

I wipe my palm across the foggy mirror, which only gives me an incomplete glimpse of my post-make out, post-shower look. Even with a layer of steam between the mirror and me, I can tell it's not my best—not my worst, but not my best.

I start to open the handful of drawers in the reclaimed wood vanity. Hmm, a bunch of unopened travel-size items. There's a wide-tooth comb in the back—score. My tangled waves are thanking me already. Behind the comb, pushed toward the back, is an old tube of mascara. From an ex? Or maybe his sister? I'm going to go with the latter. Just because I don't have names and faces doesn't mean I like the blurry picture of girlfriends past any better.

I pull out the wand and sniff it...though I have no idea what I'm smelling for. Does mascara go bad? It looks a little dry, but not unusable. I lean over toward the mirror and go for it with a couple swipes.

I'm definitely going to bed with this on, like one of those scenes in a movie where the woman wakes up in full makeup. When you're spending the night for the first time, you say *Sorry kid* to your skin and go for it.

I may have let Baron get to second base, but that doesn't mean I'm ready to go au natural yet. Give me a few dates and maybe a beer, and then we'll see.

I walk out to the guest bed in my towel and see that Baron left me an old t-shirt and a pair of sweatpants. He is quickly moving up on my list of favorite people. I pull the soft cotton against my skin. You know these clothes have been washed hundreds of times; they're thin and silky in a way only well-loved clothes can be.

There's a strong possibility I'm going to steal these and never give them back. I wouldn't even sell them on eBay, though I'm sure they would net me more than a few months' rent.

People are crazy, but I'm not about to cash in on that.

I open the door and step back out into the open air of the main living area. I don't see Baron, and I wonder if he's taking a shower himself.

I think about walking toward the master bedroom to find out, but I chicken out. I may have initiated this evening, but I'm not ballsy enough to take it that far.

Instead, I eye the weathered leather of the massive sectional and head over to sink into the deep cushions that could swallow smaller people whole. It's my kind of couch.

I almost sit down but stop when I notice a blanket covering a large lump—a large *snoring* lump. I giggle to myself. Why is my first instinct to draw on his face with permanent marker? Maybe a well-placed *I love unicorns*.

I wonder if he has any glitter glue lying around to make it really fancy. *Eh, probably not.* I give up on my half-hatched plan and sit down. In my exhausted state, this couch is too alluring to avoid any longer, even for plans of mischief.

I slowly sit down next to Baron's head, careful not to jostle him. I want some uninterrupted time to stare at his profile. Damn, it really is even better in person than it is on my computer screen. A camera can't quite capture the perfect line of stubble that runs along his cheek. High definition gives you the clarity, but 3D gives it the oomph. And when he smiles…it's over. The way his cheeks crease, it's like he's spent his whole life looking for the laughter in life, and that's even sexier than the five-o'clock shadow he wears so

79

well.

"Got a good view there?" I jump at the sound of Baron's voice. His eyes are still closed, but a smile is spreading across his lips.

"Were you asleep, or just testing me?"

"A little of both." He opens his eyes and sits up.

I have the strong urge to wiggle myself into the sliver of space next to his torso, but it feels too intimate to even attempt. Sure, you can see me half naked, but unabashed cuddling is the stuff couples are made of.

Baron yawns and blinks his eyes slowly. I think there was more sleeping than there was testing. "Sorry. I woke up early to get a training session in. Do you mind crashing here tonight?"

Something tells me it's more about avoiding an hour-long round trip on the road than getting some nooky, and I'm kind of okay with that.

"Sure. I'm pretty exhausted too." A day full of turn-your-life-upside-down experiences does that to a girl.

Baron stands up from the couch and reaches out a hand to me. I wonder if he's expecting us to go to bed together. *Crap.* I hadn't thought about that when I said yes. Cuddling with him sounds amazing, but it crosses the invisible line in my brain. Even though I know I'm toeing it, I'm not quite ready to jump over with both feet.

He pulls me in and wraps his arms around me, and I feel like someone just wrapped a warm blanket over a sky of exploding fireworks. *Oh hey there, line, we're getting to know each other really well tonight.*

He leans toward me, and I close my eyes in anticipation of his kiss…but I feel his lips hit my forehead instead. I open my eyes and see his eyes softly shut and then blink open.

How is this man, this bear of a man, so sweet?

I hum to myself. Being wrapped up in his arms with his lips to that wedge of space between my eyebrows…it isn't what I expected.

It's even better.

Baron pulls back, just enough to catch my eyes. "I want you to know that I want to take you to bed with me. I want to have you, all of you, but I also want you to know that I'm interested in you, not just in getting laid. So, I think we should sleep in separate beds tonight, because if I'm next to you...I'm not going to be able to keep my hands off you. Not for a second."

I agree with him, but that doesn't stop my body from feeling like someone just stopped the Ferris wheel before we made it up to the top. The ride's not over, but I still want to yell at the attendant to hurry up and get us moving again already.

"You're right. Space is good." The words come out like I'm trying to convince myself.

"I wouldn't say it's *good*." He doesn't take his eyes off my lips, and I can't help but bite them as I think about how good it felt to kiss him, as if my world started and stopped with every taste. "But I don't want to rush this. You're worth every single second. It won't kill us to take it slow."

"Are you sure?"

"Nope." He shakes his head with a small laugh.

I wiggle myself out of his arms and sigh dramatically. "If I die tonight, it was nice knowing you."

"Just remember, if you die tonight, you'll miss tomorrow, and I'm going to make sure it's worth sticking around for."

"I guess I can try not to combust overnight." I reach up and kiss him on the cheek. "But damn, you make it hard."

He raises his eyebrows, and my eyes go wide for a split second as I take in the double meaning.

"I mean..." I fumble.

My enflamed cheeks only egg him on. "I can make it hard all night long."

I barely hold back a snort, but even though he's making me laugh, it's not cooling me down for a second. If anything, it's the complete opposite. "Don't tempt me," I warn playfully.

"I'm just trying to make sure you come back for me, that's all."

I don't think it's coming back that's the problem here. It's the walking away that's the real challenge.

I pull out my phone as I climb into the biggest, softest bed I've ever seen. This real-life, successful grownup business is pretty damn awesome. Now that I'm getting a taste of this side of life, I wonder if my measly little twin-sized bed is going to feel quite as comfortable.

When I press the home button, I notice I have a message from Andie.

> *Hey, just finished study group. I'm 2 doors down from ur place.*
> *Girl time?*

I pull the message to the side to check what time she texted. Hmm, fifteen minutes ago. She's probably waiting for my response. *Damn.* I quickly type a response.

> *Sorry, not home tonight. Hang out soon tho?*

I don't want to say too much. This is one hell of a situation to try to explain over text message. My phone buzzes again.

> *Parents?*

Ugh—so much for avoiding the topic. I debate just replying with a flat *Nope*, but I doubt that'll fly.

> *At Mr. Sportsball's apt*

I can almost hear her squeal from forty miles away. I see the trail of dots light up my screen immediately.

> *OMFG!!!! RU SERIOUS?!!?!?!*
> *Why ru txting me right now?!*
> *GO BANG THE HOTTIE*

Thank you, Andie Bertelli. I have my own personal sexytime cheerleader, just a text away. I would tell her we're in separate bedrooms, but that's a detail best saved for the in-person debrief I know is coming ASAP as a direct result of this breaking news.

I'll get right on it.

I wish I was getting right on it—literally—but Baron is right; it won't kill us to take this slow.

YOU GOT THIS!!

Love you!

Have THE BEST NIGHT EVER!

I laugh to myself. I don't think this many capital letters and exclamation points have been used since Andie texted me that she got into Michigan's medical school. It's one of the top ten in the country, and they're notoriously picky about accepting students who went there for undergrad too.

It's odd to be on the receiving end of the excitement. I haven't exactly been living a bustling life full of daring adventure and intrigue, but I think the tides might finally be changing. Today, I'm staying with a famous sports star. Tomorrow, I could be on my way to Haiti. Who knows?

The world keeps handing me surprises, and I'm not going to complain. I'm just going to keep showing up and seeing where it takes me.

Chapter 9

I wake up to the smell of coffee, and it takes me a full minute to process where I am. *Not my clothes...not my bed...definitely not my apartment.*

Memories of last night do a quick lap around my brain. *Ah, that's where I am.* I grab my phone: 10AM. I contemplate whether or not I should beg off and head home, or stick around and see what Baron's like the morning after.

Well, the morning after a very PG-rated sleepover. I hate this anxious flutter that's growing in my stomach. I don't know why people do one-night stands. I *hate* the next morning awkwardness, the *do I stay or do I go.* You tiptoe around the conversation. Neither wants to kick the other out, even though you're both wondering if the other one really wants to stay.

Okay, game plan: I should grab a cup of coffee and scope out the other member of this equation. Granted, just looking at Baron is visual kryptonite. I should probably make all my decisions while I'm not within visual proximity of him.

This train of thought is going nowhere without caffeine.

I walk out into the main living area, and the nutty aroma of fresh coffee overwhelms any other thoughts I was planning on having for the moment.

"Morning." Baron is leaning back against the counter in a soft blue t-shirt and jeans. His hair is still half wet from a morning shower, and I bet if I walked right up to him, I'd be able to smell the scent of his body wash.

"Hi." My answer is soft, uncaffeinated.

"I thought maybe we could go out for breakfast and then walk around the farmer's market." He smiles as if his plan to take over the world is working. I don't want to break it to him that I'm not quite as exciting as the whole world. Something tells me he wouldn't listen anyway.

"I'll say yes to anything so long as there's more of that around here somewhere." I point to his mug.

He laughs and walks into the small galley hallway that's just to the side of the kitchen. I follow him and see a counter tucked in there with a sink, some cupboards, and the largest silver contraption I've ever seen outside a coffee shop.

"Um, I think I might need to go back to school to get a degree on how to use that thing."

"You should see the manual. It was taller than this mug."

No one should put that much work between coffee and me in the mornings. I'll take my ten-dollar on/off switch machine any day.

"What do you like to drink?"

I'm tempted to ask for something ridiculous. *Double venti half pump caramel extra foam cappuccino.* I decide to take it easy—on Baron and on my taste buds. "Coffee and cream please."

"Coming right up."

Less than five minutes later, I'm sitting at the counter with the most delicious cup of coffee with warmed cream I've ever had. Okay, so maybe I can't knock this whole fancypants coffee machine thing.

85

I can't knock much of anything these days. Every time I try something new, it opens up a whole new world. I feel like someone's going to hand me a flying carpet pretty soon, and who am I to say no to an offer like that?

"I didn't even know this existed. I grew up less than thirty minutes away, and I've never been here." We decided to take advantage of the gorgeous morning and walk the two miles to the market. I imagined it would be a bunch of tents set up in a parking lot.

Nope. There is a full-on brick building that's been here for over a hundred years. Mind. Blown.

I can already see that the indoor area is crowded with vendors; their stands are overflowing outside. There are flowers and produce and trinkets. It's a good thing we walked, because my eyes and stomach would walk out with ten bags of things in a matter of minutes if I knew I had a car to transport them in.

"Come on, there's this fruit stand in the back that's amazing." Baron reaches for my hand and starts to walk me through the crowds.

I have no idea what he's talking about. There are berries right out front that look like they were dipped in paint, their color is so vibrant. I see watermelons that are at least twice the size of my head, but I let Baron lead me forward. The man knows his coffee; I'm guessing he knows his fruit vendors too.

He finally stops in front of a stand where an old man with a green apron wrapped around his tall, wispy figure is greeting people as they walk by.

When he sees Baron, his face lights up, displaying each well-earned crease around his cheeks and eyes. "Bear! I wondered if I'd see you today! I saved you the best peaches. Here, let me grab them for you."

He has me at peaches. He goes to a table in the back and reaches down to grab a carton of the most beautiful peaches I've ever seen. They're a perfect ombre from red to orange, the tiny fuzz softly diffusing the brightness.

The man hands the carton to Baron and notices me standing off to the side. "Who's this?" he asks with a wink.

I reach out my hand. "Hi, I'm Monty."

He wipes his hand off on his apron and stretches it out to welcome me. It looks like worn leather, creased and battered, but when I take it in my own, it surprises me with a soft warmth.

"It's nice to meet you, Monty. I'm Chevy."

"Good name in this city." My parents met in Montgomery, Alabama; I wonder if Chevy's parents worked at the car company.

Chevy winks at me again. "I tell 'em I'm the best model yet."

I bet he is. He has to be at least eighty, and he's here working the stand like he's still thirty years old. I hope I have half as much energy and enthusiasm when I'm his age.

Baron pulls out his wallet, and Chevy shakes his head. "Nope, you're going to take our team all the way this year, and I'm going to tell everyone it was the peaches."

Baron smiles but continues to pull a ten out of his wallet and presses it under the corner of the silver cash box near the back of the table.

"You never know."

"Have you seen this boy play?" Chevy asks me, standing just a touch taller. You'd swear Baron was his own son. "He's the fastest runner I've ever seen for someone his size."

"No, I haven't."

Baron laughs. "She's not much of a football fan, Chevy. I don't think she's going to be cheering on every game like you do."

Chevy gives me a long look, his eyebrows pulled in while he

takes in Baron's statement. Is he trying to find the critical flaw that causes me to be different than the millions of Americans who can handle sitting down for four hours to watch a bunch of men run around on a field? I hope he tells me if he finds it; I wouldn't mind knowing what makes me so different.

He looks over at Baron and pats him on the shoulder in approval. "That's good. You need someone to keep you on your toes, Bear. Someone who'll push you to be a good man, not just a good football player."

I feel my cheeks flush with heat. I don't know if it's because of Chevy's support or the fact that I've barely spent a whole day with the man standing next to me and we're talking about games that are months away from now.

Baron shakes his head. "Give me a chance to win her over first, Chevy."

Chevy chuckles. "Well, what are you standing around here for? Go show her the market." He adds in a mock whisper, "And buy her some flowers for goodness' sake."

Baron reaches out and shakes the man's hand again. "Thanks Chevy. It's good seeing you."

"You too. You too." Chevy turns to me. "You got yourself a keeper with this one. He's a good man, one of the best."

I swear I see a little bit of color touch Baron's cheeks. I turn to look Chevy in the eyes.

"Yes sir."

I don't doubt that he's right. I don't doubt it for a second.

One bouquet of flowers and three extraordinarily juicy peaches later, we're walking back to Baron's apartment. I have no idea what comes next, but if it's half as good as this morning, this will be one hell of a first full day together.

I've been thinking off and on about Chevy, about the city—hell, the state—full of people that support Baron. He is a good man, but he's also a good football player. Yet, he doesn't seem like the type of person who needs the approval of a cheering section in order to be satisfied in life. The football players I've met thought they were God's gift to the world. They were good at the thing people revere. They got off on being the game-day hero, even when they were villains off the field.

"So, why football?" I've avoided the topic, as if turning the light off on the subject would make me forget there's a giant elephant standing in the center of the room.

Baron hums to himself. I'm sure he's answered this question a million times in a million different interviews, but the way he's taking his time makes me think he's giving me the real answer— not some canned version that sounds good in an article.

"My two older brothers played all the sports. Hell, my sister did too. We didn't have a ton of money growing up, but we had a lot of land, so we were constantly outside, even in the winter." He laughs to himself, and I silently wish I could see the memory that is so clearly running through his head right now.

He reaches for my hand and threads his fingers together with mine, and for a second, I can almost feel the nostalgia mingle with the pure pleasure of being in this moment with him.

"My dad loved football," Baron continues. "He always wanted to be a football player growing up, but he blew out his knee when he was in high school. So did my brother, exact same injury. But, I was good at it, quick and big. I played in high school, and when colleges started showing interest, I played even harder. It was a way for me to go to school for free. So, I pushed myself, and once I started, I just never stopped. I did a bunch of work with my brother's knee doctor in order to avoid the same issues, and really, I just got lucky. I've had minor injuries here and there, but nothing major—not yet, at least."

The way he says it...as if it's inevitable. "Not yet?"

Baron shrugs. "I'm trading getting beat up on the field for lots of money. It's not something I can do forever."

"What do you want to do forever, then?"

Baron doesn't need to think; his answer is immediate.

"Buy a huge piece of land near my family in Ohio and build furniture."

"Furniture?"

"Yeah. I built all the tables and bookshelves in my condo. My bed, too. I like being out on the field playing ball, but using my hands to craft a piece of furniture is my own personal nirvana. I could do that for the rest of my life and be happy."

The way he talks about it, the way his face is illuminated with pure delight, I believe him. I can see it, and the image of Baron standing in a huge barn working with power tools is a damn fine image. Hell, he could charge admission just to let people watch him. The clientele would be ninety-nine percent women, and they would probably demand a shirtless option, but man, I'd pay more for that too.

"What about you?" Baron's voice interrupts my imaginary vignette of him, shirtless in a barn. *Yup, I'll be coming back to that one later.*

What about me? "Umm..." A flicker of images surface, but there's no clear way to describe them.

"You take pictures of adoptable pets and events for the newspaper...is that what you love to do? Or is it something else?"

Do I love that? "Not really. I mean, I love photography. I feel the most like me when I have a camera in front of my face, but what I'm doing right now isn't exactly the type of photography I really love."

"What kind of photography do you love?"

It's embarrassing to admit the kind I'd love to do is not at all what I'm doing right now.

"The kind that ends up in National Geographic. The kind that takes me to areas of the world most people will never see in their lifetime. The kind that stops people in the middle of a grocery store to pick up a magazine because the image on the front cover takes their breath away."

My brain shifts into overdrive like it always does when I start thinking about the kind of life I really want.

If I really want it, why am I not doing it?

"What's wrong?" His tone is kind, gentle—the complete opposite of the voice in my own head right now.

"Nothing."

"Your face lit up when you started talking about the kind of photography you love, and then all of a sudden it shifted to the biggest frown I've ever seen."

I sigh. "I just hate that I'm not doing what I want to be doing."

"Neither am I. Sometimes you have to do something you're good at for a while before you can do something you love."

I scrunch my face together like a mouse.

"That's not quite it."

"What is it then?"

I bite my lip. I know what it is, but I've never actually said it out loud. I close my eyes and let go.

"I'm scared of what I love. I'm scared to travel across the world and be away from my family and my best friend. I'm scared I'm not good enough to take photos that show up on the cover of magazines. I'm scared I'll get lost, or sold to a cartel somewhere. I'm scared I'm not strong enough to hack it in the middle of nowhere. I'm scared to show up and start doing what I think I love and then figure out it isn't as exciting or glamorous or wonderful as I've imagined it. I'm scared I won't love it when I start to live it."

Baron stops walking. He's silent for what feels like an eternity. He traces the triangle of freckles on my left shoulder, and his touch softens the sharp edges of my fear.

His hand stops moving, and he looks straight at me. His eyes convey the words before he even says them. "Even if you don't end up loving it, it'll be okay. It's okay to love something in theory and then find out you don't love it in real life. I thought I wanted to coach college football after I finished playing. You know what I figured out?"

He pauses. I don't have a guess, so I just shake my head.

"Coaching sucks." Baron laughs as he says it. "Or at least coaching anything above grade school does. You work a ton. Everyone is on your case about the result of the game, when all you really want to focus on is growing your players as individuals and as a team. You never get enough time with your own family, and half the time, the fans hate you."

"So, furniture, huh?"

He smiles. "Yup. Furniture doesn't have opinions on your ranking."

"Me and furniture both."

Baron interlaces his hand with mine again. "That's part of why I'm drawn to you. You're not interested in the version of me that shows up on the covers of magazines or in headlines about last week's game. You don't care about Bear, the football player. When you choose me, you're choosing the real me, the part people don't care about come Sunday night's game."

I wrinkle my nose. "Well, those people are silly. This part of you is better."

"You think so?" The way he asks makes me think he's been Bear Richards for so long, for so many people, he isn't confident that Baron Richards is good enough for public consumption.

"I know so." I turn in toward him, pressing myself into his chest. "I'd like you even if you lived in a shack and built furniture day in and day out."

Although, maybe it could be a shack with a really, really solid coffee-making setup.

Baron beams down at me. "Good, cause I like you. Photographer, adventurer, book-reading sports-hater." He leans down, brushes his lips against mine, and whispers, "I like you a lot."

A smile blooms on my face, spreading out toward my fingers and all the way down to my toes. I feel like a flower opening up toward the sun, and I like the way the warm light feels on my skin.

If this is adventure, I'll take it. I'll take it all.

Chapter 10

It only takes Baron six hours and twenty-three minutes to text me after dropping me off at my studio back in Ann Arbor.

> *I had a really nice time with you last night.*

Yeah, I'm pretty sure yesterday wasn't a first date. First dates are supposed to be awkward and uncomfortable, and instead of trying to figure out how to let Baron down gently, I'm already trying to figure out how I can see him again.

I get now why a girl leaves her sweater at a boy's house on purpose. It's not crazy; it's giving the universe a little nudge in the right direction.

I thank my lucky stars Baron is not a typical guy who waits three whole days to say something. I would have broken down after about twenty-four hours and done it myself.

That doesn't mean I can't act cool. I quickly type *Me too* and my phone whooshes it through the airwaves. I toss it onto my bed with feigned nonchalance.

But I can't seem to focus on a single thing in my apartment. Instead, I start to bounce like a kid waiting in line for the bathroom.

I can't stop thinking about him, and as much as I wanted to write him off for being a football player, he broke through every last strand of my resistance this weekend.

I want to spend time with him, and I'm pretty damn sure a flock of cheerleaders isn't going to show up at my door and laugh in my face for believing he wants that too.

He's real. This is real. And I have the butterflies to prove it.

My phone dings again and I race to grab it off of my comforter. Thank God no one can see me right now; I'm sure I look like an idiot.

I have to fly out tomorrow for a work thing this week. Can I see you when I get back?

My heart skips across the surface of my emotions and then drops. He wants to see me again! But, I have to wait.

I know there's some dating rulebook somewhere that says I need to say I'm busy, but a full week already feels like an eternity. I don't want to add more unnecessary waiting on to that timetable.

Sounds great.

I toss my phone back on my bed and do a little moonwalk around my apartment. Okay, so my Jackson skills aren't that good, but it's a solid knockoff.

I get to see Baron again, and I am going to spend every minute of the next week dreaming about that brown-haired, blue-eyed Greek god and how my body feels like it's taking a trip around the universe when he kisses me.

Hey calendar, are we there yet?

* * *

Baron texts me on Friday night, asking if he can pick me up the next afternoon for a date.

I don't even think twice. I just respond with a yes, and my

phone immediately dings back at me. He tells me to bring clothes that can get wet.

I check the forecast. It says partly cloudy, but with our track record, I wouldn't be surprised if we started a thunderstorm all by ourselves.

The minute I see his Prius pull up outside, I race out of my apartment and down the stairs. I should probably exercise more restraint, but it's been six whole days since I saw him last. We sent a few texts back and forth every day, but nothing is as good as seeing him in person.

I open the passenger door and slip in, taking a long sip of the man sitting in the driver's seat. Damn, he's refreshing. Nothing about him is overdone, from his cropped dark hair to his plain t-shirt and hiking shorts, but everything about him makes my heart start to race and my brain release happy chemicals. My body wants more of him. Right now. Preferably in the upright and locked position.

He leans over and his lips graze my cheek. "Hi, beautiful."

"Hi," I whisper back, leaving my eyes closed for a second longer than normal.

"You ready?"

"Depends on where we're going." It's a coy lie, and we both know it. More and more, I find myself willing to go anywhere with him.

He shifts the car into drive, and I can see the hint of a smile on his face. "The best part is not knowing."

I can't help but smile back. Yeah, I guess it is.

We don't go very far before we pull up to the parking lot of a place I would know even if my eyes were closed and I could only smell and hear it. We're at Kent Lake. I used to come here all the time growing up.

The sun is starting to peek through the clouds and the chill in the air is starting to soften. Even though the calendar says it's June, it always takes Michigan a second to catch up.

We rent a canoe and within fifteen minutes, we're out on the water. Every muscle in my body relaxes. Being near water is calming; being out *on* the water is pure bliss.

"Happy?" Baron asks.

"I don't think you could have picked a more perfect spot."

"Good." He smiles to himself, and I am thankful we have two glorious hours where we're stuck sitting across from each other. Dark sunglasses are suddenly the best invention in the entire world —I can stare at him with abandon for every single second of this canoe trip.

"I have to admit though," I say with a hint of teasing, "it's kind of freaky how well you pick out dates."

His eyebrows crease together. "What do you mean?"

"Well, I grew up going here." I motion toward the lake. "And that first night, you were going to take me Pinball Dave's, right?"

He nods his head.

"When I was younger, my parents and I used to go to the same pizza joint every Friday night. They had pinball and Pac-Man and Street Fighter. I saved all my quarters for those nights. How do you know me so well without knowing me at all?" It's uncanny.

"Lucky guess," he replies with a soft shrug. "That, and Googling the best date ideas in Michigan. Google is kind of like my wingman. I mean, it got me to that animal shelter. I feel like I owe it a drink or something."

What did people do before the Internet? Miss out on the best dates of their lives, apparently.

We are both so entranced in our conversation, we don't notice the massive tree limb reaching out from the shore, right in our path.

"Baron, watch out behind you!"

He turns around with an agility I'm sure has been honed since day one of his football career. He catches the branch without thinking, but our boat keeps moving forward, sending his center of gravity off-kilter.

I lift my paddle out of the water, but he still has a hold on his and it tips our boat to the side. For a second, I think if I just lean in the opposite direction, I can keep us upright. Then, I remember that I'm sitting in a boat with a professional football player—I am a pebble to his boulder.

He lets go of the paddle and the tree at the same time, but it's too late. We crash into the water, and the entire boat flips bottom-side-up.

Just as my head pops up above the water, I see Baron swimming toward me. A second later, he wraps his arm around my waist. His feet must touch the bottom because his legs are completely still.

I automatically wrap my legs around his waist, and I don't mind my body's natural instinct here. I feel every single wet inch of our bodies pressed against each other, and tipping our canoe over suddenly seems like the best idea of the day.

"Are you okay?" His eyes are wide even though there's water dripping down his face from his drenched hair.

"Yeah," I say with a laugh. "We just can't help but get soaking wet around each other."

Baron's eyes flash with heat for a second, and I realize what I just said. My brain is stuck on a single track around this man.

"Well, I wouldn't mind a repeat of the other night, but I think *they* might mind," Baron says with a nod of his head toward the shore. There's a beach not too far from our capsized location, and there are a couple families playing on the shore with their little kids.

Fine. I guess we won't corrupt any young minds here.

"Come on, I think there's a boat launch just over this way." I untangle myself from Baron's arms and swim until my feet touch the bottom.

We get the boat out of the water and carry it back to the rental return on our way to Baron's car. This is the second time I'm drenched and without a change of clothes, but at least I brought a towel. I pull it out of my bag and wrap it around myself. Even though the sun's out, the air still has a hint of bite, and I shiver involuntarily.

Baron walks over to me and pulls me into his chest, rubbing his hands up and down my back. I wish there were about three less layers between us right now, but I'm not going to say no to this physical contact. It's heating my body up from the inside out.

"We can climb inside, turn on the heat, and have an indoor picnic?" he suggests. The tone of his voice crackles just beneath the surface. I don't think either one of us wants a console stuck in between us, but my stomach rumbles loudly before I can suggest another option.

We get inside the car, and Baron pulls out a reusable grocery bag from the back. He starts to pull out about ten different cheeses, crackers, olives, hummus, and grapes.

Ohmygod. It looks amazing. "My stomach really likes hanging out with you." I look over and catch his crisp blue eyes. I feel as if I get lost at sea every time I look at him.

"It's not dinner," he reasons, "but I figure this is kind of like an appetizer. You know, in case we don't make it that far, that fast."

I like where his mind is at, and just as I contemplate ditching the appetizer course and going straight on to dessert, my brain screeches to a stop.

Wait. Dinner. *Crap.* Today's Saturday, which means it's dinner night with my parents, and I completely forgot to tell them I won't be able to make it.

I run through my options: don't call and risk them sending out a search party, or try to discreetly text my mom.

"So do we have dinner plans or are we winging it?" I ask, creating a conversational distraction. I unwrap the towel from around my shoulders and reach back to stuff it in my bag while feeling around for my phone. *Got it.*

"I have a few ideas, but we should get dry first," Baron says with the charm of a smile pulling at his eyes.

My skin tingles. I know exactly what kind of ideas he has and I want to explore everything his imagination has dreamed up, but first I need to make sure my face doesn't show up on the side of a milk carton anytime soon. I try to unlock my phone without looking, but my fingers aren't any more coordinated than my brain right now.

I click the home button again.

"Sorry, I didn't understand that," a robotic voice echoes in the car.

Shit buckets. I'm pretty sure I'm all dry now because my face is on fire.

Baron chuckles. "Trying to find an escape route with your phone already?"

My face only burns hotter. "God, no. I just…I was so excited about today, I forgot I had dinner with my parents tonight. I was trying to be sneaky about texting them, but apparently, I suck at covert operations."

"You don't have to cancel on your parents."

"No, really. We do this every week. It's no big deal."

Baron gives me the look I was expecting when I bashed football during our very first conversation. "Well, I'm not going to let you break your record. Besides, family time is sacred. I'll drive you there, and then I can come pick you up when you're done and we can have dessert."

I try to think through a way to call my mom and Jedi mind trick her into canceling dinner.

"Trust me, I'll make sure dessert is well worth it." Baron's smile is light, but his eyes are intense.

Damn, I don't think I'm going to win this one. *Fine.* "There better be some whipped cream involved."

He laughs to himself as he starts up the car. "Don't worry, I've got you covered."

I like the sound of that. I like the sound of that a lot.

Chapter 11

We pull up the long driveway up to my family's old farmhouse. Some families pass down jewelry or china settings; my family passes down a house. My great-great grandparents on my mom's side built it, and it's stayed in the family ever since.

Baron slows down and rolls down his window. I start to ask him what he's doing, but then I look over and see an arm waving at us from one of the massive flowerbeds that bookend each side of the driveway.

So much for making a quiet entrance.

My mom gets up and walks over to the car while peeling off her thick green gardening gloves. She's wearing an oversized sun hat, but even with the shade, her skin is kissed with freckles. She's in her fifties but still looks thirty-five; whenever I tell her that, she gives me a great big hug and tells me it bodes well for my future.

She reaches a hand out to the window and gives Baron a welcoming smile.

"Hi." She leans to the left and catches my eye. "Who's your date?"

Thanks, Mom.

"Umm, this is my friend, Baron." Is it okay that I just called him my friend? *Football player I met in a bar* doesn't fit, and it is way too early for any remotely romantic labels.

Baron jumps in to help my fumbling. "It's nice to meet you, Mrs. Bell. I was just dropping Monty off."

My mom crinkles her nose at the formal name. "Please, call me Elaine, and tell me you're staying for dinner."

I jump in before Baron can react. "Mommmmm." I draw out the word as if I'm sixteen and she won't let me have the keys to the car.

She raises her eyebrows at me. "What? We have plenty, and you can't let a boy drive you home and not feed the poor guy."

Baron laughs under his breath. He isn't looking at me, but I'm sure he can see me squirming out of the corner of his eye. It feels as if little spiders are crawling all over my skin, and I don't know whether to close my eyes and wish them away or to send my body into a full-blown shake attack to try to fling them off.

"It's okay. I need to get home anyway," he says casually.

My mom stops looking at me and shifts back to Baron with a pure mom face. "Do you have any plans tonight?"

He shakes his head. I want to yell, *You're walking into a trap!*

"Well, you do now. Pull up to the house and park. You're staying for dinner."

Yup. Baron, you just got mommed.

My parents are fascinated by the fact that Baron plays professional football—they've been asking him questions nearly nonstop about the rules and tactics. I zone out and focus on the smoked brisket my dad made instead. I love it when he makes barbecue in the summer. He spends all day slow-cooking the meat, and he makes three different homemade sauces to go with it: classic, mustard, and vinegar.

I look over and notice that Baron's barely been able to get through half of his plate. This is one of my dad's best briskets to date, so I'm pretty sure it isn't for lack of trying on Baron's part.

"Come on, you guys. Let the man eat." Baron looks over and gives me a small grin of thanks. I give him an apologetic smile in return. Sorry dude, you thought you were just driving a girl home; you didn't know you were going to have to explain the ins and outs of American football to two sports newbies.

I didn't even realize my parents cared about sports—it wasn't a topic of conversation growing up. I don't think I realized sports were a thing people did outside of recess until I was in third grade and somebody brought in a signed football from the Detroit team for show and tell.

I still didn't understand it was something you could get paid to do until well into middle school. I thought people still had jobs at desks in offices and then went to the stadium on the weekend and played because they were good at it and enjoyed doing it.

I know. I was strange. Everyone liked to point that out.

My mom's focus falls on me. "So, how did you two meet? Did the paper send you out to do sports coverage?"

I almost snort. Olive knows better than to ever send me out for a sports assignment. She tried that once, and all she got were blurry pictures of people running. I'm a photographer, but that doesn't mean I have any idea how to take pictures of people moving fast and doing something I don't remotely understand.

"No. We, uh, met at a bar." It's such a normal start to a meet-cute story. Two kids meet in a bar…and that's where it stops being normal. Two kids meet in a bar. One of them plays sports. One of them hates sports. The story should have ended there, but it kept going. It's still going.

I'm as surprised as anyone.

Baron finishes his bite and jumps in. "I was intrigued. Your daughter was reading a book in the middle of a loud sports bar."

I feel the need to defend my position. "They have the best wings, and I was meeting Andie there."

Baron smiles. "I had to talk to her."

"What book?" my mom asks—it's her professional obligation as a librarian.

"Oooh, *Hidden Bodies.* You'd like it. It's dark and twisted." My mom stands up and goes to the hutch behind the dining table to write down the name. There are sticky notes all over our house with her thoughts. She's a director for the local library system, so even though she's around books all day, she doesn't actually get paid to sit and read them. I'm constantly sending her new book recommendations.

This is my world. I look over at Baron and see him smiling. I've pulled back the curtain, and he likes what he sees.

Something vibrates against a chair, rattling the wood. Baron's hand darts to his jeans, and he pulls his phone out of his pocket. He looks down, and his eyebrows crease together.

"I'm sorry, but this is my agent. I need to step outside and take this." We all nod, and he quickly gets up and darts out the kitchen door. I hear it clank shut, and I wonder why his agent would be calling him in the middle of a weekend in the summer.

My dad leans back in his chair, resting his clasped hands against his chest. "He's a nice kid. Not what you'd expect from someone who has so much at such a young age. Must have a good family, good parents."

I want to reach out and hug both of them at the same time. I'm lucky to have both of my parents. I might have already traveled around the world twice over if they weren't so wonderful. Every time I think about leaving, it feels like getting out of the car in the winter just after the heat kicks in. There's a whole world out there to explore, but it just feels so nice to stay huddled up inside for a moment longer.

I stand up to start clearing the plates, and my mom joins me. We're on dishes duty since Dad cooked today.

"I know that look you got on your face when I invited him to stay, but I'm glad I pushed you both. He's a good man. I'm glad we got to meet him. It's nice to know you're spending your time with someone who's worthy of it."

It's not the first time I've heard that sentiment, but it feels even more meaningful coming from my mom. I set down the plates in my hand and wrap my arms around her with a squeeze. She's never judged who I spend my time with, but she did instill in me the idea that it's better to surround yourself with a few great ones rather than waste your energy trying to pile in the okay ones.

I've done pretty damn well for myself so far in life. I have a handful of extraordinary people in my life, including my parents. It looks like Baron is another one to add to the list.

When Baron walks back in, I can tell his phone conversation was draining. His hair is ruffled, like he's spent the last twenty minutes weaving his hands through it. There are tiny lines planted firmly between his eyebrows, like grooves of thought he's walking back and forth in.

He doesn't need the parental brigade to launch an investigation into his current state.

I give my mom another hug. "I think we better get going. Thanks for dinner."

My dad walks in and joins the goodbye. "It was nice to meet you, Baron. I hope we'll be seeing more of you again soon. You're welcome any time."

Baron smiles, but it looks as if it's taking significantly more effort to hold the corners of his mouth up now. "It was nice meeting you too, sir. That brisket was phenomenal."

My dad beams with pride. I don't think there's anything he loves more than feeding people and feeding them well, except maybe science. He can't ever really turn off his inner neurobiologist.

My mom shoves two huge containers of leftovers into my hands. "Good. You're going to be eating it for a week."

"Mommm," I say with a hint of whine. "You don't need to send us home with the whole pig."

Baron laughs. "I'll eat it if you don't."

My mom reaches up and gives him a hug. "I knew I liked you. Have a safe drive."

My dad follows up with a handshake that turns into a hug, and when he pulls away from Baron, his eyes are faintly wet, even though his smile looks full and effortless again. He doesn't have this anymore. I make a mental note to bring him back for another family dinner. I'll happily share, both my leftovers and my family.

We finally make it back out to his car and start to drive away from the house. We're both quiet, and when I look over, I notice that Baron's face is pinched in thought.

I would leave it. I should...but I'm starting to care about him, and when I start to care about people, I want to help carry whatever load they're hauling around on their shoulders.

"Are you okay?"

He nods wordlessly, but the movement is slow. It's as if he's trying to convince himself that his head is supposed to be moving up and down and not left to right.

I let him process, and we continue driving down the dirt road I grew up on. I've been down it a million times before, but it suddenly feels like new territory. He jerks the car to the right and pulls over into the empty lot of a corn stand that's closed up for the night. He shifts the car into park and turns in his seat to face me.

"That was my agent. Everything just went through. I'm getting traded."

I have a vague idea of what that means, but I feel like I need to be sure it is what I think it is. "To another team?"

"Yeah. A different team."

"In a different state." I realize as soon as the words run out of my mouth that I have no idea if states have more than one team. Is there some other professional football team in Michigan? Are states even allowed more than one team? It's a stupid question, but I'm at a loss here.

"Yeah." He stops and looks down at the center console. "Seattle."

Oh. My heart and stomach grab hold of each other and race off the cliff together like two suicidal maniacs. I feel weightless and heavy all at once.

"Seattle." I repeat the word, just in case I got it wrong. Baron nods, and I know I didn't. I wish I had.

I didn't even realize how many blocks we had stacked until the world beneath us shifted and every single one came tumbling down.

Chapter 12

Baron and I barely talk on the way home. We're both silently trying to process what just happened. I have a million questions. *Did you know about this? When do you have to move? Are we still going to talk?*

I could barely figure out where I stood on this whole not-a-relationship-but-spending-time-together situation. Throw a four-hour plane ride between us, and all I can do is throw my hands up in defeat.

Baron is completely silent. He grips the steering wheel with both hands the entire way back to Ann Arbor. I'm convinced there are going to be permanent indentations on the leather.

I can't even imagine what he's thinking about, how he feels. He's already a couple hours' drive away from his family; this will move him much farther away.

I get that. I so get that. I haven't taken off on my own adventures because I can't quite wrap my head around leaving the state I've spent my entire life in. It's my adult security blanket, and even though it desperately needs a spin cycle, I'm still clinging to it with everything I've got.

It's a relief when he finally pulls up to my building, and I'm relieved when he doesn't turn off the ignition. We both need time to process.

I step out and look back, completely unsure of what to say.

Baron leans down so he can see my face. It looks like every feature of his face is pulled toward the center in concentration. It really does make him look like a bear. "I'll, uh…call you."

"Yeah, don't worry about it." I want to let him off the hook. I don't want him to call just because he thinks he has to.

His concentration releases for a split second, and I see the Baron I sat in a canoe with this afternoon. "No, I'm really going to call you, as in this week."

"It's a date. A phone date."

"Good." It's such a simple word, but he packs it with meaning. "And I'm sorry about dessert."

"Another time," I offer with a small shrug, trying to downplay the emotions that are punching me in the gut. I didn't realize how much I wanted more until the possibility of it got pulled out from under me.

I say goodbye and head up to my apartment. I'm standing in the same place I was just a few hours ago, but everything's different.

I spend Monday in the office doing photo placement for the articles running that week, online and in the paper. There's still no news on the big changes that are coming, which makes it feel like my entire world is in limbo. I still haven't heard from Irene Collins, and I'm starting to think the worst. Maybe she did pass on my resume, and the HR director didn't like my application enough to even respond.

I can't bring myself to look at their website to see if they currently have photographer positions available. I don't want to know. Whoever said ignorance is bliss is my kind of person. I'd take them out for a beer and give them a high five if I could.

My phone buzzes, and I look down to see Baron's name flash across the screen. The man keeps his word.

I swipe right to answer. "Hi, can you hold on a sec?"

I quickly work my way through the nearly empty building to head outside. It's so close to five, and on gorgeous summer days like today, everyone tries to escape the office to catch the extra hours of sun. I don't blame them. The only reason I'm still here is to avoid thinking about the man I'm on the phone with now.

I step outside, and background traffic noise floods in. *Ah, that's better.* "Thanks. Hi. Um, how are you?"

Or, you know, are you still moving to Seattle? That too.

"I'm good. What are you up to right now?"

"Just finishing up work. Why?"

"Up for a short road trip tonight?"

I wonder for a split second if he's planning on kidnapping me and driving me out to Seattle—except that's anything but a short drive. Baron doesn't exactly seem like the kidnapping type, and I'm pretty sure most girls would go along with it willingly anyway, even if it involved riding in the trunk of his car.

"Monty?"

Oh, right. Road trip. "Sure. When do you want to leave?"

"Um, well, I just parked in Ann Arbor. I can wait until you're ready though." Well, I guess I'm escaping the office early today too.

"Do you know where the Ann Arbor Daily office is? I can grab my bag and meet you out front."

Baron confirms and ten minutes later, I'm sitting back in the passenger seat of his little blue Prius.

"So, where are we headed?" I'm half tempted to keep it a surprise, but the look on Baron's face is a complete 180 from when he dropped me off at my apartment. I have to know why he's so excited about this trip.

"Well, first, where any good road trip starts: food."

We pull into the gas station just outside the city, and Baron cajoles me into picking out my favorite junk foods: Doritos, Twix, and Vernors. My parents would always let me pick out one treat whenever we went on a road trip when I was younger. It feels oddly mischievous to grab all three today, even though I'm a fully independent adult with access to whatever junk food I want, whenever I want it.

I guess that's how you know you're really an adult. You could walk around eating Oreos and chips all day, but you suck it up and eat your vegetables because you know you'll feel a million times better if you get some carrots in your stomach.

We also grab some tacos from the drive-through one parking lot over, and I'm starting to seriously wonder about the length of this road trip.

When we get on the road, Baron lays down the ground rules. "Okay, passenger gets DJ privileges, but the driver has veto, but only three vetoes per hour. Singing participation earns one extra veto per hour."

"As in singing one song earns you an extra veto, or singing for the full hour earns a veto?"

"Good question, DJ Monty. One song."

I'm immediately determined to overpower him with all the late 90s, early 2000s music I can. *Oh hey, Backstreet Boys, nice to see you again.* I barely notice when we pass the *Welcome to Ohio* sign; I'm too busy laughing at Baron's interpretation of Britney Spears' hair flipping and boy band dance moves.

Two hours later, we pull into a parking lot, and Baron shifts the car into park. It's almost 8PM, and the sun is just starting to work its way down toward the horizon. I step out of the car and can smell the hint of moisture in the air. Are we by the water? I wasn't even paying attention.

Baron grabs my hand, and we start to walk toward a paved trail. I see a sign that says lighthouse, but the print is so small, I can barely read it. Hmm, we must be by Lake Erie.

We don't have to walk very far before my suspicion is confirmed. Waves crash against the flat slab rocks of the beach, and there's a bright white lighthouse with a red top like a little beret. There's something so romantic about it, like a steadfast love that's always beaming light out for its soul mate to come home. It's an oddly beautiful idea, the idea of lonely love. You're so sure of it that you never take your eyes off the water, no matter how long it takes for it to come back to you.

Baron sits down on one of the raised rocks and motions for me to come sit by him. I smile to myself; maybe I've found that. I won't know until I sit down and wait.

I squat down and swing my legs out and around, curling them into my chest and leaning my whole body into Baron's side. He wraps his arm around me, and we sit for I don't even know how long, just listening to the gentle waves lapping against the shore.

Baron is the first one to speak. I knew he would be. There's so much on his mind, and I desperately want to hear what it is before I come to any conclusions.

"My dad brought me here when I was a kid. It was one of the only times it was just him and me. I had just lost a football game. I missed a pass and the other team intercepted." He stops and shakes his head. Whether it's due to the memory or to the fact that I have no idea what he's talking about, I don't know.

He takes a deep breath. "I wanted to quit. I felt like I had let everyone down, and he brought me here and told me you don't ever let people down by trying. You let them down by giving up. He passed away a few weeks later from a heart attack. Every time I've had a big decision to make, I've driven back here. It's always felt like it's my direct link to the man that knew me better than I knew myself."

I lean into him with every fiber of my being. He's showing me a part of him the rest of the world doesn't get to see, and that feels monumental.

He rests his head against mine. "I wanted to bring you here with me. I wanted to immediately, right when I got that call… which is crazy. I know it's crazy, but I feel like you fit. You see the side of me no one takes the time to notice."

I know what he means, and when I turn to look up at him, I feel like I'm staring at the face of someone who is already imprinted on my heart. It *is* crazy, but I can't say I don't feel it.

"I want you to come with me, and I know that's insane. You don't have to answer me now. I just want you to think about it. I'm not asking you to move in with me, just come out to Seattle with me and spend a few months at least. I can find you a month-to-month studio to rent, or you can stay in my guest room. Whatever the details are, it doesn't matter."

My heart is swelling out and pushing against my lungs. Neither organ is able to function. Everything stops.

"I don't want to give up on us. I want to spend time with you. I want to see where this goes, and I know it's asking a lot of you. I'm hoping you see it as an adventure rather than just some crazy guy asking you to do an impossible thing."

It does sound impossible, but it also sounds crazy to say goodbye to him right now. I don't want to walk back to his car, have him drop me off, and never see him again.

And I'm not naive enough to assume that once football season starts back up, we would be able to continue seeing each other if we lived in different states. He wakes up at 5am in the off-season to push himself through workouts every day; I'm sure when he's in full-on go mode, it's a whole different level of commitment.

We sit and stare at the water, and the sky begins to take on a watercolor hue. The sun may be setting on today, but I have the option in my hands of whether it's going to rise on a life in Ann Arbor or a life in Seattle.

I take a deep breath, letting myself feel the warmth of Baron's profile against mine. "I can't say yes, but I can't say no either. This is a really big idea. A crazy one." I can feel his muscles pull tight underneath my touch. I draw my hand toward the center of his chest and stop, feeling his pulse race. "But, it's not completely insane. I keep talking about how I want to live a life of adventure, and what better adventure is there than the possibility of pursuing love?"

It feels crazy to say that out loud, and I blush at how easily the word love slipped out. I almost want to scoop it up and swallow it back down. I'm not in love with him, but I can't say I won't be someday. Every single hour I spend with him makes me want a hundred more, and isn't that how the seed is planted?

"I'll take it." I can feel Baron's smile as he presses his lips against my temple. We sit and watch the sun slide toward the horizon, and the lighthouse beams out into the indigo night, endlessly casting out hope that its soul mate will find their way home.

Chapter 13

I step out of the driver's seat of my car and head toward my parents' house. Andie gets out of the passenger seat and follows me.

Just before Andie started med school, her parents moved back to New York. All of her older siblings are spread out across the country, and her parents wanted to be back close to their extended family on the East Coast.

She's become a regular at our family dinners, and it's kind of the best having all my favorite people together in one room.

Well, all of them minus one. A hesitant but trending addition to the favorites list, Baron moved out to Seattle days after he got the call. Training camp had just started, so he needed to get there ASAP.

Andie and I walk in through the side door of the house that opens up into the kitchen. The sweetly spicy smell of my mom's chili tickles my nose. Oh, dinner is going to be so good.

Mom walks over to us and wraps us both in a giant group hug. "My girls! It's so good to see you, Andie!"

My dad walks into the kitchen and beams when he sees the two of us. "How's school going, Andie?"

I grab a cold can from the fridge while she tells him about her rotations. My dad the science guy is in heaven.

My mom works on mixing together ingredients for cornbread muffins, and I pop up onto the counter to watch.

"So, have you talked to Baron lately?" she asks while she stirs the ingredients together. I don't have to see her face to know her eyebrows are betraying any impartiality she thinks she has. She's mentioned him every week since he was here for dinner. She never presses too hard, but she always asks. He made an impression, and it was a good one.

"Yeah. We talked last night. He's coming home next weekend. His loft here is all packed up, and he just wants to make sure everything works out with the movers and getting it listed to sell."

My mom hums under her breath. "Well, you're more than welcome to bring him over for dinner. I understand that he'll be busy, but he is *invited*." There's emphasis on the last word. My parents mostly keep to themselves. We're a quiet family, and we're kind of like the libraries my mom oversees: there's a lot going on, but we don't go running around screaming about it.

She's implying that I am going to see him though, and even though he and I haven't directly talked about it, I realize it's true. It's just assumed that Baron and I are going to spend time together, and it finally hits me that I'm going to have to stop straddling the line. I need to pick up one foot and drag it over the border so I am firmly planted.

Yes, or no. I have to pick one.

"So, how's work going? How did the shoot at the concert go last week?" My mom pivots into an entirely new topic, but it does nothing to settle down the rhythm of my heartbeat.

We talk for the next twenty minutes about our jobs, but my mind is on next weekend the entire time.

I'm going to have to say yes or no. Stay or go.

If I haven't figured it out by now, how am I ever going to decide?

"Monty?" Andie's voice breaks through the deep gray fog of my thoughts.

"Yeah?"

She laughs, and I wonder what the joke is. "Can you pass the muffins?"

I pick up the bowl next to me and hand it over, confusion tucked into the creases of my frown. I've gotten away with being zoned out for the majority of dinner, but I can feel three sets of eyes glued on me now. The jig is up.

"Are you contemplating how to achieve world peace over there?" Andie asks with a teasing smile, and it snaps me back to reality.

"Yeah. I think it comes down to free doughnuts and easy access to romance novels."

I get a *Hear, hear* from my mom, and my dad just shakes his head.

"How's the romance section of Montgomery Bell's life doing these days?" Andie pries. She had to study on the way over tonight, so she's taking the opportunity to best friend me now.

I fidget with the ties of the seat cushion, unable to look her in the eyes. "Umm, I don't know, exactly. It's kind of at a crossroads."

My parents are silent, but I see them both cast a knowing glance at the other. I wish they would tell me what they know, because I feel like I'm staring at a massive decision and my pro and cons list is way too short.

"What kind of crossroads?" Andie asks as she leans in, resting her head in her hand like we're on a talk show and she's both intrigued and intent on extracting information from me.

I take a deep breath. I haven't mentioned Baron's proposal—*ugh, that makes it sound even more serious*—to anyone yet. I've barely been able to process it myself, let alone process other people's thoughts and feelings about it.

But, considering I'm potentially going to have to make a decision before I see them next, it seems kind of important to get an audience vote here.

"He asked me to move out to Seattle—not move in with him." It feels important to clarify, as if asking me to move somewhere for him but me still having my well-defined space is a key point. "Just move. And date. Like normal people. Or, I guess like one normal person and one person who has an entire country following him on the Sports Network news page."

Everyone nods together. Why the hell is everyone so calm about this? I was expecting something more than nodding. This feels like an exclamation point sort of thing, and all they're giving me is stupid little periods.

"Um, you guys, he asked me to move across the country."

"Sure," my dad says, like it's something a person does on any ol' day. *Oh hey, want to move with me to a state that you can't feasibly drive to in less than several days?*

"What do you mean, sure?" I need clarification on their nonchalance.

"You two haven't known each other for that long, but it seems reasonable that two people who like each other a great deal would want to be in the same city. I'm not surprised he asked you to go with him, especially given your flexibility with work."

"It's reasonable? I think it's kind of crazy." That's the problem I keep battling: the idea of moving across the country for a man I barely know seems absolutely insane.

"I think it's romantic," my mom chimes in.

"So do I." Andie piggybacks on the sentiment. "I vote yes."

"I'll cast my vote with Andie's," Dad announces with a twinkle in his eye. He loves having two daughters; I think he'd go along with just about anything we say.

I look at my mom, and her lips are drawn together in thought. She's not going to tell me her vote—I already know that. It's part of what makes her such an amazing mom. Ever since I was old enough to know the difference between stupid and just flat-out dangerous, she took a step back. She's still there in my periphery to jump in if I ask for it, but she doesn't try to steer me one way or the other.

I think it's been part of the reason I haven't been eager to leave. I *want* someone to tell me it's okay to step outside my comfort zone. I don't feel like I should be allowed to be an adult. Wasn't there supposed to be some skills test we had to take before we got handed our legal adult card? I took a driver's test, but that didn't do jack to help me understand how to steer my life.

And I'm in the driver's seat here.

My mom finally sighs, and it's an audible reminder that I need to breathe too. "You can't make the wrong choice here. You can go explore a new city and a new relationship, or you can stay and focus on building the wonderful life you have here. Either way, you're going to figure out what works and what doesn't work for you, and either way, if it doesn't fit, you can always fix it. It's not a permanent choice that locks you in forever."

Andie turns to my mom and raises her fist for a bump. "Nicely put, Elaine." My mom raises her fist to meet Andie's and gives her a small shrug, as if what she just said was the simplest thing in the world.

And it kind of is.

You stay or you go. It doesn't mean you have to keep going in the same direction forever. That's the beauty of adventure. You get to try out a new route and see if it works, and there's no shame in rerouting if you figure out it doesn't work for you.

It's even more beautiful if the risk you take pans out. You have to travel to the edge of the world to find your cliff, and when you do, if you time it right, you might just be in for the best sunset of your life.

After we leave my parents' house, Andie gets a text message about a grad student party in the house next door to her apartment building.

"You up for it?" she asks hesitantly. This is her kind of deal, not mine.

Even so, I wouldn't mind a bit more noise in my life to drown out the thoughts in my head. It's like a racquetball shooting across an echoing court in there: do I stay or do I go?

Do I stay or do I go?

"Yeah, let's do it."

Andie perks up. "Really? You sure?"

I nod. Besides, it's not like med school gives her a lot of time to be a normal single lady about town.

We pull into my parking spot, and I head upstairs to change into my most comfortable but still going-out-acceptable jersey dress. I make sure to tuck my Kindle into my purse.

You know, *just in case.*

By the time we get to the house party, the music is already up at least two notches higher than it should be. I have a feeling I'm not going to like this, but I try to keep an open mind.

We walk in the door and are greeted by the typical college house rented by boys, meaning it hasn't been cleaned since they moved in nine months ago. I could dye my dress black just by rolling around on the floor.

Yeah, my open mind just closed up shop. I am so done with the college boys scene.

Someone offers us red cups full of cheap beer, and I'm thankful this experience at least comes with an alcoholic buffer. I'm going to need some beer goggles before I can sit down on any surface in this house.

Andie scans the room. "Well, it's not a penthouse in Seattle, but at least my options are kind of cute."

I follow her line of sight and decide that her beer goggles must be better than mine. None of these guys compare to Baron, penthouse or not.

"You can do better."

"Don't worry, I'm not planning on taking any of these boys home to Mama Bertelli, but that doesn't mean I can't *take 'em home*." She adds a wiggle of her eyebrows to make sure I catch her meaning.

Oh Andie. I roll my eyes while I laugh under my breath. Andie is two parts ridiculous to one part fierce badass. She could walk up to any one of these boys and have them wrapped around her finger in a matter of minutes, but she wields her power wisely, which makes me love her even more.

My phone starts to buzz in my purse, and my hearts flips. I quickly grab it and see Baron's name.

Andie notices and nods toward the stairwell off to the side of the room. "There's a bathroom up there. Go chat with your sportsballer. I think I see a guy from my class."

I can tell she's lying, but I take her excuse anyway and head up toward the quiet of the second floor.

I still haven't figured out what I'm going to do, and Baron hasn't pushed me. He has called me though—every single day. We've spent hours on the phone with each other these past few weeks, and the distance has forced us to get to know the important things. He takes bacon on his pizza; I'm more a green peppers and sausage fan. We both agree that pie is the most magical dessert in existence, and that there's nothing quite like corn on the cob fresh from a farmer's stand in the middle of the summer.

It's the most utterly confusing non-relationship I've ever been in. I want to be the person Baron calls when he gets home from training, but I am so absolutely terrified of life outside our bubble.

I am not target material for a football player's girlfriend. I'm not the girl they pan the camera toward in the stands who's cheering her boy on and looking fierce while doing it, and I don't see how you can be in a relationship with someone and not support them. It's not like I can sit at home and edit photos while Baron has a game; even if he said it was okay, it wouldn't sit right with me.

Watching my parents all this time has taught me that you need to live and breathe two ideas: be loyal and be kind, always.

In Baron's case, that means showing up and supporting him, even if it's not my cup of tea. I just can't figure out if it's an over-steeped green tea I can swallow or a cup of pure piss I wouldn't touch in a million years.

I lock the bathroom door just as my phone stops buzzing. I hit redial and bite my lip while I wait.

Baron answers on the second ring. "Hey, I was just leaving you a voicemail. I'm glad I didn't miss you tonight."

"Me too. I'm just hanging out with Andie." *And wishing you were here.*

My feelings are bubbling up to the surface, and it's everything I can do to keep from saying too much, too fast. I like this guy. I like him a lot. But, I worry about getting pulled into the whirlwind—I don't know if it will lift me up or rip me to pieces.

"Tonight was family dinner, right?" he asks. It kills me that he remembers the details.

"Yeah. It was nice." I debate telling him they asked about him. "How was your day?"

"Just some extra training and hanging out with some of my new teammates. It's different out here, more intense. It's good to hear your voice, helps balance it out."

I close my eyes and sink back against the door. "Ditto."

"Next weekend…" I can hear the tempered optimism in his voice.

I get to see him next weekend, but it's up to me whether I get to see him every day after that or not.

Someone bangs on the door. "Hey, you done yet?" a female voice barks from the other side.

I cover the microphone with my hand. "Yeah, one second." I move my hand. "Sorry, I need to get going."

"Sure, no problem. I'll call you tomorrow. Have a great time with Andie."

We hang up, and I feel as if I just chugged a glass of water and my body is still screaming out for more. I can't get enough of him. Five minutes isn't enough time.

Five hours isn't enough.

Hell, I don't know if there even is a point where I will be satiated with him. I feel as if I'm always going to crave more.

I have no idea if I can move out to Seattle and be the perfect girlfriend, but I know I can't stay here and be happy knowing there's someone out there that I can't get enough of.

And that he feels the same way about me.

I unlock the bathroom door and slip out past the girl waiting for her turn. I start back toward the stairway, but an arm reaches out and blocks me.

"Whoa, where you going, hottie?"

I turn to face the guy blocking my path, and he's exactly what I would have guessed: a popped collar jerk wearing reflective sunglasses like he's trying to give us a soundtrack to his night.

"Downstairs to meet my friend." I don't owe him an explanation, but it's an automatic reflex.

"What? Stay up here. I can be your friend."

Charming. "Really, I need to get back downstairs. She's waiting for me."

I start to duck under his arm, and he shifts to stand in my way. "Come on, I know you want me."

Wow. Sometimes I forget how far college guys can wedge their heads up their asses.

"Not a chance," I say with a tight smile. In what universe do jerks think this actually works?

I see Andie at the bottom of the steps, and she must recognize my barbed edges because her eyes narrow in on this idiot before she even makes it to the top.

"Excuse me, you're going to need to step away from my best friend and take yourself back to the cave you came from," Andie warns as she pushes him to the side and reaches out to grab my arm.

Mr. Sunglasses stands there for a second. "Whatever, you're not that hot anyway."

Andie stops mid-step and starts to turn around.

"Stop," I whisper. "He's not worth it."

"Oh, I think the entire female population would thank me if I kneed him in the balls right now."

"He's still going to be an asshole, balls intact or not." I slide past Andie on the stairs and keep moving back toward the main floor, hoping she'll follow me.

"Well, at least I could potentially stop him from procreating."

I turn around and see him trying the same exact move on the girl who used the bathroom after me. "Trust me, I think he's got that covered all by himself."

We slip back into the party. Andie tries to introduce me to a few of her classmates that showed up while I was talking to Baron, but my mind zones out after I catch their names.

Everything about this makes me miss Baron. He's so far past this phase of life. He doesn't need the approval of some girl who's hit the bottom of her red cup.

Frankly, I don't think Baron needs anyone's approval.

My stomach flips, and it's not from the alcohol. I hate that football is pulling him away from me.

You can do something about it. You can say yes. That tiny voice in my head is getting louder every single day.

I keep coming back to the list of pros and cons, and the logic behind why I should stay in Michigan keeps getting fuzzier while the reasons I should move to Seattle keep getting clearer.

I want to go, and I'm finally realizing there's nothing stopping me but my own damn fear.

Chapter 14

I walk into the office on Monday, and I can smell the change in the air before I even get to the bank of desks reserved for freelancers. It's crackling with heat, even though the A/C is on full blast.

I peel off my cardigan and head in for my regular 9:30 with Olive.

There are three mugs of tea already on her desk when I sit down, and I wonder how long she's been here this morning. I don't actually know what time she normally gets to the office, but I'm pretty sure it's not three mugs worth.

My butt hasn't even touched the chair before Olive starts. "So, there are some changes happening to the Daily." Her voice reminds me of those bad robotic voices that were so popular in the late nineties.

I desperately want to skip to the meat of the conversation. I want to know if I'm getting a plate of bacon or a plate of Spam, but I feel bad for Olive. It doesn't take three mugs to tell me she's already had this conversation, and she's going to have it again and again. So, I just nod politely.

"We've been bought by American Free Media." You don't have to work in publishing to know that name. AFM is one of the largest media conglomerates in the country, and the free part of their name is wildly inaccurate. Their business model is all about monetization and turning profit, making more with less.

I know where this conversation is going without having to hear another word. "They're not keeping us on." Maybe they'll keep the Olives of this company, the managers who know how to keep it running, but they're not going to keep the long list of freelancers, certainly not the photographers. They'd rather grab stock images from a site they own and run it with headlines that grab your attention but make you climb through ten levels of ad hell before getting anywhere close to the actual content.

Olive sighs. "Yeah." Her voice has lost its metallic edge, softening to show her exhaustion.

"And because we're freelancers, there's no contract, so no severance or layoff package." I should be upset. I should be livid right now at the injustice of corporate America being complete and utter dicks, but I can't muster the enthusiasm. I feel bad for Olive. I feel bad for my coworkers who have bills to pay. I even feel bad for the ones that have to stick around. The Ann Arbor Daily was still home to the journalism we all studied and revered, the kind we looked up to when we first fell in love with the field.

There's no way AFM is going to let that kind of anti-sensational, unbiased work stand. Hell no. That doesn't stop people while they're scrolling through their Facebook feed. Hell, it doesn't even show up on their Facebook feed because the vast majority of people don't share it. I mean, it doesn't even have a top ten list.

"We'll pay for the photos we've already asked for, but beyond that, no." Olive runs her fingers along the edge of her notepad without looking up.

"Okay." I don't know what else to say. It seems pretty cut and dry. My job is gone, and there aren't a lot of legal loopholes for either party to get lost in on the way from employed to unemployed.

"I'm happy to be a reference for you." Olive stops staring down and looks me in the eye. "You've been an outstanding asset, both as a photographer and as a colleague."

I mumble a *thank you* and start to stand up. I have the sudden urge to hug her—this might be the last time I ever step foot in this office—but Olive doesn't really seem like the hugging sort. I reach out my hand like an awkward end to a first date.

First and last date, apparently.

She stands up and shakes it. That's it then.

I am unemployed. There's a whole swamp of emotions I should be drawing from. Instead, I want to skip out of the building, but I hold back. It's kind of like wearing neon floral to a funeral—it's a statement, and not the kind you want to make.

I'm going to move to Seattle. I knew it before I even walked in the door. I knew it when I left that party Saturday night. I felt the tectonic shift of my bones in that direction. They were on their way, even if my brain was working to catch up.

But the past half hour? It's as if the universe is saying *Nice job, Monty, I approve of your life choices.*

Now, I'm going to walk out of this office building and go straight home to message every single human under the sun I know that might have a job lead.

It's funny how that happens. When you stand still, the world whips around you like you're standing in the middle of a tornado. You have no idea which way to turn. Everything is a kicked-up, dusty mess whirling about. When you finally step forward, when you finally make the decision to move, you see there's a path right in front of you. And oh hey, your favorite flowers are growing up ahead, and no shit, there's totally a rainbow just beyond that. *Ohmygod, double rainbow? What?*

The universe rewards taking action, and that's what I'm finally doing.

I'm finally moving forward, and it feels damn good.

Somewhere between Main Street and State Street, I have the grand idea that I should wait to tell Baron. The image of surprising him with my packed boxes on Saturday morning is already a sepia-toned GIF in my brain.

That thought carries me through fourteen hours of packing and emailing about potential jobs, but as soon as I see his name flash on the screen of my phone, I know I can't hold it in.

I swipe right and press the phone to my ear. "I'm moving to Seattle!" I shout.

There is stunned silence on the other end.

"Baron?" *Wait, did he butt dial me?*

"Yeah. I'm here, just shell-shocked…and excited. Holy shit, you're moving out here?"

"Yes!" My life is an exclamation mark right now: upright and full of energy.

"I can't believe it. I hoped you'd say yes, but I kept my mouth shut. I didn't want to push you…"

"Well, I'm saying yes. I already found some free boxes on Craigslist, and I am drowning in a sea of piles."

"Monty. You're moving here." The pure happiness in his voice as he processes the news makes my heart race.

This is the right decision. I'm moving forward, and everything in my view is like a picture-perfect sunrise.

"I get to see you in five days." He sounds like a little kid before Christmas. "And then I get to take you home with me."

"If I ever finishing packing. I've been at it all day, and I don't know how I'm going to get it all done."

"Packing sucks."

"You should have told me that before I said yes."

Baron laughs. "I'm not an idiot."

"Of course not. You snagged me."

"Yeah. Yeah, I did." I hear him take a deep breath. "Monty, I can't wait to have you here. I want you in my life, and I'm really glad I don't have to let you go."

I wish I could curl up into him and kiss him right now. "Me too."

In five days, I can, and I won't have to stop.

Everything is packed. My life fits neatly into thirty-four boxes and two suitcases. I thought it would be harder. When I left the office on Monday, my excitement was quickly tempered by a swift get-shit-done mode.

End lease. Mourn the loss of a chunk of your savings for breaking said lease. Pack things. Go spend three hours with Andie while she studies. Don't talk to her, just be in her presence and try to soak in as much wonderful BFFness as you can through osmosis. See parents. Try to not bawl your eyes out.

Andie's sitting outside on the front concrete steps of her apartment building with me, waiting for Baron to drive up. My legs are bouncing wildly, but I don't want to stand up. I want to take her with me, even though that's not a remotely feasible option. I don't have a ticket for her, and while she's tiny enough to fit into a piece of luggage, I don't think she'd take too kindly to being hauled through the air in the cargo hold of an airplane. There's also the whole pursuing her dream to become a pediatric surgeon thing. *Geez, stop being so selfish, Andie. The sick kids of the world don't* really *need your genius.*

I've avoided this for so long, this bittersweet feeling of change. Nothing will be the same again. Even if I come back in three months, life will continue moving along here without me, and I won't be the same person for having had this experience.

"Earth to Monty?" Andie nudges me.

"Sorry, just a little distracted. What were you saying?"

"Just that I'm going to add hospitals in Seattle to my list of residency programs to apply to, so at least I can fly out for an interview and visit."

"Right, matching. That's coming up?" Everything she's saying is skimming the surface like a rubber ducky floating along a lazy river. I am in Baron la-la land. It's been three weeks, six days, and five hours since I last saw him—well, since I saw him in person at least. There are just certain aspects of video calling that don't really measure up to real life.

Andie shakes her head. "I get it. You're finally going to get laid. It's cool. I'd be thinking about that too if it were even a remote possibility in my world. As it stands, the only thing that's screwing me is my current rotation schedule."

"Aren't there like hook-ups in the on-call rooms or something?"

"Real life is not Grey's Anatomy."

"Well, maybe you should change that."

"With who? One of the other exhausted, extremely overworked med students? Please, I'd have better luck getting an attending in bed, and trust me, none of them look at all like McDreamy or McSteamy. So, I'll just stick to living vicariously through you." Andie starts to sing. "Someone's gonna have sex toniiiight."

"It's gonna be really late when we get there."

My cheeks are bright red, but my lady parts are blue. I have been thinking about this for way too long, and the anticipation is unbearable. I keep telling myself I can handle another six hours, but horny waits for no one.

"Whatever. Drink some coffee and suck it up. I want details. I mean, the man's got some big hands." Andie waggles her eyebrows playfully.

Yup. Just add more kindling to the fire here.

A black sedan pulls up and parks. Speak of the devil.

Baron's Prius is already out in Seattle and I sold my car to help pad my savings account, so he got a rental for the weekend. I've been sweating bullets waiting for something, anything in response to the ten thousand emails I've sent out over the past few days. One finally came through today: an old professor of mine set up an interview for an assistant gig out in Seattle. I go in on Monday, and I'm pretty much willing to hand over my soul, my kidney, and my old Polly Pocket collection in order to land it.

My heart starts to race, and not because I'm thinking about Baron's glove size. I pull Andie in for a hug. "It's not goodbye, okay?"

"Nope." I hear the crack in her voice. "You're going to see more of me on video chat in a month than you saw me in person for the past year."

I don't know how people moved across the country and left their family and friends before the Internet. Being able to still see their faces is going to keep me sane, and my heart needs more than a static JPEG saved on my computer's hard drive.

Baron steps around the front of the car and walks toward us. He's wearing a t-shirt and jeans, but the way my brain reacts, you'd think he was wearing a three-piece tux. It's one part hubba hubba mixed with three parts knee-buckling swoon.

He reaches out and pulls me into his broad chest, and I feel my lungs expand to twice their original size, as if simply being around him gives me more air to breathe.

"Hi," he whispers against my forehead as his lips brush my skin. I sink into the feeling of having him close, and it's heaven.

We pull away and Baron turns to Andie. "Hey, thanks for

letting me steal your best friend."

"No problem, Bear—I mean, Baron." Andie fumbles. She has fielded my nonstop texts for the past few weeks like a pro, but I know she's still awestruck over the celebrity status of my boyfriend.

Baron looks down at me. "You ready to go?"

I reach out and pull Andie in for a group hug. I think she might be squeezing Baron harder than me, but she also doesn't get to take him home tonight.

Shit. *I'm* taking him home tonight. It still doesn't feel real.

None of this does. My eyes start to sting and I let go of Andie.

"Call me tomorrow and tell me about your, um, flight?" She nudges me awkwardly.

I laugh under my breath. "You got it."

Baron grabs my bags and puts them in the trunk while I give Andie another hug. I can't say goodbye, but I also can't stay.

"Go. You've got a flight to catch and a boy to board." She smacks me on the butt, prodding me to get in the car.

I close the door and she walks back to the stairs of her apartment building. She waves at me wildly, but I know her throat has the same lump in it that mine does.

Baron shifts the car into drive and looks over at me. "We'll be back before you know it."

My life is pulling away from the station, and even though I'm excited about where I'm headed, I can't help but stare out the window at the scenery of what I'm leaving behind as it slowly fades into a blur.

Chapter 15

Baron passes out the moment the plane starts to pull away from the gate, and I can't blame him. As hard as my week has been, I had one job: neatly fit my life into cardboard boxes. Baron was pushed to his physical limit in practices all week, hopped on a red-eye, and worked on the last ten percent of moving that takes forever.

Seriously, screw that ten percent. The random can of plant food from a fern that died two years ago. The excess amount of hair ties you find EVERYWHERE. The stack of magazines you promised you would get to but still sit in a pile untouched.

I'm so glad to be done, especially when I'm sitting in a first class seat to Seattle. Baron told me he'd have his personal assistant take care of booking my ticket and finding a kickass studio apartment in my price range. I tried to argue, but I was too stunned by the fact that he had an assistant. Is this even real life?

Still, even in a seat that could fit two of me plus a mini fridge at my feet, I'm struggling to relax. I'm sitting next to a man I've known for a little less than two months, and I'm moving across the country with him.

Oh, I know. I'm moving toward the call of adventure, but in

this case, adventure has a seriously nice ass that puts on glorified tights to go to work. It's kind of obvious that I'm not just doing this for the hell of it.

I've tried to let *Game of Thrones* distract with me with its Drogo sex appeal and plot twists galore, but I just keep looking over at Baron. He's even better than Drogo, and it's all I can do to not wake him up and find a quiet corner of this airplane to take advantage of that fact.

The familiar ding of the seatbelt light flashes like an ugly yellow omen, and the captain's voice clicks on over the PA system: "We're heading into some turbulence. Please return to your seats while the fasten seatbelt sign is turned on. Thank you."

Welcome to the other reason why my travel dance card is a sad misfit standing at the side of high school prom while everyone else is out on the dance floor. I hate the roller coaster feeling—not the emotional, *I'm so happy, oh my god, now I'm so sad and nothing will ever be fun again* feeling, no; the literal riding-on-a-roller-coaster feeling.

I despise it, especially while I'm strapped inside a metal tin can of recycled air as it flies thirty thousand feet in the air and could tumble down in a fiery crash at any moment.

Yes, I recognize that I'm more likely to die in a car than an airplane. Does that mean my brain suddenly becomes rational when we hit the pockets of wind that turn my stomach into a gold-medal Olympic gymnast? I didn't ask for a double back handspring back tuck; I don't care how talented my stomach thinks it is.

The plane starts to jostle, and my hands fly out to hold on to the arm rests. I look over and see Baron sleeping as if the flight attendant slipped him an Ambien with his water. I mean, if that's first class service, sign me up.

Considering I didn't get the same offer, I'm assuming this is just another reason his nickname is Bear. He certainly sleeps like one.

Game of Thrones is still playing on my laptop, but I don't have the mental capacity to pay attention. No, I use all my energy on silently repeating *Please don't fall out of the sky* over and over, as if it will actually help the two pilots sitting up front do their jobs. One thing's for sure: I'm not stopping.

By the time the light dings off thirty minutes later, my knuckles are white, and I bet my face matches them. I'm a walking corpse. *Thanks air travel; let's do this again sometime.*

I have been sitting in my seat with my legs crossed so tightly, I think my calves have lost circulation for life. I've had to pee this whole time, but there was no way I was going to stand up while the light was on. I still don't want to, even with it off.

I slowly lift the clasp of the buckle and stretch out my legs. My bladder expands into the extra room, and rather than making the situation better, I feel like I'm going to pee my pants—not exactly the look I'm going for to entice Baron into bed tonight.

I pop up and race to the front cabin restroom, quickly shutting the door. I thank my past ingenious self for deciding to wear a dress, and I squat over the toilet. I look around, and I swear it's not just the first class cabin that gives you an extra two feet of legroom —the bathroom is bigger too. I could have a tiny dance party in here and bust out my grossly underrated grocery cart move.

I flush the toilet and recoil at the aggressively loud noise; it sounds like it just shot its entire contents halfway out the plane.

Someone knocks on the door, and I quickly glance at the latch to make sure it's firmly secured in the 'occupied' position.

"Monty? Are you okay?" Baron's voice sounds like it's up against the other side of the folding door. I quickly finish pulling my dress down and shift the latch to 'unoccupied.' I open it and am six inches away from a wide chest of pure sex appeal. *God, I want to take you home right now.*

"Yeah. Are you okay?" I ask. His hands are pressed against each side of the doorway, and he's leaning in with a concerned look pulling at his face. I can't figure out why my bathroom break has him in a panic. He pushes into the bathroom, and my suspicions are confirmed—it really is bigger than a coach bathroom. You couldn't fit the two of us into the bathroom at the back of a plane if you had ten sticks of butter and a crowbar.

"Yeah. One of the attendants woke me up when you rushed to the bathroom. She said you looked like you were having a tough time in the turbulence. I didn't even notice it. I was out. I'm sorry. You can always wake me up if you need me."

The worry hasn't left his face, and I reach up to touch his cheek, trying to ease his concern.

My heart skips a beat. How many men would have gotten up to check on me? Maybe half of them. How many of those men would have walked right into the bathroom to be there for me? A verbal check through the thin accordion door would have satisfied their need to help.

Baron is the kind of man who steps up. It doesn't matter who he is or how many people are following his stats right now.

I take a deep breath and roll my shoulders back down. "I'm okay. I was a little freaked out, but really I just had to pee." I want to add *because I drank two cans of ginger ale and a bottle of water while you were sleeping*, but there's a line, and that's dipping the toe on the wrong side.

Baron leans in and presses a kiss to my forehead. I close my eyes and relish the sensation of my world slowing down while I'm cruising hundreds of miles per hour through the air.

He lifts his head up and tucks a piece of hair behind my ear. "I know today is a lot. It's a big deal, and I appreciate how much you're changing your life to take a chance…"

On us. Those two little syllables are silent, and yet it's as if someone took them out of their vacuum-sealed bag and they inflated to fill the entire space.

I don't think I've ever wanted a man more in my life. It's about so much more than sex. I feel connected to Baron in a way that makes me want him on every single level.

Preferably right now.

I press a quick kiss to his lips, and then bend my knees and let them drop softly to the floor. I am going to have to wash this dress in the hottest water known to man, but it is going to be so worth it.

"Montgomery." I love the way he says my name, as if he has to use each and every syllable to communicate his need for me.

He moans as I weave his leather belt out of the buckle and through the metal clasp, slipping it loose and quickly undoing the button and zipper of his pants. I press them down and reach in to grasp the hardening length of him, feeling the blood pulsing to meet me. I pull him out to meet my mouth and run my lips over the long stretch of soft skin. I want to taste every inch, to find the spots that make him stop and close his eyes, the parts that stop his world wholly and completely.

I slip him in and out of my mouth, and I can hear his breath jump every time I catch that small ridge of skin that sits on the bundle of nerves that crackle like the burning end of a stick of dynamite.

My own breath shortens. This kind of power is more intoxicating than a free drink in first class. I have complete and utter control over the man standing in front of me, and even though I'm the one on my knees right now, we both know I'm the one who is holding the reins in this situation.

I meet my mouth with my hand and move them together. Baron slams his hand against the door of the bathroom, and I start to build my momentum.

"Monty, I'm gonna..." His voice trails off, unable to form a complete thought. I know enough to finish it for myself. I normally take a step back, let my hand do the work, and let my mouth sit out for the final touchdown.

But, this is different. Baron is different. I look up and lock eyes with him. This is a climax for both of us, and I want to see him.

I build momentum, and I see his eyes roll back a moment before I swallow. I take him in one more time, and then pull back. I shift back up onto my feet and try not to look too hard at the bathroom floor. No regrets if I don't look too closely.

Does this earn me my Mile-High club wings? Because I'm pretty sure kneeling on an airplane bathroom floor should do it.

"Monty, that was..." Baron's eyes are still half closed. I giggle to myself. *Badass.* That was badass.

A knock interrupts the second half of Baron's fill-in-the-blank. "Excuse me, um...the fasten seatbelt light is turned on. We've begun our descent. We're going to, um, need you both to take your seats."

I turn every shade of red a crayon box has ever dreamed of having. How long has the attendant been standing outside that door?

I bury my head in my hands, and Baron wraps his arm around me. I can tell by the soft jumping of his ribcage that he's laughing. "We'll be out in just a second."

I shake my head back and forth. I don't think I'm going to be able to look anyone in the eye for the rest of this flight.

Baron sneaks his pointer finger underneath my chin and tips it up softly. "That was fucking incredible. Let's go move to Seattle, baby."

I smile. My face is still flushed, but it's been downgraded to a Pepto-Bismol pink instead of candy apple red.

I sure am starting this move off with a bang.

We pull up to a high-rise building in the middle of what I assume is downtown. Baron presses a button clipped to the visor, and a gate I hadn't noticed opens. We pull into a garage, and I notice fancy cars I only saw every so often back in Ann Arbor parked in nearly every spot.

Well okay then.

Baron pulls in, shuts off the car, and turns to me. "So, my assistant found you an apartment."

I knew that much. She had emailed me the address and some pictures, along with her rave review of it. It looked better than I had imagined for my tiny budget. I hadn't even looked up where exactly it was.

"It's on the ground floor of this building." I open my mouth to speak, but Baron continues. "I bought the condo on the top floor, so she got you a good deal. I hope that's okay. I just figured it would be easier if we didn't have to run across town to see each other."

There are so many thoughts fighting for top billing right now. So, Baron got a deal on my rent because he already gave them buckets of cash? Am I okay with that? Is it okay that we're living in the same building?

I'm too tired from traveling to filter through it all. It's already dark here, and that means it's well past a reasonable hour back home. My brain can't process this right now.

"I can take you to your apartment, or you can come home with me tonight. It's up to you." Baron shifts toward me, and I can see him holding his breath. He just flipped all his cards over on the table and is letting me read them and decide for myself.

I don't have to think it through. "I'm coming with you."

We take our bags over to the elevator and head up to his condo. I snuggle up to him, but after our little jaunt in the airplane earlier, I'm going to let the small public spaces have a break—even though the only thing my mind can focus on is what it means to go home with Baron tonight.

I don't know how we've spent the last month away from each other. I don't know how I existed out of his arms. It doesn't make sense. I haven't known him for that long, and yet, I feel like I didn't exist before he came along.

The elevator chimes and the doors open to a long hallway with two doors. It's so similar to his last place, and yet I know the moment he opens that door, it's going to be entirely different—about 42 floors different.

When he swings the heavy metal door open, I nearly drop my bags. The lights are off and all I can see is the outline of the city sparkling against the dark velvet backdrop beyond. I think it might be the sound; I could see its soft outline while my eyes were glued to the airplane window during our descent into the city.

Baron flips a switch and illuminates the large open living area of his apartment. It doesn't have quite the same industrial vibe, but his weathered rustic furniture warms up the straight lines and all-glass space that might otherwise feel sterile.

I already know I'm going to be spending more time up here than in my studio downstairs, but I don't regret getting my own space. I may have moved here because he asked me to, but that doesn't mean I'm going to jump right into being a full-time, move-in ready girlfriend.

Maybe I can kick Baron to the ground floor when we need some space—I'm pretty sure these views and I were made for each other.

I feel Baron's warm breath tickle my neckline as he sidles up behind me.

"I'm so glad you chose option B." He slowly trails kisses up my neck, and my eyes close involuntarily as I shiver underneath his touch. None of the men I've been with have done this to me. They haven't taken their time to get to know every inch of my skin like Baron is right now. It's like he's trying to make a mental map of every cell so he can plot the best routes. I hope he takes the scenic one tonight.

"Hmm, why's that?" I hum under my breath when he nibbles

142

on my earlobe.

"This apartment needs a christening." I can hear the smile in his tone. I hear how it curls up like a whisper of smoke from a fire that's been burning for far too long.

"And what does a christening entail?"

Baron skims his fingers along my waist toward the hem of my dress, catching the edge of the fabric and lifting it up to tease my skin with his touch. I want more of this. *So much more.*

He reaches to the other side of my waist and grabs my hand, pulling me toward the kitchen. I follow him, curious where this is leading and entirely sure I'm going to like where it ends up.

He opens the fridge and pulls out a bottle of champagne. *Oh, I like this a lot.* He pops the cork and pours us each a glass. I take a sip, closing my eyes to relish the taste of sweet bubbles skipping across my tongue and down my throat.

I used to hate champagne. It didn't match my years of built-up expectation. It wasn't as sweet as I expected it to be, but once I tried it a few more times and gave it space to be something I hadn't expected, then I finally started to love it.

It was proof first impressions aren't always right. Sometimes, you have to try things a few times and learn how to let go of your preconceived ideas in order to really find out what you do or don't like.

Baron leans his glass toward mine. "Cheers, to exploring a new city with the woman who was crazy enough to move across the country with me."

"So you sent this invite out to more than one crazy lady?"

"Just you, but I thought my odds were pretty good."

"You're lucky I'm insane." I give him a cheeky grin and take a sip of the champagne.

"Yes. Yes, I am," he agrees. He reaches out and grabs my hand, pulling me gently toward the door at the far end of the open apartment. "If you think the view is amazing in here, just wait until you see it from the bedroom."

When we walk through the doorway, the lights are off. The whole far wall is glass, and I can see the blue lights on the Seattle Great Wheel. There's a hint of reflection on the dark water, and just a little farther out are the small twinkling lights of more of the city.

I want to get naked and keep the lights off, but for a reason completely unrelated to my confidence level—I want to revel in the glow of this gorgeous city.

"This is incredible, Baron."

"It's even better with you here." He steps up to me, wrapping his free arm around my waist and pressing my lower back so I arch against him. "I missed you."

I could spend hours right here in this bedroom with him and still not get enough. My whole body is alive, as if someone just plugged me into a charger. The energy is pulsing through me, filling me up.

I set down my champagne on the bedside table. I need both hands for this. I reach up, weave my fingers through Baron's hair, and pull his lips to mine.

It's sweet at first—I can taste the hint of champagne still on his lips—but as Baron walks us back toward the bed, his kiss deepens, his mouth demanding more of me.

"Take your dress off and lie down," he instructs. My heart beats wildly at his request, but I do as he asks.

He takes a sip of his champagne then holds the glass over me and tips it slowly, trailing tiny drops that fizz against my skin. He leans down and follows the trail from the bottom of my chest down to my stomach with his mouth while his hand grazes the inner edge of my thigh.

He traces the edge of my panties and moves the damp fabric aside. I close my eyes as he starts to explore. My skin is coming alive beneath his touch, and I want to feel every single breath of its existence. His fingers slide up and down, and I shudder at each and every change of direction.

God, if this is what I get for going down on him in an airplane bathroom, I'm going to become a frequent flier for life.

Baron stops and pulls his hand back, and my eyes fly open. He pulls my panties off in one smooth motion and then he reaches for the glass of champagne.

Oh, I like where this is headed.

He centers himself between my legs as he takes a sip, and then he leans down and flicks his tongue against the spot his fingers just left. The fizzing bubbles pop against my skin, and it travels through my nerves like bursts of light hitting every edge of my body. He lifts up to take another sip; half of me doesn't want him to stop, half of me will do anything to repeat that feeling.

He circles his tongue around me, and my hands clench at the sheets underneath me. I can't handle this feeling. It's like someone just lit the long rope on the end of a stick of dynamite, and I'm feeling every single crackling lick of the flame running along its path. Baron matches its speed, lick for tantalizing lick, and I see it cornering the final bend.

When it hits, I close my eyes and sink into the feeling of being ripped apart and pulled back together in one extraordinary burst.

I open my eyes to see Baron pulling his shirt and pants off, and I understand his urgency immediately. I need him inside me. Now. I peel off my own bra.

Baron stops. "You're so goddamn beautiful. I can't get enough of you. I don't ever think I'll be able to get enough of you."

I crawl toward him and wrap my arms around his neck. My face is just a breath away from his. "Ditto."

I kiss him with everything I have, every fear, every joy, every need. It all mixes together like cream poured into coffee, the smoothness balancing out the acidity.

He runs his hands along my legs and grabs my ankles, pulling them out and wrapping them around his waist. He turns us around and shifts us back toward the head of the bed, reaching into the drawer of the bedside table to retrieve a condom. I grab it from him and open the foil packet, and then reach down to feel the length of him in my hand. It sends a flash of excitement rippling down my spine. This, all of this, is going to be inside me.

I roll the condom on, and I watch his eyelids flicker with pleasure. I lift my hips up, still holding him in one hand, and I position myself, just seconds away from sliding down onto him.

Our eyes lock, and I wonder how the world existed before I knew him. Everything was smaller. Dull. Ordinary. It's like my whole life just knocked back a glass of champagne.

And I'm so damn glad it did.

I slowly slide down, inch by glorious inch, and then I lift my hips up and down, exploring the feeling of having him inside me. It's like I'm finding corners of myself I never knew existed, and I want to take the time to note each and every one.

Baron lifts his hips up, moving us from sitting at the edge of the bed to lying down. He grabs my hips, lifts me up, and spins me around slowly. "Lean back, baby."

I lie down, pressing my back to his chest as he reaches down to tease me with his fingers. Our hips rock together and the angle hits me in a way I've never felt before. It feels like a train is barreling at me and I am powerless to stop it.

When climax hits, it takes us both out, and we collapse, motionless against each other.

I finally summon the energy to roll off of him, and he slips the condom off before turning back to me and wrapping me tightly into his chest.

I trace the lines of his chest with my finger, my eyelids heavy but my brain buzzing. "Well, if you were trying to start this move off on the right foot, you succeeded."

"Just trying to win you over, one orgasm at a time," he says with a yawn.

"That'll do it." I bury myself into him, reveling in the feeling of saying yes. I said yes to Seattle. To Baron. To adventure.

And right now, it feels like the best decision I've ever made.

Chapter 16

Baron gives me a kiss goodbye when he gets up at the butt crack of dawn to run sprints before he heads in to actual practice. The man never stops. He's constantly trying to improve his speed. He could outrun a cheetah at this point, but he'd still tell you he could go faster if he kept working on it.

I roll over and fall back asleep with a smile whispering across my face. As far as a first twenty-four hours in Seattle goes, this is off to a pretty damn good start.

When I wake up to my alarm forty-five minutes later, I sprint out of bed to get ready for my job interview.

I practically bounce my way down to Pioneer Square with my thermos of coffee and overeager smile. I am so grateful that my former professor emailed me back. If he hadn't, I would be sitting in Baron's apartment huddled on the couch with my computer, applying to every position known to man without knowing if anything would stick.

This may not be a surefire thing, but at least it's forward motion.

It helps that the interview is with Stewart Grant—he's a legend.

I've seen his photos show up in all the big magazines. I don't care if he pays me in pennies, it would be an honor to work for him.

I swing the heavy metal door of the studio loft open. I have to remind myself to close it, my brain is so in shock. The giant space is sectioned off with different backdrops, and the floors and tables are littered with all sorts of props—sheets, clothing, a giant metal wheel. I don't see anyone in here, but Mr. Grant's name is stamped in metal just to the side of the door so I know I'm in the right place.

"Hello," I call out.

I hear shuffling from a door that looks like it goes into a kitchenette.

Mr. Grant steps out and scowls at me before walking over to a row of desks at the side of the room. "You were supposed to be here last week."

WHAT? My body goes rigid. "I'm sorry, the dates must have been mixed up. I just flew in this weekend."

He doesn't acknowledge my apology. He shuffles through a stack of papers and shoves a paper-clipped set at me. "Fill these out and send them to my accountant who handles taxes and payroll."

I feel like I have mental whiplash. "Um, Mr. Grant, I thought this was an interview."

He doesn't bother to look up, just sits down in front of a massive desktop and starts to click through a bunch of images. "You need to know three things about this job: I take my coffee black with one teaspoon of coconut oil, I will not eat sandwiches with avocados on them, and you are not to touch the equipment under any circumstances."

I don't know whether I'm more shocked that I just got a job without answering a single question or that my new boss is apparently an asshole. My gut is trying to scream out a warning, but I stifle it.

I need a job, and even if he's going to treat me like some fresh-faced new grad, I have to take it. I can't afford not to.

Fine. I'm not going to scoff at putting in my time to prove myself. "Okay, what do you need me to start with today, Mr. Grant?"

"Clean up this mess." He waves his hand behind his head, in the general direction of the giant prop disaster covering every surface of the loft.

I want to ask him if he wants me to sing "The Sun Will Come Out Tomorrow" while I do it, but I'm not stupid enough to lose my job on the first day. Give me another month of menial labor, and I might be singing a different tune.

I should have waited to see my salary before booking a blowout and makeup appointment, but I am a nervous wreck about tonight. I need all the help I can get.

Baron asked me to join him at this banquet after I told him I was moving, and it finally hit me that I am the girlfriend of a big fucking deal—which is about five thousand degrees past how much of a deal I can handle. I said yes to Baron, but the fine print on this is making me feel kind of nauseous.

Which is why I'm here. Nothing like a little liquid courage to help you walk into a room of people you don't know, and this liquid courage is courtesy of little bottles called foundation and a red lip.

I walk up to the counter and check in, and then I wait until a woman named Leslie comes out to get me. She's the same height as me and has equally deep brown hair, except she has a wide streak of purple on one side. I spot a stud tucked into the outer curve of her nose, and she's rocking a red lip better than Dita Von Teese.

Thank you, Seattle. This is exactly what I imagined when I pictured the city: fancypants with a touch of sass. I like it.

"Hi! You're Montgomery, right?" Leslie asks.

"Yeah, I'm Monty. Nice to meet you."

She gives me a full smile. "Can I get you anything: water, tea, glass of bubbly?"

Umm, champagne? If they're offering, I'm taking. While it would be the better life decision to refrain from boarding the alcohol train until the event tonight, my willpower is shot after dealing with my new grouch of a boss all day.

I accept the offer, and two seconds later another woman walks over with a flute in hand. She hands it to me and introduces herself as Dhrea, the woman who's going to handle my makeup. Considering that her gorgeous terra cotta skin looks dewy and flawless while also looking product-free, I know I am in good hands.

I sit down in a plush black leather seat, and Leslie examines my hair while Dhrea starts to pick colors out of the drawer in front of me.

"Okay, lady, so what are we thinking today? Subdued updo? Wild, voluminous curls? You tell me, and I'll make it happen."

I have no doubt this team could transform me into a Victoria Secret model—at least from the neck up—if I asked them to.

When I said yes to attending the event, I set aside a black strapless cocktail dress while I was packing up. It's not fancy, but it'll fade into the background well, and that's my game plan: don't stand out, just ride the wave, and don't get pulled under. I think it's a winning strategy, even though Andie sent me about ten sad face emojis when I texted her a picture of what I was planning to wear.

If she were here, she'd be doing it up big—full sequin style with va-va-voom hair and an attitude to match.

"Umm, can you do some beach-y waves?" It's more than I could ever attempt to accomplish myself. I may be twenty-three years old, but I still don't know how to do my own hair. I top out at messy buns and side braids.

"Done. What do you think, Dhrea?" Leslie turns to her partner in crime while continuing to weave her fingers through my hair, getting a sense for its texture and fullness.

"Peachy undertones with a bit of bronzer. We'll pull off sun-kissed California girl like pros." They give each other a high five, and it's kind of exciting to have this lady power team working on me.

Leslie and Dhrea start talking about a recent restaurant opening and the few Seattle celebrities that came out for the event. Apparently, some wives and girlfriends of Seattle's football players came in for this whole primping service before it.

While they're busy talking, a woman with gorgeous red hair comes in and sits down in the seat next to me, and a stylist starts to cut her hair. The redhead has her phone in hand the whole time, not even acknowledging that there are people around her.

I wish I had enough guts to do the same sometimes, but I always worry about being rude. So, instead, I sit and sip my drink, trying to pay attention to the back and forth of the conversation.

Leslie mentions a name that sounds familiar: Cameron Holt. I feel like I've heard Baron mention it, or maybe I've just heard it in passing.

"Who's that?" I ask with my eyes closed while Dhrea paints on my foundation. I may not be able to see their faces, but I can feel their surprise rattling through the air like a rubber band that just snapped.

"He's the quarterback of the Hawks," Leslie explains. Then she adds in a stage whisper, "And a fine piece of ass on wheels, at that."

Right. Football. I should pay attention, even though the idea of trying to memorize the players and their positions sounds on par with memorizing names of battles and the years they occurred for history class.

"Mmm, have you seen the new trade? If he plays even half as good as he looks, we're going to the championship, baby," Dhrea adds.

I turn bright red, but Dhrea must have really done the foundation well because they keep going.

Leslie frowns. "Yeah, he has that animal nickname."

I can't handle it any more. I jump in before we get too much further down this road. "Bear?"

Dhrea snaps her fingers together. "That's the one! Damn, he's hot."

"Yeah. He's my boyfriend." I try to say the words without any hint of jealously or possession. He's a public persona; if I start getting upset that random strangers find him attractive...well, I'll be angry forever, and it would be way too awkward to sit here and pretend I don't know who he is.

"Good job, girl. He's a catch." Leslie says it like I nailed a job interview or scored a sweet apartment.

I blush again, but this time for altogether different reasons. I am the girlfriend of a professional football player. There's a certain amount of spotlight that naturally deflects to me simply because of where I'm standing.

"What position is he playing? I forget," Dhrea asks.

"Umm..." I should know this. I really should. He's told me before, and I can't for the life of me remember the string of words he put together. "Wide running backer?" My tone tilts up at the end.

Both of the women laugh lightly. Leslie unhooks the curling iron from my hair and pats me on the shoulder. "Oh honey, that's not a position."

I quickly fumble to cover up my mistake. "I don't know much about sports. We met at a bar and I didn't realize he was a football player."

"No shame in that," Dhrea says with a comforting smile.

"So, was it love at first sight? I mean, I love him, and I haven't even seen him in person yet," Leslie teases.

"Umm, not exactly." I swallow another sip of bubbly and then tell them our story. My rant about football. How Baron pursued me even though I hate sports. About how we fit in every other way. How I wanted more adventure in my life and that moving to Seattle came up at just the right time to be a crazy but not unrealistic option.

They're enraptured with every detail while they continue to work on me like the fairy godmothers they are, and before I know it, they're doing the final touches. They both give me hugs like we've been BFs forever and start to work on cleaning up the explosion of hair and makeup products around me.

I take a look at myself in the mirror, and I'm pleased to see that I still look like myself, just a version that's walking around with perfect lighting and some flawless brows. I could get used to this.

I pop out of my seat, ready to check out at the front desk. The woman sitting one seat over looks up from her phone and gives me a dazzling smile. I look behind me, positive she must be looking at someone else, but it's just the entrance behind me, and the only thing there is open air. *Huh. Strange.*

I give her a tentative smile, and she hops out of her seat and extends her hand. "I couldn't help but overhear—did you say you were going with Bear Richards to the team event tonight?"

I nod tentatively, unsure of how to react. I thought this woman was absorbed in her phone the entire time she was sitting next to me, but she must have been paying attention, which makes my brain start to rewind through my last hour of conversation.

"Well, that's so exciting." She glances down at her phone. "I didn't catch your name."

"Um, I'm Montgomery." As soon as I introduce myself, I wonder if this is a situation where you use a fake name. I mean, is that tactic only reserved for creepy guys at bars, or is it acceptable to become Ashley or Melissa when a stranger is coming across a little…well…strange?

The woman taps something into her phone, and I decide I am thoroughly weirded out by this encounter.

"Um, I have to get going. Nice, umm, meeting you." I know I'm being overly polite, but I am awful at extracting myself from awkward situations. I let myself off the hook and don't wait for a response. I head over to the main counter and thank Leslie and Dhrea before ducking outside.

I can't shake the strange feeling that my life is about to get a lot less normal. It follows me back to my apartment three blocks away, and it doesn't budge when I peel off my clothes and change into my dress.

At least I have Baron. I quickly fill my clutch with the tiny containers of extra makeup Dhrea gave me with a wink and advice about reapplying if my makeup got smudged, and then I walk out of my studio toward the elevator to Baron's condo.

My life is going up, but I'm still worried the cable might break and send me hurtling back down to the ground level I started on.

Chapter 17

We've only been at the Columbia Tower for fifteen minutes, but I've had enough socializing to last the next five years.

My cheeks are piled high into tight balls, and they're starting to cramp from all the effort. They're not secret powerhouse muscles; they're tiny mounds of fat that have never seen this much unrelenting physical activity, and right now they're screaming at me to put them out of their misery.

But, I'm here on the arm of the new player, and apparently that makes us both fresh conversational meat. I'm about to start rattling off my name, Social Security number, and ATM PIN to the next person who asks who I am and what I do.

Baron's face lights up when another couple starts to walk toward us, and I turn to see a man who's at least a foot larger than Baron in every direction holding the hand of a woman who is at least a foot smaller than me in every way. They're a striking pair. His deep brown skin is a perfect shadow to her bright ivory. The way they lean in toward each other is so absentminded, you can tell they've been together for so long their bodies naturally pull together, curving into their own ying and yang.

"Monty, this is Zane, one of my best friends, and his wife, Georgie. We all went to college together, and I never thought we'd ever get to play on the same team again, but here we are!" Baron and Zane clap each other on the back, sharing wide, easy grins. It's the first time I feel like I can breathe easy tonight.

Georgie turns to me and opens her arms out wide. "I'm sorry, but I feel like I need to give you a hug right now. I've heard so much about you, and I'm sure you already know this, but Baron is one of the sweetest guys in the world. I am just so glad you two found each other."

I let Georgie step in and hug me, and even though the forwardness feels slightly foreign in this room of fake smiles and awkward introductions, I'll take any ounce of genuine kindness I can get.

Baron and Zane start talking about video games and when they're going to get together to play some new one that just came out, and Georgie rolls her eyes while grinning from ear to ear.

"These two. They are so far past the bromance stage, it's a full-on man-and-wife situation going on here. Zane might be my husband, but I am without a doubt his second wife."

"What does that make us?" If we're the significant others of two man-wives, then are we sister-wives? Or in-laws? This is new family tree territory.

"Comrades." Georgie flashes me a grin. She pulls her phone out of her purse and hands it to me. "Here, put your number in. We have to hang out, and not just at games either. You're family now."

There's nothing like being in a room full of strangers to make you miss your best friend. Even though I don't have Andie here, I'm grateful for Georgie tonight.

As I finish tapping in the last digit into her phone, I hear someone shout *Zane* across the crowd. The two man-wives standing next to me break their conversation with frowns, and Zane looks over to find the voice that is interrupting their wifely conversation.

Zane's head drops with a tiny shake. "Sorry dude, it's Rick. I'm sure he has something completely useless but incredibly important to tell me, and I have to walk all the way over to him to hear it."

Georgie gives me a soft, apologetic smile. "Hang in there. These are tough at first. They get easier. We'll find you later, k?"

It's good to know I'm not the only person who finds conversation with people I've never met before to rank below getting a deep clean at the dentist—and not some little *use the swirling brush for a little longer* sort of appointment, the *hack at plaque on your teeth with the world's smallest ice pick* type.

Zane and Georgie grab hands and make their way back toward the dense part of the crowd. I barely know them, but I feel like my security blanket just grew legs and walked away from me.

Baron wraps his arm around me and tugs at my waist, turning us away from the crowd and toward one of the back walls. I know by the way the cotton pulls against my skin in his tight grip, he would much rather there be fewer layers between him and me right now.

I don't think that's really the right way to start off the introductions to the rest of the room—*Hi, here's my full Monty.*

He leans down and grazes his lips against my ear. "I'm sorry about this, baby. We only have to stay for another hour, and then we can head home."

My smiles fades into pleasure. I would so rather be home right now, for so many reasons, but when Baron pulls away, I press my lips back up into place. I came here to be his girlfriend, and I can tough it out for another sixty minutes. Too bad I didn't wear a watch; I wouldn't mind a countdown clock right now. We're at a football banquet—isn't there a scoreboard around here somewhere?

"You must be Baron and Montgomery," says a new voice, catching us from behind. I turn around and see a swirl of tight blonde curls that graze the top of a long, sequined red dress. I'd noticed it from across the room a few times, and it looks more like something Jessica Rabbit would wear to a movie premiere than a football team event, but I can't say this woman doesn't pull it off flawlessly. She may be overdressed, but she wears it like a badge of honor, as if she'd be offended if anyone tried to outshine her.

I don't think that's happening any time soon. The sun is starting to set, but I'm pretty sure her dress is giving it a run for its money.

Baron stretches out his hand. "Yup. I'm Bear, and this is Monty." The woman takes his hand with a giggle, and I have the sudden urge to sucker punch her.

I mumble a greeting instead and reach out my own hand.

She glances at it like I just finished a shift at the local auto shop and quickly looks back up at Baron with wide eyes and a bright smile. "It's so nice to meet you. I'm Rochelle."

She says it without mentioning what player she's attached to, even though it's painfully obvious from the rock she's sporting on her left hand that it's not some low-level rookie. I look up and see Baron smiling back at her like she's any one of the other people we've talked to.

Seriously, dude. This woman is gorgeous with a side of pure evil; take that smile down a notch.

I keep my eye out for Georgie, hoping she and Zane come back and crash our conversation—*soon.*

"...and you decided to tag along, huh?" Rochelle's voice crashes into my thoughts, and I realize she's looking straight at me.

I give her a weak smile, unable to decipher if she meant tonight or to Seattle or what. I get the feeling Rochelle is not the sort of person you ask to repeat herself. I don't want to move my name higher up on her shit list any more than I somehow already have.

A small *ting ting ting* cuts through the conversation of the room, and everyone looks over to see Coach Naylor standing up at the front stage.

"Oh shoot," Rochelle says with a puppy dog whimper. "I was going to get champagne before Joe started his speech. Would you be a dear?" She looks over at Baron with eyes wider than a billboard of the word please. It's obnoxious, and even though I know I'm going to have to see this woman again, I have decided I do not like her, not one single bit.

Baron responds like a gentleman and says, "Sure thing," before quickly wading across the room to the bar to grab a flute for the stupid woman.

Rochelle turns to me, her eyes pulled into tiny, unsympathetic slits. "You're not going to last two weeks here. You should just pack up your bags and go home."

My jaw drops. Did I just experience a weird lip-reading misinterpretation? She couldn't have actually just told me to give up and move home. That's absurd; she doesn't even know me.

"You're not team material, and that's what this is." She glances around the room and adds a dramatic little twirl of her pointer finger. "We're a team, players and wives, and you are not marriage material. So, I would walk away now before we chew you up and spit you back out like the trash you are."

What the actual fuck is happening right now? I can't jog my brain into working. I have no words to form a coherent reply to this woman's crazy. I don't even know what triggered her, let alone how to handle it.

Baron walks back over with two flutes, one for Rochelle and one for me. Normally, I would spend this moment being grateful for dating such a keeper, but right now, I think I might puke into this glass, and it is way too tiny to catch the entirety of this spew. I quickly excuse myself and race down the hall to find a bathroom.

I turn left and get out of eyesight of everyone, and then I stop. My breathing is jumping erratically. What the hell is going on right now? I feel like I just walked onto the *Mean Girls* set and didn't even realize it.

An arm reaches out and pulls me two steps into the bathroom. I stumble in and look over to find its owner, and Georgie is staring back at me with wide eyes and her phone screen turned toward me. Its neon glow is starkly white against the soft light of the women's restroom. She quickly glances back and leans down to check the space underneath each of the wooden stall doors.

When her head pops back up, her lips are pulled down into a frown. "We have a problem."

A problem? I can't figure out how I've already created such a scene that Rochelle is coming after me like a vulture pecking at soon-to-be dead meat. "What do you mean?"

"Did you talk to a reporter today?" Georgie asks, her tone laced with concern. At least she doesn't seem to be upset at me about whatever this is.

I am so confused though. I didn't talk to anyone today except for the people at the salon. "No."

"Are you sure?" she asks again.

I pinch my eyes closed and try to think through my afternoon. It was just Leslie and Dhrea, but they aren't reporters. There was that one woman sitting next to me... *No, that's crazy.*

I open my eyes slowly, trying to figure out what comes next. "Maybe accidentally... Why, what's going on?"

"This." Georgie hands over her phone, and I look down to see an article in the sports section of a local news station: *New Player Brings Hatred of Sports to the Team Spirit.*

I want to vomit. I don't want to keep scrolling, but my thumb has other plans.

I skim my way down the article. There's barely a word about Baron himself, just me, Montgomery Bell, the sports hater and all-around killjoy who's going to drag the team down, one anti-sports sentiment at a time.

There are a few semi-unflattering photos of me pulled from

161

online. I don't even want to think about what else is sitting in the dredges of the Internet, just waiting for some entrepreneurial reporter to dig up. I've never had a crazy streak, but I went to college in the age of social media. There are untagged photos of me doing things that would have been better left tucked away on someone's memory card rather than uploaded to the great wide web.

"Ohmygod." My knees buckle, and I crumble down to the floor. I don't even care about modesty right now. Georgie getting a flash of my black panties is so much less upsetting than the feeling of someone ripping my clothes off and making me dash through the Internet streets against my will.

Georgie kneels down next to me, puts one hand on my shoulder, and gently pries the phone away with the other. "I thought you should see it. One of the other wives mentioned it to me just a few minutes ago. I ran over to tell you and saw Rochelle talking to you like she was a lion and you were a wounded warthog. This is why Rochelle is being a complete and utter bitch—well, more than normal, at least. She's not exactly Glinda around here, but she's playing the Wicked Witch to a T today."

"I don't..." There are so many ways for me to finish the sentence: I don't know how to handle this, I don't know why this is happening, I don't know how to fix this train wreck.

"It's going to be okay," Georgie says gently. "This is gonna blow over, and Rochelle always has a stick up her ass. She'll figure out something else to be angry about in no time."

I look over at Georgie, tears brimming at the edges of my eyes. "What's Baron going to say? I really screwed up, and I didn't mean to."

"Oh my goodness, Baron is a sweetheart. It's going to be fine. He doesn't care about this attention. It's not his style. So, you'll tell him and you'll move on. Don't worry about that for a second."

I nod my head, willing to believe what Georgie's saying, simply because I have no energy to send myself in any other direction.

Georgie squeezes my shoulder as she stands up. "Okay, I'm going to go get Baron—I'll tell him you're not feeling well. It's getting late; no one really pays attention to who sticks around at this point. I'll have him meet you downstairs in five. Take a second, and then sneak out and meet him downstairs. I'll cover for you."

I am overwhelmed with appreciation. I came in tonight without knowing anyone but the man I moved here with, and I feel like I'm leaving with another person firmly planted in my corner— although I didn't realize I was walking into a boxing ring in the first place.

Baron meets me downstairs, and we hop into a cab to head home.

He slides into the center seat and starts to rub my knee. "What happened? Are you okay?"

I can't open my eyes. I don't want to look at him now and see the change on his face when I tell him.

"I unintentionally talked to a reporter, and she ran a smear story about us." I swipe open my phone, knowing the article is the last thing I looked at so it'll be the first thing on the screen.

I hand it to him and lean my head back against the headrest.

"Shit." The word comes out under his breath. I know he didn't mean to say it out loud, but it still stings.

He reads for another minute and then I hear the click of my phone. He's silent for another moment while he processes it. "You didn't know it was a reporter?"

"No." The word is flat, but I know that if I picked it up, it would be the long edge of a sharp blade.

"And she didn't tell you either?" I can hear his breath pressing heavy on every word.

I finally look over at him, and I can see the anger in his eyes. I know it's not directed at me, but I can't help but bristle that it's even there.

"It's not like reporters give you a heads up," I argue. "*Oh hey, I just wrote down everything you said, and now I'm going to print it in a way that makes you look like a huge jerk.*" I hate the way my voice sounds, but I can't seem to stop it.

Baron just shakes his head, skipping over my frustration and moving back to the point. "That's not ethical."

I shrug. This isn't about logic. "It sucks, but there's nothing we can do about it."

"You have to be more careful," he says with a long sigh.

It makes me feel guilty, and that sends me into an emotional tailspin. "I didn't know she was going to write down everything I said and twist it into this stupid article."

"I know that. I'm just saying you have to watch what you say in public."

"God, why do you care so much? You don't even love football." The words come out so fast, my head lurches forward as if it's trying to swallow them back.

I feel Baron's muscles contract beside me. "This may not be my forever job, but it doesn't mean I'm not loyal. This is my team, Monty. I can't turn my back on that."

I want to stomp my feet, but I don't get to be a toddler in grown-up shoes. He's right.

So, instead, I take a deep breath. "I didn't do it on purpose."

His muscles soften. "I know that. I didn't mean to imply you did. It's not a normal thing, but I'm under a microscope, especially here, being a new player on a popular team. Even if it sucks, it means you are too."

My heart clenches up at that thought. I don't like it, but I'm going to have to get used to it. "I'm sorry." I have to push to get the words out, but as soon as I say them, I know I mean it.

"I'm sorry too," Baron says as he wraps his arms around me and pulls me toward him.

It's not a perfect situation, but I didn't move here because I thought it would be perfect. I moved here because I thought it would be worth it.

Chapter 18

By the time I get to Friday, I can barely flex my social pleasantry muscles. I give the doorman the briefest of smiles and pray he doesn't try to ask me about my day when I walk through the door and take the elevator up to Baron's condo.

At least I have the afternoon off. One bonus of working for a crazy man: he refuses to book anything after 11AM on Fridays.

I dump the stack of photography magazines I snagged from work down on the counter. I still haven't unpacked my camera or any of my gear. I'm hoping that getting lost in some inspiration with a cup of coffee for an hour will do the trick.

That, and a run.

Minutes later, I lace up my running shoes and head back out to the elevator. I slip in my earbuds and let my playlist give my feet a rhythm to follow. I don't care where I go; I just need to get out of here.

I make my way down toward the waterfront, eager for some comfort from being close to the water. My heart starts to relax as soon as I turn the corner and see the Puget Sound on the other side of the street. The street is completely empty, so I immediately sprint out into the intersection.

Just as my feet cross the third white pedestrian crossing line, I hear a loud whistle. I stop, mid-stride, and pop my earbuds out.

I see a police officer walking toward me, and I look around to make sure there isn't something else going on. It's not like I have a headlight out. Both headlights are working fine these days—just ask Baron.

He walks up to me, a pad of paper in his hand. "Excuse me, miss, but you were in the middle of the street."

"Um, yes?" It's not a question, but I don't know how else to respond.

"Well, that's jaywalking. The light was green, and the walk sign was red."

I squint at him. "But, there weren't any cars coming."

His jaw clenches. Obviously, he's not a fan of being argued with. "You were still jaywalking."

I open my mouth to point out again that there weren't any cars coming, but that's clearly not working here. I didn't realize jaywalking was a rule that could actually be broken. It's like the rule of thirds in photography: it's a nice idea to consider, but no one is going to rip up your picture if it doesn't follow it exactly.

Apparently that's not the case here. The police officer starts to scribble on his paper.

Ugh. I do not want a ticket. I have no idea what that would even cost me, but I really don't need to add it to my list of expenses this month. "I'm sorry, sir. I really didn't know. I just moved here from Ann Arbor, Michigan. Jaywalking isn't a violation there."

I'm not actually sure if that's true, but I'm running with it.

The police officer stops abruptly and looks up at me. *Shit.* Maybe it is a violation there, but there are just too many unruly college kids to do anything about it.

"You said Ann Arbor?" he asks.

I nod my head.

"What's your name, miss?"

"Montgomery Bell." I add a smile, but he turns his head back to the paper and keeps writing. I don't think my Midwestern charm is working very well at the moment.

He rips off a piece of paper and hands it to me. "Jaywalking is in fact a violation there, Miss Bell, but apparently they don't teach you how to follow rules any more than they teach you to play football ."

"Football?" ...*what?*

"I went to Ohio. We beat you all four years." He finally smiles at me. "Have a nice day."

Are you fucking kidding me? I got a ticket because I stepped one foot over the line and then told the officer I'm from Ann Arbor?

I want to scream *I don't even like football* at him, but I bet he would just love to slap some cuffs on me and make my day that much worse.

Stupid football rivalries—they take no prisoners.

I put my earbuds back in and wait a full thirty seconds for the silly little walking man to light up on the sign across the street. There isn't a car in sight, but my run is ruined now. I could have run another three miles, but this isn't the kind of energy you can run out. No matter how fast I move my legs, it's going to stay twisted into a knot in my stomach. Running will only screw it tighter. I need to figure out how to let it go, and that sort of release is harder to come by.

I get back to our building and make my way up to Baron's condo. I unlock the front door, set down my stuff, and walk over to grab a Gatorade. My phone rattles against the countertop. I pick it up and swipe right when I see Georgie's name at the top of the screen.

"What are you doing right now?" Georgie asks with a hint of mischievousness bubbling in her tone. From what I can tell, this girl is straight steel covered in a layer of kindness. She's been on the football player-spouse train for years; Zane has been a top player since he was in high school. I don't think there's a scandal, injury, or bad hair day you could send her way that would break her.

She's my kind of woman. I grab a banana out of the wire basket on the counter and start to pull the peel back; my muscles are aching and I know the potassium will help. "Nothing, why?"

"Okay good. You're coming to the beach with me."

Being near the ocean does sound like exactly what the doctor ordered right now.

I look around at the condo. There are dirty breakfast dishes still in the sink, and the counter looks like it got mauled by the stack of magazines I borrowed from the office. I think my sweaty stench might clear everyone in a ten-foot radius, so I need to take a shower too.

I formulate a game plan. "I need to clean up and then hop in the shower." I'm still sort of conscious about the fact that Baron seems to live in a clean, organized bubble while I live in a tornado of mess. I'm trying to hide that fact until I'm a little bit more sure he's not regretting the fact that he invited a girl he barely knew to move across the country with him.

"Okay, I'll be there in fifteen to pick you up!" Georgie chirps into the phone, and then I hear a click.

I don't know what world she lives in, but cleaning and showering is not a fifteen-minute endeavor. I guess the tornado recovery mission is going to have to wait until later.

I walk into the penthouse for the second time today after Georgie drops me back off. It was good to get out and relax, but I'm still having trouble shaking the emotional knots that are coiled inside of me.

The lights are on, and I hear the spray of the shower. *Shit, Baron's home.* I know everything is still a mess, but I'm so emotionally depleted from the week, I can't rally the energy to pick it up.

I crawl my way onto the deep leather couch and start scrolling through my phone. It's not making me feel better, but it isn't making me feel worse either.

I hear the wood softly creak beneath Baron's feet, and I poke my head up from the couch. "Hi."

He glances over for a second and then continues to the kitchen. He turns on the faucet, and I hear the clang of dishes. *Crap, I really should have at least cleaned those up.*

I hop off the couch and quickly walk over, nudging up next to him. "Here, let me help."

He doesn't respond. He just steps away and opens up the fridge. *Okay, not very talkative.*

"So, what's your plan tonight?" His tone is as straight as a tightrope, and I'm not sure I want to walk out onto it.

"Um, hang out with you?" I answer cautiously.

"Think you could pick up? It's a disaster in here." His request is reasonable, but his tone feels like boar bristles against my skin.

"Fine." Isn't that what I'm doing here already? This is so not what I need right now.

He turns around toward me. I can hear the shift in his feet, but I don't turn around to face him. His voice hits my back.

"This is my place, and it drives me crazy when you trash it like some college dorm room."

Jesus. I left some work stuff and dishes out, and maybe some clothes in the bedroom.

"I'm sorry." My tone, however, is not apologetic at all. It's packed with heat and edged in frustration.

"I had a long day. I don't need to come home to more shit."

He means the stuff, I know that, but I can't help but replace *more shit* with the word *me*. He doesn't want to come home to *me*.

I rinse my last dish, and my fingers claw at the edges in frustration, letting out a piercing screech as I place it into the dishwasher. I slam it shut, and the dishes rattle angrily inside.

"Fine. I'll take my shit, and you can have *your place* to yourself." I stalk over to the coffee table and quickly load everything up into an unsteady pile. I don't care about being careful; I just care about getting the hell out of here.

Baron sighs loudly, but he doesn't move from his spot at the counter. "That's not what I meant, Montgomery."

I hate that he's using my full name now, like I'm a child throwing a temper tantrum.

"It doesn't matter, *Bear*. I think it's better if I spend the night at my place tonight." I'm at the door before I even finish the sentence.

I precariously balance everything in one arm and push the door handle down, pressing my back to the thick metal door. Baron still hasn't moved. He's just leaning against the counter now with his chin resting on top of his interlaced fists.

He's not even looking at me. I walk out the door without another word, and I wonder if he'll follow me, if he'll snap out of it and race down the hallway.

When I walk out of the elevator down on the ground floor and set my stuff down so I can dig through my purse to find my keys, it's clear he's not coming after me.

I called his bluff, and we both lost that game.

Chapter 19

I'm sitting in the middle of the floor, eating pizza at the coffee table because I don't actually own a dining table and haven't bothered to buy stools for the kitchen counter yet. I decided to drown my boy sorrows in the sweet embrace of carbs tonight.

My phone vibrates with a text from Andie.

Ugggh, this semester is killing me and I'm not even halfway through.

I immediately text her back.

Yeah, I'd give anything to grab a beer with you tonight.

My phone rings within seconds.

"Well, lucky you, I'm drinking a beer right now," Andie answers as soon as the call connects.

I look down at my second can. Yup, it's one of those nights for both of us. "Man, I miss you."

This is the part about going out on your own no one ever tells you about, but I always had a sneaking suspicion it existed. You're always going to crave home, no matter how far you get from it. There are going to be days that make you want to find your old security blanket and curl up with them until you feel safe and loved again.

Tonight is one of those times, and it aches. I can't get to my security blanket; it's sitting three thousand miles away right now.

"So tell me about life. How are classes? And the cute future doctors of America? And living with crazy med students who study twenty hours a day?"

I want to get absorbed in everything that isn't football right now, and talking to Andie is the perfect answer to that.

I spend forty glorious minutes getting the Andie update. The handsome boy who keeps sitting next to her in class who has a killer smile and strong hands. The stress of knowing exactly what you want to do but having five hundred million steps to finish before you can get from here to there.

I keep hitting her with questions and devouring pizza like carbs can cure my emotional overload. The muscles that were clenched around my chest start to loosen.

"What about you? Does Baron have a work thing tonight?" I can hear the hesitation wrapped around her words like cotton balls, trying to soften the impact. She knows me. She knows the tones of my voice like a pianist can tell you the notes of the keys without even having to look at them. It's innate knowledge, carved into our souls.

I swallow my last sip of beer, ready to put it down and let it out with the only person I know how to do that with.

I take a deep breath and tell Andie about it all. The awkward-teenager-in-braces-at-prom feeling I had at the banquet. The stupid article. Our fight over my mess today.

She just sits on the other end and listens. I close my eyes as I'm talking, imagining her sitting right across from me in front of this coffee table with her legs twisted into a pretzel, her favorite Michigan sweatshirt inevitably stained with tomato sauce because the girl is going to be the best damn pediatric surgeon in the country but is hopeless when it comes to not spilling food on herself.

When I finish, the last of my muscles that were twisted up inside me finally work their way free, but it feels like an empty victory. I'm not anxiously holding it all in, but now that it's out, I don't have any more clarity on where I go from here.

"Ugh, that sucks, Monty. That really sucks. Rochelle Holt sounds evil."

"Stupid cheerleaders messing with my life."

The line is silent for a second. "Rochelle isn't a cheerleader though," Andie points out.

Could have fooled me. "She's like the grown-up version of Sabrina Lang from high school. I feel like she's messing with me just because she can."

"Well, don't let her." The way Andie says it, the amount of strength in her voice, I know she wishes she could stick up for me. She regrets not being there years ago at the field house when Sabrina took me down a notch, and she would be here now if she could. But, this isn't her fight. It never was.

"Even if I had your nerves of steel, this woman is like football royalty." I looked her up after the banquet: her dad owned a team out on the East Coast, and she's the wife of the most revered member of the team, at least in the public eye. Everyone loves Cameron Holt. Everyone.

"Who cares if she's royalty? She doesn't get to bash my best friend."

"I can't do that to Baron," I whisper. As much as I don't understand it, his life is tangled up in this, and getting into it with Rochelle has repercussions for him out on the field.

Andie takes a deep breath, and I know she gets it.

"Fine. Doesn't mean I won't sucker punch this chick if I ever meet her."

"I would expect nothing less."

I hear Andie's yawn fill the silence. I need to let her go and handle my crazy on my own. "We should hang up. It's super late there."

Andie agrees, so we wish each other love and hang up.

I know I need to get some sleep. I always feel better in the morning.

I just seriously hope tomorrow doesn't prove to be an exception to that rule.

I wake up to a soft pounding on my door, and it takes me a second to remember where I am. My bed is familiar, but everything else feels decidedly foreign. I've spent all my time in Seattle spread out in Baron's king-sized heaven, so my bed feels like the only piece of me in this apartment.

I climb out of bed, wondering if package deliveries come straight to your door here. When I unlatch the lock and pry the door open, I see Baron standing in front of me, a bright bouquet fresh from the market in hand.

I pull the door wide open and motion him on in. As soon as he walks through the doorway, it's quite clear that he looks out of place in my little studio apartment. He's a giant walking around in a dollhouse.

I grab the flowers, desperate to find something for my hands to do. I pull open my half-unpacked kitchen, trying to remember if I have a vase or if I only think I have a vase. There are about a dozen boxes it could still be in.

Baron walks over and leans against the kitchen counter. I can't look at him; I'm still not ready to process what's going on with us.

Obviously, he doesn't have the same problem. "I'm sorry, Monty. I was an ass. It's been a really rough week. Yesterday's practice annihilated me, mentally and physically, and I took it out on you."

I finally look up and see the way his eyes are heavy at the edges, like his penance is pulling them down with its weight. I selfishly hadn't even considered that he might have had a tough day. I was so wrapped up in my own day, it wasn't even a thought. I feel like a jerk.

"I had a rough day too." I don't have it in me to say sorry yet. He didn't chase after me, and that still rubs me the wrong way.

He perks up at my skimmed-over explanation, and his eyes narrow as if he's trying to find something in murky water. "What happened?"

I don't know how much to tell him, and I hesitate to open up about Rochelle. Men don't get female drama. Men bash their helmet-clad heads together on a field and scream at each other, and then walk back into the locker room and pat each other on the back with a *good game*. Whatever happens on the field gets cleared up before they even make it back out to their cars.

With women? It's long-term subterfuge. There is no line drawn for field versus home. Nothing is off limits as long as you don't get caught.

No, this isn't worth mentioning. Andie can understand the jumbled mess of an explanation and be on my side, no questions asked, but Baron? I have no idea.

So how do I explained to him what happened? What undercurrent lit the match on our fight yesterday?

"Life hasn't been easy out here. I don't know many people, and my job is less than stellar. I haven't even taken my camera out of the box." The last sentence comes out as barely a whisper.

"We can go out and find something...photo-worthy?" he offers as he walks over to me.

I wish it was that simple, but it's like a part of me is missing. I don't know if I'll find it by putting a camera back in my hands. I shake my head, unable to put my thoughts into words that would

176

make sense to him.

He rubs his hands up and down my arms. The hair rises like an automatic reflex, my body reacting to his touch even if my brain is holding out.

I can't stand next to this man and stay angry at him. It feels like there are still frayed edges on this rope, but I'm willing to tie a knot in it and hope it's strong enough to hold.

I mentally sidestep my broken pieces and turn back to the part I can fix. "We both had bad days. It's gonna happen."

Baron stares at me like he's trying to decipher a foreign language he's never encountered before. A moment later, he presses into me and leans his lips against my forehead, and I feel the knot tighten. I want to put all my weight against the thick twine and test its strength. I press my hands to Baron's chest, running my fingernails lightly across the cotton that's stretched across the wide breadth of his chest.

The anger flickers for a moment, but it's licked by an entirely different flame. They burn brightly together, and I can't tell where one begins and the other one starts. I press harder against him.

Baron weaves his hands between the waterfall of my hair draping across the back of my neck and the sweet sliver of skin behind my ear.

"It's nine in the morning, and all I want to do is take you back to bed right now." He lifts my hair and replaces his hand with his lips, sending shivers through the cords of nerves running up and down my back.

I don't want to think about this stupid argument for another second. I stop trying to find the line between anger and lust and let the feeling of need that's already starting to ripple through my body run free.

"Who says we need a bed?" I ask with a hint of mischief in my tone. I jump up and wrap my legs around Baron, and he catches me instantly—perks of dating a professional football player.

He looks up at me, and I know I could spend years mapping the way his blue eyes crackle like they're ice that's been tossed into tap water.

He nips my bottom lip with his teeth, and I kiss him back with a need that's picking up like the beginning of an epic windstorm. Instead of running for the basement, I'm opening up the windows and letting it in. Tear my world apart; the thrill of the chaos is worth the aftermath.

Baron turns toward the counter and sets me down, catching the waist of my pajama shorts and pulling them down as I lift my hips up to help him. His hands reach back up to explore the exposed skin, and his fingers find the lace edge of my thong.

"Baron..." It escapes as a whisper. I can't handle the tantalizing sensation of his fingers outlining the edge of the fabric; it's too close to my edge. I want to jump off and savor the weightless feeling, but when I look at Baron and see the way his eyebrows are pulled up, I know he's not going to give me what I want. Not yet.

He kisses the inside of my knee, where I have a scar from cutting my leg open on a jagged branch while climbing up a tree to get a better view of a sunset. He smiled when I told him that story, and he's smiling again now. He likes that part of me, the one that can't see the details of the ascent when I'm climbing toward the summit.

I'm headed toward an entirely different summit right now, and I'm just as eager to get there.

His mouth trails up my inner thigh, releasing tiny bursts of pleasure behind him. He kisses skin that's hidden behind lace, and I lean back, my breath like thick stripes of candy being bent back and forth.

When he finally peels the fabric down, I stop breathing altogether. His tongue sends shockwaves through me with every sweet, twisting taste.

I grip my hands against the hard counter, and I feel the stone vibrate underneath me. My eyes shoot open. I wonder if Baron suddenly brought a vibrator into this equation. I wouldn't object, but where the hell was he hiding it?

He looks up and shakes his head. "Phone. This is more important business." He leans back down with a smile.

I close my eyes and let him get back to it—I'm not going to argue with that. His fingers find their way inside me, and I lose all sense of time and space. Every thought merges together into one unintelligible flash. Black holes do exist on Earth, and they're called orgasms.

I open my eyes and hear the ring of my phone coming from my couch cushions. My brain is foggy, but I swear I can see a thought forming beneath the white haze.

Someone's calling both of us. Who would try both of us?

Georgie. The thought breaks through. We have brunch plans with Georgie and Zane.

I push myself back up and give Baron a kiss. He looks like he just won the championship. His smile is lopsided and goofy, and I want to tell him that everyone wins in this game.

I'm pretty sure using your tongue has nothing to do with football, but Baron is a pro.

I hop off the counter just as my phone goes silent, and I race over to the couch to quickly press redial. Georgie picks up on the first ring, and we agree to meet up at Lola's in fifteen.

I'm always agreeing to timetables with her that are way shorter than I actually need, but after that morning wake up call...I could show up in pajamas with bedhead and I wouldn't give a damn.

I try to brush aside the lingering feeling of unease as I slip into a sundress that's at the top of a pile of clothes I haven't bothered to hang up yet.

I try not to look at the box marked *Gear* in the corner. I'll find that piece of myself again.

I have to.

We slip into a booth at Lola's a few minutes late, and Georgie and Zane already have a French press of coffee waiting for us.

Best. Friends. Ever.

"Late start this morning?" Georgie says with a wink.

I focus on pouring my coffee like it's highly flammable rocket science. "Yup, super tired."

"It's cool," Zane says with a laugh. "I don't think Georgie and I showed up anywhere on time when we finally started dating in college."

"How did you two meet?" I ask, grateful to steer the conversation out of the territory of this morning's delay.

Zane and Georgie are already practically sitting on top of each other. There's at least two feet of room on either side of them, which is not easy when one of them is a professional football player-sized.

Georgie leans her head against Zane's arm, and he leans down to kiss the top of her head. I can't help but melt. It's like the relationship goals hashtag is sitting right in front of me.

"Georgie was in one of my freshman math classes, and I pretended to need help studying," Zane starts to explain. "She couldn't resist my charms and good looks for long."

Baron laughs. "More like you practically flunked that class because you paid more attention to her than you did to the actual professor."

Zane shrugs, but his smile says it all. "It was worth it."

I don't doubt it for a second. I want to be like them when I grow up. I don't think there's a single force on the planet that could separate the two of them.

The server comes over to take our order. Georgie asks for some made-from-scratch doughnuts for the table to start, and I'm immediately grateful Baron and I made it to brunch.

Sex is good. Doughnuts are even better.

We get lost in conversation, and I find myself soaking it in like life-sustaining oxygen. Moving to Seattle hasn't been all sunshine and butterflies. It's felt like I walked into the cafeteria at a brand new school and have no idea where to sit, but this right here? Sitting at the table with Baron, Zane, and Georgie…this feels like home.

"We'll have to have a sleepover for one of the away games," Georgie suggests while Zane and Baron are busy talking strategy. "Maybe we could binge on girly movies? You know, balance out all the testosterone."

I know she secretly loves all the testosterone. Georgie breathes football, and not just because she's married to it.

"I'm in for girly movies for sure." I won't turn down that offer. She may not need the break, but I will. I still don't know how I'm going to sit through games every week without going completely insane. A little rom-com motivation can't hurt.

"Thank God." Zane turns his attention back to us. "I don't think I can sit through another one of those *ten different characters with overlapping plots and bad dialogue* movies."

We all have our things. I know the look on Zane's face, as if watching those movies is like hanging out with someone after they've had a fiesta's worth of Mexican food. There isn't enough air freshener in the world to help that stench.

"They're not *that* bad," Georgie argues. "If you had your way, we'd only watch action movies. Don't get me wrong, the Chris's of action are doing well for themselves these days, but I need a little laugh and chill time too."

"The superhero movie circuit has been killing it lately," I comment. I've never gotten into comic books, but all these major reboots along with pulling obscure heroes out of the back catalog and making them funny makes me want to shift my literary roots in a more graphic direction.

"Exactly." Zane extends his hand across the table to me for a fist bump.

"Ugh. I get to watch hot guys play football—that's enough action in my life." Georgie wrinkles her nose at Zane and me.

Baron just shakes his head with a smile. Something tells me he's heard this conversation before.

"That is so not the same," I argue playfully. I would take watching a two-hour movie about adventure and saving the world over a football game any day of the week.

"Football is so much better," Georgie argues back. "You get beer, camaraderie, *and* men in tights."

I just shake my head. "I can get on board with the beer and men in tights, but I think I missed the camaraderie train."

Baron wraps his arm around me just as the server walks over with our fresh doughnuts. He leans in and brushes his lips against my ear. "It's okay, my train's more fun to ride anyway."

It's a good thing Zane and Georgie are preoccupied with doughnuts, because I'm pretty sure I'm a deeper shade of red than the cherry filling.

Maybe I was wrong before. Doughnuts are good, but sex is better.

Way better.

Chapter 20

There's nothing to phone home about over the next couple weeks. I can still count the number of people I know in Seattle on one hand, and I spend my days working for the human form of Grumpy Cat. His coffee is always too hot or too cold. I never respond to emails fast enough, and when I do, he says my responses *appear rushed.* I'm a glorified scratching post for a man who knows photography better than anyone I've ever met but can't be bothered to teach me a damn thing. I can't figure out if it's more upsetting that he's a jerk or that I put up with it.

At least it's Friday. I'm sitting on Baron's bed in the middle of a gorgeous condo overlooking the sunlit water of the Puget Sound, so I really can't complain.

Baron is walking back and forth between his suitcase and his walk-in closet. His first preseason game is tomorrow, and all the players have to stay in a hotel the night before a game, regardless if it's at home or not.

I'm scrolling through my laptop, looking through my boss's photos from this week, when a text comes through iMessage and dings in the upper corner.

I see Andie's name and a link, so I open up the messaging app to read it. *Huh.* She's asking if I saw this. I click and see the local news header load first.

I have a feeling I'm not going to like this. I see three dots blinking next to Andie's name.

This woman is insane.

She doesn't even have to clarify. Now I really know I'm not going to like this.

It's a profile on Rochelle, something about her latest work with some charity. I wonder what this has to do with me. I almost scroll right past it, but my eye briefly catches a capital B, and I quickly jump back up.

It's a Q&A style interview, and the reporter asked her about how the football families support each other.

"Oh yeah. We're all really close, even the new ones. There's a new player and his girlfriend, Baron Richards and Montgomery. Everyone's started calling them Beary, like the fruit. It's our little team nickname for them. It just caught on."

Ugh. *Beary*—are you serious? That makes me want to vomit. What's even worse is I can't completely justify wanting to knee her in the ovaries. I know she's not being nice, I just can't figure out why she's pretending she is.

Either way, I can't stop reading.

"They're so sweet together. You just hope, you know, they can make it through. This is a crazy life, and Montgomery's not used to this kind of attention. It takes a lot of dedication to be a professional athlete's wife. We've got to be team players."

Well, that I can kick her for, maybe a quick one as I call out *Hey, what's that, a dinosaur?* and everyone turns the other way.

I know what she's saying is a jab, and she knows it's a jab, but the rest of the Internet is going *Awww, she takes in the new couple and makes them feel at home.*

I tab back over to the conversation to respond to Andie.

I don't know exactly how to justify how much I hate her,
but I figure if I give her time, she'll give me a good reason.
I see the three dots appear across the screen.
I know, right? She's crazy, but smart crazy.
Watch out for this one, M.
She's the kind that will sneak into your room at night,
stab you, and plant the knife in your BF's locker.
Lovely. I'm going to think about that every single time I go to
bed now.

Baron comes out of the closet, throws a shirt into the duffel
bag, and shuts it. "Okay. I think I've got everything for tomorrow.
I'm really sorry I can't stay with you, babe. It's just a thing we have
to do. At least it's not an away game, so I'll be back home after we
play. We can even walk home together." His smile is apologetic. He
knows I didn't know exactly what I was signing up for. I don't think
it was a lie of omission, I just don't think he gets it yet that he grew
up with this. This culture is ingrained in him like a second
language while I'm still learning its alphabet.

"It's okay, it's just one night." The words feel hollow, but I can't
justify telling him how much it sucks. What? So he can feel bad
while he stays away? It's not like it's his choice.

He walks over and gives me a kiss on the forehead. "It is, and
you can hang out with all the other players' wives and girlfriends
tomorrow."

The way he says it, it's like he's completely forgotten I'm an
introvert who would rather stay home and read all day. Being
around a group of people I don't know sounds like getting stuck on
the "It's a Small World" ride for three hours with that same robotic
melody repeating on high the entire time.

I give him a thumbs up with just a touch of sass, but he
interprets it as enthusiastic approval. I don't bother to correct him.

Instead, we get ready to walk the waterfront together for an
hour before he has to go check in and grab dinner with the team.

I message Andie that I have to go. I don't mention that I have to go spend at least five hours with Rochelle tomorrow. I make a mental note to make sure my phone is fully charged so I can stand in the corner of the room and text my best friend the whole time.

This is what I signed up for. I might not have known all the details before I put my name on the line, but I knew it wouldn't be all puppies and burritos.

I knew I'd have to suck it up and watch some football, and tomorrow, that's what I'm finally going to have to do.

Well, this is hell—privileged hell, but hell nonetheless.

I'm hiding out in the ladies' bathroom in the owner's private box where half of the team's significant others are hanging out. I'm still trying to figure out where the other half are and if they somehow got to stay home and chill while the rest of us are stuck here.

Because if that's an option, I am so in.

At least Georgie's here too. She keeps introducing me to the other wives and telling them I'm a photographer. Part of me wants to spit in her drink, but I know she's just trying to look out for me.

I've been asked if I do headshots. Newborn shoots. Modeling portfolio work. When I say no, the conversation quickly flips to the safe zone—their safe zone: football.

My head is so tired from bobbing up and down with a giant smile plastered across my face, I think it might just roll off by itself and look for shelter.

I find myself trying to actually pay attention to the game, just for something to do that isn't talking, but I seriously can't make sense of anything except for the fact that men in different-colored jerseys run to opposite ends of the field, and they keep stopping to do squats.

No wonder Baron's ass is a freaking rock. You could carve metal with that thing. I thought it was because he's constantly running sprints, trying to improve his speed. That helps, but kicking off from a half-bent position is absolutely a contributing factor.

I'll take it. I'll take it all day long, preferably naked and with good lighting so I can appreciate it in its full, jaw-dropping glory.

I crack open my purse to text Andie. I haven't had a chance to tell her I'm stuck in the owner's suite.

She'd kick me if she were here. She would absolutely hyperventilate if she stepped foot in a suite on game day, and here I am, wishing I was anywhere else. I'd even take a wickedly uncomfortable stadium seat for four hours over being stuck in here with a bunch of people I am forced to talk to despite having nothing in common with.

But I'm the one who's here, because I'm the one who fell for Baron. Love certainly has a sense of humor.

And I'm not entirely sure I think it's that funny.

I hear the main bathroom door swing open and a set of heels clack against the stone floor. I swear I can feel the air being sucked out of the room, and I know who I'm going to see before I even open the door. I'm tempted to stay hidden in my stall, but I know she can see my feet. I wouldn't put it past her to know it was me just by my Converse.

I swing open the door to face the she-devil. Her naturally tight curls are coiled to perfection, and part of me wants to ask how she does it. I can't get my hair to look that good with a natural wave; it either comes out crispy, flat, or greasy. Why do evil people always have good hair? Is it to distract you while they reach into your chest, rip your heart out, and crush it beneath their perfectly buffed leather Manolos?

Because I'm definitely distracted right now. I'm staring at her perfect hair instead of exiting this bathroom like a live grenade was just tossed in.

"Well, well, well…if it isn't the lesser half of the Beary equation." Rochelle side-eyes me while she touches up her lips in the mirror. She can't even be bothered to take the time to insult me to my face.

I want to throttle her. I want to find her Achilles heel and twist it just enough that she tumbles to the ground. It's a lovely image in my head, but I'm not sneaky or conniving enough to figure out her weakness. Even if I did, I don't think I could use it. I'd want to, but there's no way I could follow through.

I think she's evil, but I don't have the guts to try to do anything about it.

I walk toward the door. I'm not going to confront her. I'm not going to take her down. I might as well get back to the outrageously uncomfortable social situation I managed to get myself into.

Thanks love, you're a real jerk sometimes.

I reach for the door handle, and I see Rochelle move out of the corner of my eye. I lurch to the side, thinking she's going to reach for me, but when I move and catch a better glimpse of her, she's leaning casually against the bathroom counter.

"You don't fit here, Montgomery. I know it, and you know it. You're not one of us, and you're never going to be. You don't have it in you to make it in this world. I'm doing you a favor by telling you now—you should be thanking me."

"Thank you for what? Being a bitch?" The words tumble out before I have the forethought to catch them. I have the urge to cover my mouth in case any more try to race out after them.

"Hate me all you want; I'm right. You'll figure that out eventually." She turns back to the mirror and continues to check her flawless makeup. She dropped her knowledge bomb, and now she's on to more important things.

I want to be sick, but I'm not walking back into a stall. I pull the door open, and the sound of the polite chatter mingling with the low roar of the game hits me like a thick wall of smog. I can't breathe through it. It's not what my body needs. I need fresh air. I need quiet. I need solitude.

I turn the other direction and head out toward the large concrete hallway of the stadium. I pull out my phone, find Georgie's number, and fire off a message.

Sorry, need some fresh air. Be back in a bit.

I open up my maps app and do a scan of the area. Waterfall park in the middle of the city, and it's only two blocks away? Sold.

I walk there as fast as my legs will carry me, which is nearly a sprint. There are a bunch of drunk fans chanting loudly all through the streets, and their cheers only make me go faster.

I make it to the park, and I'm dubious of this whole waterfall business, but as soon as I walk through the zigzag entrance, I see it. It's not big, but it drowns out everything else, like a sound machine oasis in the middle of Seattle.

There's no one here. Everyone else in the world cares about the game that's happening two blocks away, but my universe is happy to reside in this little half-block space for the moment.

For once, I'm not thinking about my crappy job, or if I should buy a plane ticket home for Thanksgiving. I'm thinking about if Rochelle is right.

And I hate her even more for that.

I know I don't fit in Baron's world. That was clear from the moment I knew what his world was. I guess I just thought maybe our worlds could overlap. I mean, how many relationships are built on having the exact same interests?

Rochelle keeps planting seeds of doubt, and I know exactly what she's doing. It's not like she's grabbing rat poison from a pouch labeled *rosebush seeds*. No, she's grabbing from a bag that has a skull and bones stamped on the front.

I know what she's doing, and yet, I can't brush it off. What if she's right? What if I'm not cut out for this? Will Baron and I survive if I'm a girlfriend who isn't involved in the world he lives in?

I stare at the water cascading down and slamming against the rocks below. I wonder if the rocks mind the pressure. They just sit there, unflinching, silently eroding away under its weight.

My phone chimes in my purse. I pull it out and see Baron's name. Shit, the game must be over.

I'll be done in thirty. Meet me at the locker room?

I don't even know how the hell to find the locker room, but I'm too chicken to admit I ditched out of his first game early. I want to scream *It's not even a real game,* but I think someone might shank me. I'm in Hawk country here. You don't insult the home team on its own turf.

I head out of the park, saying a silent goodbye to the peaceful bliss of this urban refuge, and make my way back to the stadium. I quickly pull up the results of the game. *Thank you, Internet.*

Whew, okay, at least the Hawks won. I'm not ready to deal with the inevitable depression of a loss. I know I'm going to need to be understanding, but all I'm going to want to do is roll my eyes because *Dude, you had a fifty/fifty chance.*

He knew who I was. I laid out my cards the moment I met him, but will he still love me when he sees that side of me in real life?

Chapter 21

I find the locker room entrance without too much trouble.
Apparently, everyone and their mom knows how to get there.
Getting in is the real problem. The man standing in front of the
open-air entrance looks massive, and that's saying something
considering I just watched—okay, glanced at—a pro football game.
I don't use the word massive lightly; I think this guy was ready for
professional sports when he was ten. Now? He could crush tree
trunks with his bare hands.

"Hi, um, I'm with Baron Richards." Is that how this works? Do I
need to pull my shirt down, show some cleavage like I'm trying to
get into the VIP section of a hot club?

"Your name, miss?" Okay, no cleavage required.

"Montgomery Bell." I add a charming smile for emphasis, but
his face stays in the same stoic line. Is there a list or something?
This guy doesn't seem to be holding any clipboards, but he could
hide a house behind him, so who knows.

I'm about to ask about how this process works when Baron
walks out of the entrance and right over to me.

I turn back to the bouncer as if to say, *See, I'm supposed to be here*, but he doesn't seem to notice.

Baron wraps his arm around me. "I missed you."

"I missed you too." There's so much wrapped up in those words, but I don't know how to tell him everything hiding underneath the surface.

Instead, I let him grab my hand and we head out of the stadium toward the street.

When we stop at the crosswalk, I lean my head into his chest and breathe him in. I notice that his hair is just a little wet, and he smells like Old Spice. He must have showered after the game, and for a second, it feels like I could be walking with a normal guy. We could have had brunch this morning and then gone for a walk down by the pier and decided to check out Pioneer Square.

But he's not a normal guy. People just paid serious money to sit in the stands to cheer him and his team on. Baron Richards is my normal boyfriend. Bear Richards? He's the country's boyfriend.

"So where are we going?"

I can see the hint of a smile playing on Baron's face. "I thought maybe we could have our first date."

I crinkle my eyes and nose together in confusion. "But..." We had our first date. It was kind of the first date that never ended; we had puppies and burritos and his apartment and then my parents. It spanned days.

Baron laughs as he stops and turns toward a door in a block of old brick buildings. This doesn't look like a restaurant.

I turn to face the front of the building, and my eyes are overwhelmed with flashes of light. It takes me a full ten seconds to even find the sign among all the neon color: Pioneer Pinball Museum.

He remembered. I lean in and feel the weight of him beside me, wanting to touch the person that keeps surprising me day in and day out. I turned him down in front of Pinball Dave's back in Ann Arbor, but at some point, I admitted how spot on he was with that idea without even knowing it, and he held on to that detail. Now we're getting another shot at it.

He reaches out and grabs the handle of the door, pulling it toward us. "After you."

I grab his hand and weave my fingers with his. I want to feel his skin on mine. I want to wash away any lingering anxiety from today with the intoxication of his touch.

Baron pays the admission and we head in. There are only a couple of people in here, but the walls are packed with more machines than I've ever seen in my life. My eyes stop when I see the *Lord of the Rings* machine, and I'm done. Just done. I don't even have to feed it any quarters to play to my heart's content.

It's taken me years to craft my nerdiness, and it runs deep to my core. LOTR is more than a movie that showcases Orlando Bloom's piercing eyes; it is a standard all other fantasy books are held to. Mix that with some balls, bumpers, and flashing lights, and that's my kind of sport.

Baron kisses his favorite spot of skin where my neck dips to meet my shoulder. I shiver at his touch, and I can feel his smile respond to my physical reaction. He loves doing that to me. He loves making me tingle and ache for him almost as much as I love feeling that way.

"I'm going to go grab us some beers," he says with only the slightest hitch to his tone. I know better though—he's just as affected by me as I am by him.

He walks away, and my thoughts speed back up into real time. Wait, beer? This museum is focusing on all the right things.

I barely even notice when he comes back five minutes later with two plastic cups of beer. I finally look up when the machine eats my ball. I don't even care. It's not eating my quarters. I can play this all night.

I stop and turn to Baron, grabbing the cup he hands to me. I can tell by the crinkle around his eyes that he's happy I'm enjoying myself.

"Good date?" he asks.

"Great date." I take a sip of my beer. "Although this isn't what I expected when you asked me to meet you at the locker room."

He stuffs his hands in his pockets. "Yeah, some thought went into this."

I can't figure out why he's shy to admit that. It makes me feel even more special to know he's spent time and energy trying to find something he thought I would enjoy. Obviously, he hit the nail on the head with this one.

I take another sip, letting the cool liquid hit the back of my throat and cascade down. It feels good, relaxing. The beer I drank earlier today felt like medicine to get through a prison sentence. This feels like a beer to relish in letting go and enjoying the moment. It's strange how different life is outside the stadium.

"I'm not gonna lie, I was kind of expecting you to show me the locker room."

"Yeah." He stops and scrunches his eyebrows together while he sorts through his thoughts. "I guess I would have done that before."

"What's that?"

"Show a girl the parts of the stadium most people don't get to see—the locker room, the empty field…get my best friend's wife to take them up to the owner's suite." He adds the last item to the list with a sheepish smile.

He did that? It's sweet when he says it like that, but I can't believe I endured three hours of torture because he thought it would be something special.

Still, it's the thought, right? He's trying to make me feel included at an event where I feel entirely out of place.

Instead of trying to show me those parts of his life, after a day full of it, he brought me here. I appreciate it, but at the same time, it stings a little to know I don't fit into his life like any of the girls before me did. Something about that makes me nervous.

Can it really work when I don't want to immerse myself in this life? It would be like stepping into a pool full of pink paint. When I stepped out, my outline would still be the same, but it wouldn't look like me. I am the freckles running across the bridge of my nose regardless of how much sun I get. I am the scar on my eyebrow from when I ran into the dining room table and cut it open when I was three.

I am books and photography. I will never know how to do the sports thing, and I don't really want to learn.

But, I want Baron, and he's a football player. I have to take the good with the I'd-rather-pull-my-hair-out-than-sit-through-this side too.

He leans over and kisses my forehead. "What's going on in that head of yours?"

I shrug, unable to take the words in my head and let them wander about in the world around me. They're little bits of my soul, and I don't know how to let them go without exposing myself too much.

I take the easy path. "Well, I've never seen an empty stadium."

"I didn't think you'd be interested," he says with a tilt of his head.

"I'm interested in you." That's the truth, no caveats.

Baron presses against me, and the blood rushes out of my head and into every crevice of my body. I love that feeling. It's as if every blood cell in my body is clambering to the edge, reaching out to feel his touch.

He runs the tip of his finger along the curve of my jaw. "Even if I play football?"

"You're Baron Richards to me. You aren't football. You're just the man I want to spend my time with." Because when you peel away the layers, I want what's at the core. It's the sweet, thoughtful man that brought me to a pinball museum.

Baron opens his mouth, but I can't tell if he's going to say something or kiss me. I hold my breath waiting for the answer.

He closes it again and grabs my hand, leading me toward the back of the museum. There's a flight of stairs I hadn't noticed before. Baron nods at the guy standing behind the counter serving beer and buckets of popcorn, but they don't say a word. He just takes me up to a second story.

There are a dozen more machines up here, but the space is tighter. It feels like the end of a shrinking hallway, and even the ceilings feel lower. On a normal day with a bunch of strangers, it would feel claustrophobic, but tonight? Tonight, I would rather have Baron in a closet than a grand ballroom.

And I have him. All to myself. There isn't another soul up here. It's just us.

I try to take a second and appreciate all the classics sitting up here, but even if the dizzying amount of flashing colors packed into a relatively small space wasn't enough, I am standing next to something that is turned on. Way on.

As soon as he climbs the last step, he wraps his arms around my waist and kisses my neck, and my muscles contract at his touch. I want him, but the wall at the far end is only a half wall. This is basically a second story balcony, so any noise we make is going to mingle with the pinball soundtrack and make its way through the whole building.

Baron's hand skims down the outside of my leg, dancing over the fabric of my skirt, and when he finds the edge of it, he follows it in toward the line of my inner thigh, pulling the fabric up with it.

"We can't…" My words come out as a moan. There are people downstairs, and any one of them could walk up those stairs any minute.

"What if I told you I gave the bartender a twenty to 'rent' the top floor?"

"Oh." My eyes are wide.

"I don't know about you, but I'm a fan of Arabian Nights." His fingers graze the lace of my panties, and I can't figure out how he can focus on anything in this room while it's spinning in Technicolor motion.

He lifts his hand, my skirt drops, and I'm stuck like a hung ball. I need him to slam the machine a few times to get it rolling again.

"Come here. I want to watch you play again." He walks over to a table and stands to the side.

I have no idea how I'm going focus long enough to play a game, but I'd play any game to get the feeling of Baron inside of me right now. I step up and press the button to start, and the machine rattles to life.

"In an ancient land, a young princess was imprisoned by an evil genie," a deep voice bellows from the game. The ball loads with a flourish of the sitar, and I pull the lever back, releasing it and feeling the whole table vibrate with the shock of the mallet connecting with the metal ball.

As I shift my fingers to the buttons on each side of the box, Baron steps up behind me and grabs my waist. I can feel the hard length of him against my low back, and I close my eyes for a second.

When the ball disappears under the blue genie at the top of the table, a female voice begins to speak. "The tale of thieves. Spell sesame, and my ruby will be yours."

A laugh tumbles out of me. This game is stunning, the lights and colors like walking through a market in the middle of a desert. The colors wrap around you like windblown silks. Standing here with Baron pushed up against me and need building between my legs, the woman saying to *hit me once more* is like my own voice found its way through the machine and decided to take control.

I'll play this game. I'll play it all night long.

The ball comes flying down the center of table, and I punch the flipper. It connects with the ball and sends it flying back up, hitting the S-E-S-A-M. One more letter, and it's mine.

Baron runs his hands from my waist, down my hips, to my thighs. He leans his chest against my back, pressing his lips to the side of my ear.

"Open sesame, baby."

I shift my legs wide, and he lifts my skirt and pulls my panties down. They're soaked already, and he hasn't even touched me. I hear the familiar sound of a zipper and the condom wrapper ripping open.

He presses right against me, and I close my eyes just as I hear the ball hit the golden lamp, sending it spinning and releasing a whirl of melody.

The ball comes tumbling back down, and I miss it. It runs straight down and hits the peg at the bottom of the machine, just as the princess's voice tells me to *try again*.

I would give this game all my quarters to keep playing right now. Baron is pressing against me, and I can barely pull in a breath. I hear the sound of the ball reset, but all I can think about is how much I want him inside me right now. I need him and I don't care if everyone in this museum hears it.

"Show me what you want," he whispers.

I run my teeth against my lips as I pull back the handle. "This is what I want."

I release it, and the whole table vibrates underneath me as the music builds like wild horses running across the desert and Baron presses into me. The ball hits a bumper, and Baron pulls back and slams into me, sending shudders reverberating through my bones.

"Are you ready to obey me?" It takes me a second to realize it's the game talking and not Baron. I hit the flippers and send the ball back up to the lamp. It hits its target, and Baron matches its shock. I have every incentive to keep this ball in play; I don't want him to stop.

Every time the ball hits a post, Baron pulls back and hammers into me. It's an intoxicating game, watching the ball and wondering when it's going to hit its next target.

It comes racing back down to the bottom, and I slam the buttons so hard, the whole machine vibrates. The ball drives up toward the blue genie lamp near the top of the game, disappearing underneath.

Baron stops, and I let out a whimper. *Please don't stop. God, ball, why did you have to disappear?*

It comes flying out, and Baron rewards me with a slow thrust, which hits all of my trigger points. This is the best fucking game of pinball I've ever played in my life. I never want it to stop.

I hit the ball when it comes back down, and it goes flying all the way to the top and starts bouncing from one wall to the next between the genie and the lamp, like a magic trick that keeps on giving. Baron matches it hit for hit, and I can feel the pull of my release building with every single bouncing hit.

Just as the ball is captured by the genie, I lose it, tumbling over the edge into a mindless oblivion. My muscles contract and release in tiny spasms as delight swirls through my body like a snake spiraling up out of a basket.

"Turn around," Baron whispers again, just as my brain is starting to come back online.

The genie still has a hold of the ball, and part of me is reluctant to let our high score go to waste, but I'm sure as hell not going to say no to more of this.

I do as I'm told and turn around. Baron lifts me up onto the glass, pressing one hand against my stomach, leaning me back against the length of the machine. I wrap my legs around his waist as he enters me again.

"Don't let go," he asks with a devilish glint in his eye.

I hook my ankles and squeeze, and he grabs each side of the pinball machine. I reach down, pressing my hands on top of his. I know he can't see what's going on, but every time I feel him hit the buttons, he slams into me.

I hear more balls rush into the playfield, every cling of metal ricocheting off metal sending us further along in this game.

"Hurry!" the princess cries out.

Baron keeps driving into me, but his hands stop working, and I can tell by the flutter of his eyelids, he's racing toward the jackpot. I slip my hands underneath his and keep pressing the bumper buttons, as if it was the sole force pulling Baron up the hill. I can feel him release inside of me, and I hear the last ball slide down the peg at the bottom of the lane, dropping down into the unknown abyss below the machine.

He leans over on top of me, the weight of him heavy on my torso. I want to stay here forever, but my bare ass is hanging out on top of an arcade game in the middle of an open alcove of a museum.

This isn't exactly a cuddle and chill sort of moment. I kiss Baron's shoulder and then start to press up onto my hands. He pops up off of me and adjusts himself back into his jeans.

"I think I'll rent this place out next time, see if we can slam tilt any of these games."

I look at him in mock horror. "And potentially damage some of the greatest pinball machines known to man?"

"They would want me to. Even a pinball machine would sacrifice itself for that kind of action."

I turn back around and pat the Arabian Nights machine lovingly. "Thanks for your service, Mr. Genie."

My wish was certainly granted tonight.

Baron wraps his arm around my shoulder. "Want to play some more downstairs?"

"Dude, no pinball game is ever going to live up to that one. Let's quit while we're ahead."

"It was a high score, all right," Baron says with a laugh.

"Nerd."

He shakes his head and points back at the board of the

machine. Oh. Twenty million. Yeah, that's pretty damn good. Pretty damn fucking good.

Chapter 22

Well, this is my kind of game. The guys are gone for the away game this week, so Georgie invited herself over. We're having a slumber party in his condo, since he actually owns a television—which is kind of required when you want to watch a football game.

Well, *want* might be a bit of an overstatement, but I figure if I'm going to dip my toe in the water, it might as well be in my pajamas with a ton of carbs in front of me. Georgie is one hundred percent on board with the idea. We order a massive pizza, bread sticks, and a side of mac and cheese. Life is good.

We sit and veg for a while as the teams are announced and the game kicks off. I try to pay attention, but even in the comfort of Baron's tricked-out bachelor pad with a world of carbs sitting in front of me, I can't focus for shit.

Fortunately, that's what phones are made for. I tuck mine against the side of my leg, stealing glances at my current read on my Kindle app while Georgie yells at the screen.

I get so wrapped up in a high-tension scene I don't notice when Georgie goes silent. When I look up at the television, I can see her staring at me out of the corner of my eye.

"What you got over there?" she asks with one eyebrow raised.

"Just a little supplemental reading."

"Football is really not your thing, huh?"

"Sports really aren't my thing. I didn't grow up with it—we didn't even have a TV—and the people who were into it at my high school...well, they were jerks. So, I just got turned off, and nothing ever changed that," I explain.

I've never really tried to sit down and understand what's going on, but I've come to realize it doesn't matter if someone meticulously describes the rules and motivators behind the game. It's still like asking me to read *Moby Dick* page by tedious page. I can do it, but I'm not going to enjoy it—even if it does have the word dick in the title. Worst literary bait and switch ever. Football players may be absurdly attractive men in tight uniforms, but I'm not fooled for a second.

Georgie assesses me, and I wonder if she's going to make me sit through a lecture on the ins and outs of the game. It wouldn't be the first time.

She purses her lips. "You're not like any of the other girlfriends or wives."

I can't tell if she means it as a compliment or an insult. Either way, it's the truth. I'm not. I don't follow the game. I'll support Baron, but I'm not going to become a serious Hawks fan overnight.

"Eh," she finally says with a shrug. "I don't think Baron would have gotten along well with someone who was super into this whole thing." She fans her arms around in a big circle, like jazz hands. The inner football circle is kind of like a big Hollywood production—game days and banquets and articles and sponsorships. It's so much more dramatic than real life.

I've never thought about why Baron would have been attracted to someone who didn't love the world he lives in. He's attracted to me, and I never really considered the root of it. "Why do you think that?" I ask.

"Because he's a great player. He loves his team, but he's not someone who lives for the limelight. Hell, he's not even someone who lives for the game. Some of these guys, they have this hunger for it that never fades. It's like they need to suit up every week and get out on that field to prove who they are. Baron knows who he is, and he's going to be okay when he doesn't get to strap on that helmet every Sunday."

"I guess you're right." He knows what he wants after this career ends, and that's what this is—a job that pays well and that he kicks ass at. He enjoys it. Hell, he loves football, but he doesn't define himself by it. It would be like me defining myself as only a photographer.

I'm so much more than that. I'm a book nerd and a dog lover and a wanderer at heart. You can't strap me down with one description, even though we do that to our sports stars.

"So, it makes sense," Georgie continues. "You're not going to drop him when he's done being a football player. What is it about football that you hate so much?"

I flip through the reasons like I'm shuffling a deck of cards. There's a whole pile of reasons, but I keep coming back to the queen of hearts. "I feel like it brings out the worst in people, the competitive, catty side. It's like it's a beacon for the Rochelles of the world."

"The Rochelles of the world don't actually play though."

"Yeah, but we turn our players into gods, and they turn around and pick people like her to stand by their side. We all know who turns the heads of gods; women rule the world whether anyone acknowledges it or not."

Georgie thinks for a second, and then tilts her head to the side. "But, Baron picked you."

"I don't know why."

"Because he's one of the good ones. There are men like him and like Zane who play this game for the right reasons, because football is their family. It's the people who showed up on the sidelines when they were fifteen and dropping every other pass like it was a stick of butter just as much as it's the hordes of fans that scream their faces off every week. It's about the community, and they get that. They show up because they get that they're playing for their team and their city and their sport. It's bigger than them, so it's an honor to play, not a privilege. The men who see it as a privilege are the ones to watch out for, because they do pick the Rochelles, and they play for the glory of themselves. Sports aren't about a singular person. They're about all of us together."

The idea hits me like a lamppost that came out of nowhere. It's always been there. I can't pretend it didn't exist just because I didn't see it. It was there before me, and it'll be there long after me.

I've been throwing out reasons left and right about why I hate football, but it was never really about me. It doesn't matter if I like it or don't. There is a whole group of people that love it, and I don't have to understand it. I just have to understand that those are the people Baron plays for. He shows up because he's loyal. I hug my legs into my chest, trying to grasp the idea that maybe I've latched onto my hatred of the sport because of the wrong people.

If I hate it for the wrong reasons, does that still make it true?

I walk over to the kitchen the next morning, eager to use Baron's super fancy-schmancy coffee machine to brew me up something delicious. It's like Christmas morning every morning here. Should I try a latte today? Or maybe an iced macchiato. I don't even know if macchiati are iced, but I bet this machine does and will make it for me.

I'm scrolling through my options when I hear Georgie. I can't tell if she just sneezed or gasped, but I can hear her mumbling to herself, phone in hand.

Part of me wants to bounce on over and be nosy. The other part of me is not caffeinated enough for bouncing and wants to smack the other half for even thinking about.

I let the second half win, and I start to brew an iced Americano.

"Um, Monty, you should come see this." Georgie's tone is somber, and suddenly, I wonder if maybe the whole team lost their jobs. Can that happen? Could the owner lose all their money and ditch the team? And would I really be upset about that?

I grab my coffee mug and saunter over in my fuzzy slippers. "What's up?"

She just hands me her phone, and I see a familiar website logo splashed across the top, one of those stupid celebrity gossip sites that posts grainy photos of people going to the grocery store without a speck of makeup on, because obviously the world should be shaming people who decide not to spend an hour primping for errands. That's definitely what we should be focusing on.

I want to find all those photographers and point them in the direction of things that actually matter.

I scroll down, mostly skimming the article. It's some football player and a cheerleader. I don't get why I should care about this, but I scroll down to the end and see the full photo: it's our jersey colors. Oh, well that's why I should care.

I see the player from the back, the cheerleader's arms wrapped around his neck while he leans down. Her lips are brushing his ear, and the way her eyes are closed, you know she's enjoying her current situation.

I scroll down farther, and then I stop. I nearly drop the phone, as if I finally realized I'm holding a dead rat.

That's Baron. The cheerleader has her arms wrapped around Baron. The next set of photos makes it look like he's wrapping his arms around her waist.

I can't look. I quickly hand the phone back to Georgie, and I plop straight down on the floor, sloshing my coffee over the edges of the mug on my way down.

I don't care that it's dripping down my legs and soaking into my slippers, and I really don't care that it's pooling on the wood floors of Baron's apartment.

"Men are idiots," Georgie says as she props her chin on the side of the couch. She looks like a puppy, but I know she would turn into a vicious attack dog if anyone pulled this on her.

I agree with her, but whether Baron is an idiot who is going to cheat on me or an idiot who will get himself into stupid but harmless situations because he's quicker to oblige than to push away, I don't know.

I do know this could happen to anyone. Just go to a bar and chat with someone who isn't your significant other—someone will take a picture and tag it on Facebook. Boom. The Internet is an equal opportunity relationship destroyer.

So, I can't quite put my finger on why this feels like I'm stuck sitting in a box that has a thousand nails pounded into it. Every flinch, every breath feels like sharp metal piercing my skin.

I guess it doesn't matter if it's Facebook or some celebrity gossip site: no woman wants to see another woman's arms wrapped around her boyfriend. I just got the pleasure of seeing it along with the rest of the public on the Internet.

This sucks.

I'm sitting on the couch with a half-empty pint of Ben & Jerry's when I hear the lock start to turn. I was planning on taking a shower and looking like a million bucks, but the fact is I don't actually give a shit that I have a trail of ice cream spilled down the front of my shirt.

And into my lap.

And probably on the couch too.

Nope. I could care less what I look like, because I'm pretty sure my outsides are matching my insides right now, which seems appropriate. There's no use fighting misery, even if she is an ugly bitch.

"Monty?" Baron's voice is soft and low. There's a beat of hesitation. He knows.

I take a deep breath. I'm not ready to have this conversation, but I know I'm not going to be ready even if I finish this pint as well as the bottle of wine that's sitting on the table.

This is not one of the times in life you want a football player whose main objective is to improve his speed. Nope. This is one of the times you want a lazy boyfriend who thinks getting up from the couch to get a bag of potato chips is a marathon. Baron walks over to me within seconds, and the conversation is staring me right in the face.

I'm going to continue focusing on my ice cream. I don't want to see his face. I don't want to see the guilt. I want to live in the space of self-pity and misery for a second longer before I move on to really, really pissed.

"Monty," he pleads. Points for him though—he doesn't try to sit down on the couch. "I'm so sorry. I don't know how that happened."

My head shoots up, and my eyes narrow on him. His face is long and heavy. *Good.* Because that's exactly how I feel right now.

I finally gave in and drudged through the Internet trenches last night. I typed in his name and went to town.

I can't decide if it was sillier of me to go this long or to break my streak.

It doesn't matter much now. I've seen the string of beautiful women Bear Richards has been attached to, and the list is long. Even if he only dated half of them, the final count would still rival the VIP list for a Taylor Swift birthday party.

And thank you, Internet. You so kindly provide me faces for *all* the names. We have brunettes and blondes. Cheerleaders and models. Famous actresses. Even a pop star. There are pictures of dates walking hand in hand out of clubs and restaurants. Arms linked in front of the sponsored backgrounds of red carpet events. Grainy photos of beach vacations.

This whole time I thought I didn't fit into the world of sports, but the real problem stared back at me from the endless results pages. It's not about whether I love Baron Richards or Bear Richards, or some combination of those two personalities.

No. It's about the fact that I am Montgomery Bell. I'm still the same person who showed up at a football field when someone told me the star football player had a crush on me. I'm willing to show up on the edge of the spotlight and wait for them to walk off and grab my hand.

And who wants to be the person waiting off to the side?

You want to be the person that takes a step into the light and owns it with them. If you're constantly standing off to the side, you're not living your own life.

And that's not me—not anymore.

I hit the end of the pint just as my sadness rolls over into a wave of anger.

"Are you going to say something?" I press. I finally want to hear it, whatever it is.

"They got the worst of it—the photographer. Nothing happened. That cheerleader walked over and asked me if I'd take a selfie with her to send to her little brother who loves the Hawks."

I watch his face with every single word, and my anger wants him to be lying. I want to unleash it on him because if I don't, I feel like it might consume me. But, he's not lying. The way his eyes crinkle at the edges with sadness and fear…it's not an act, and it makes me want to punch a wall.

"You should be more careful," I spit out, letting the flames of my anger lap at his ankles.

He nods his head slowly. "You're right. I give people the benefit of the doubt, but I live a public life. There are people waiting on the sidelines, ready for me to screw up."

"And you did screw up." I know I'm being hard on him, but I can't stop myself.

Baron drops to his knees and grabs my hand. My resolve weakens, and I hate myself for that. "I fucked up, and I'm so sorry. I didn't mean to hurt you, but I did, and it's not going to be the last time, but I love you. I'm yours. You have to know that."

My breath catches, and the fire that has been building inside me loses its oxygen. "You love me?"

He kisses each of the knuckles on my hand, and my breath skips with each tender touch of his lips to my skin. "Yes." His voice is low and soft, and it's like a thick blanket that stifles any of the lingering flames.

I close my eyes. I don't know how to keep myself and love him at the same time, but that doesn't stop the second part of the equation from being true. "I love you too."

He sees the white flag I just raised and pops up onto the couch. The cushion I'm sitting on dips toward me, as if physics wants to give me a little nudge. I sigh and move in toward him, and he immediately wraps his arms around me. I close my eyes and lean my head against his hard chest.

"I'm so sorry, Monty," he repeats tenderly, and then I can hear his smile almost before he continues. "Do you think six feet is enough for the restraining order?"

I lift my head up and see the laughter playing on his face. "What restraining order?"

"Against the opposite sex. I mean, I've got you. Between my family and you, I think I'm all set. So, six feet for the rest of them," he teases.

I can't help but let a smile peek through. More like six feet *under* for anyone who tries anything like that cheerleader did. I lean back into his chest.

He's mine. It's messy and confusing, but it's my mess, and I'll take that for now.

Chapter 23

The next game comes way too fast—like six days later too fast.

I get a call from Georgie in the morning, and I'm only halfway into my coffee, so my resolve is only halfway up its daily rollercoaster.

"Come to the owner's box with me today? Please." Georgie adds the last word with a lingering puppy dog whine.

I press the warm ceramic mug to my lips. I smell the coffee, willing it to work its willpower magic, but it's caffeine, not pixie dust. "Fine," I mumble.

Georgie squeals, and we make plans to meet an hour before the game starts.

I still don't understand how people do this on a regular basis. Sitting at home or at a bar watching a game is a four-hour event. *Going* to a game? That's at least six hours of daylight. Shot. Gone. Poof.

And I'm dating a player. Attending games is practically written into the unofficial code of conduct rulebook for relationships. People who do this for fun? Color me baffled.

Hours later, I'm standing in the box. Again. Listening to the people around me talk about the game, the team, their little kids' travel teams.

Does *everything* involve sports? If it does, please tackle me now. I'll take the concussion.

Georgie walks back over to me after getting sidetracked by conversation when she went to grab a snack. I've been trying to pretend I'm enraptured by the game below us for the past twenty minutes, and I don't know how much longer I can keep it up.

I tucked my Kindle in my purse just in case, but something tells me whipping out a book in the middle of the owner's box is more than just abnormal behavior, it's downright offensive.

"Sorry about that. Daphne was asking about my dress from the event a few weeks ago. We got talking and..." Georgie pauses. "You know, I should just introduce you. She's super nice. Come on." Georgie reaches out to grab my hand, but I pull back.

"Umm, that's okay." It's an awkward response, but it's the best I've got. I'm at my max, which seems to be getting lower and lower every time I show up to one of these things. I am peopled out, and we're not even halfway through the game yet. I need a bubble bath and like five hours all to myself to recover.

I'm already wedged into a corner in an effort to make myself as off to the side as possible. This isn't my cup of tea, and I would rather sit over here like an outcast than walk around pushing myself to my breaking point by trying to fit in.

Georgie nods, but her mouth is pulled tightly to the side. You could throw her into a room full of vampires, and she'd not only walk out with her porcelain skin intact, she'd have business cards and favors lining her pockets.

"We can just stay put. That's fine." The way she says it, I know she doesn't mean it, but she's not going to drag me around by my ponytail, trying to pull the extrovert out of me.

Which is good, because I don't think there's any sneaking around in there. The introvert strangled it and buried it out back years ago.

We turn back to the game in silence. It's a heavy truce, but it'll hold.

We hit the end of the third quarter, and my legs are starting to ache from standing for so long. I wiggle my knees, realizing I've kept them locked this whole time.

"I didn't know the third quarter came with a dance break."

I grimace at the voice, turning around to see Rochelle's halo of blonde curls. I swear her hair is a weapon of mass destruction. It makes you think there's an angel standing in front of you when it's the devil instead.

"Hi Rochelle." And so we begin our next round of social torture. *Kill me now.*

"You're still here, Monty? Hmm, I would have thought you'd have run off by now." Her voice is sweet like honey, but it's laced with poison.

"Still here."

"Well, geez, Baron better put a ring on it soon. If you want to have any chance of getting your body back after having his offensive line worth of kids, you better get moving."

The way her eyes sparkle when she speaks, I know she's just swinging to see if she can hit a mark. Little does she know, she just threw the ultimate sucker punch.

I don't know if I want kids. I'm not the type of girl who's dreamed of being a mom since she was old enough to ask for dolls for Christmas.

I feel like an idiot. How could I have moved out here without knowing the basics? *What's your mom's name? Most embarrassing story? Do you want to have kids?*

The signs were there. They were staring me in the face like a stop sign outlined with Christmas lights. What kind of man wants to buy a house on a bunch of property and build furniture? The kind that wants to have a litter of children—not one or two, a whole friggin' team of them.

He came from a big family, and everything he's ever said about his childhood has been filtered in sepia-toned nostalgia. Of course he would want to replicate that experience.

I don't know if I can sign up for having a big family, and my vagina is *definitely* not along for that ride.

I'm so lost in thought, I don't notice Rochelle staring at me like I'm a wounded swimmer in her shark-infested waters until I've handed over the keys to my destruction. They're written on my face.

"Oh, you didn't know Baron wants a big family?"

"Um, we haven't talked about all the details." I should walk away from this conversation, but I'm trapped in the corner— literally. Rochelle is standing directly in front of me, and Georgie's on the side with a frown taking up half her face.

"I mean, what's there to talk about? You either want kids or you don't." She stops and looks at one of her nails, and I wonder if it's to decide if it's sharp enough to spear me right now. Newsflash: I think even her collarbone is sharp enough to cut me. "You don't want kids, do you?" she asks with one eyebrow raised.

"I don't know," I answer sheepishly.

Rochelle turns to Georgie, and I take a deep breath when her gaze turns off of me. I would be scared for Georgie, but I know she can hold her own. Instead, I grasp at the momentary reprieve like it's a glass of cold water. I'll drink every last drop, and hopefully it'll help my brain figure out an exit strategy.

"What do you think, Georgie? Should someone who doesn't know if they want kids be with someone like our dear Bear?" I want to smack Rochelle. I'm not a second-class citizen because I'm on the fence about my procreation status. I am not any less of a woman because I may not want kids, not one single ounce less.

Georgie doesn't look at me, and it's my first clue that something isn't right. I start to step in. I don't know what's going on, but

215

Rochelle doesn't need to drag Georgie into this. "Lay off it, Rochelle. This isn't your business."

Rochelle doesn't even look at me. She stares at Georgie like she's trying to snap a branch with the power of her mind.

And Georgie breaks. I hear the soft snap in her voice. "No."

I only have to turn an inch to face Georgie, but my head moves so fast, I swear I have whiplash. "Georgie?"

"I'm sorry. He wants kids, Monty, really wants them, and you can't do that to a man—not a good one like him." I see a tiredness in her eyes I've never noticed before. Where did that come from?

Rochelle turns back to me with a victor's grin. "See, Monty? Even your *friend* agrees."

I hear the emphasis she places in that sentence, and it's like a rusty nail hammered deep into my open flesh. I feel like that sophomore in high school; I vowed I would never feel that way again, but here I am, standing by a football field, just as tormented as the first time around.

Probably more. I don't belong here, but this time, I made the mistake of letting a crush turn into a full-blown romance. It's not just embarrassment anymore.

It's devastation.

I have enough dignity left to flee. I can't stand up for myself, and no one else is going to stand up for me. Honestly, I don't know which hurts more right now.

A cheer ripples through the box. I don't give a shit what just happened, but everyone else does, including Rochelle. She turns back toward the wall of glass to see what everyone is so excited about, and I take the opportunity to slip to her side, bumping her slightly as I exit my corner.

The Hawks may be winning, but I feel like I just lost everything.

*⋆ *⋆ *⋆

I walk out of the stadium and head straight for my apartment, wrapping my arms around myself. I feel as if the only way I can hold myself together is if I physically brace myself with my own two arms.

I am an idiot. The phrase repeats itself in my head over and over again, like a bad soundtrack to an afterschool special.

Girl meets boy. Boy shows interest. Girl reluctantly lets him into her life even though they are polar opposites. Girl ignores warning signs and falls head over heels. Girl finally realizes they want fundamentally different things. Girl feels like someone just took a picture of her heart, ripped it into tiny confetti pieces, and blew it right out the window.

I can't believe we never talked about having kids. It's just not something I think about. I'm twenty-three, not even remotely close to the shriveling-ovaries years. I'm not trying to find someone to pull the goalie with before I run out of time.

My thoughts about procreating are limited to a daily alarm to take my birth control and the feeling of relief when Aunt Flo appears on the dot every month.

I don't look at kids and think *Oh man, I can't wait to have you someday.* I don't even look at them and think *Oh man, I hope I don't have you someday.* I generally think *Oh man, cute kid, wish I could get away with wearing a fox on my ass too.*

I'm twenty-fucking-three. I am way too selfish to think about having a family. I'm so wrapped up in steering my own life in the right direction, there's no time to think about being the captain of someone else's.

But, I have to admit, there's always been a tiny voice tucked away in a deserted little corner of my brain. I imagine that voice is rocking a Mohawk and a *Live Free* tattoo on her forearm. She's shaking her head and saying, "I don't think you're going to have kids, ever."

217

And she's okay with that, but she's a loner. There's nobody else standing in her corner. No one even wants to acknowledge she exists, let alone agree with her, and that's always been okay because the spotlight's not on her anyway.

But Rochelle just brought in all the gear—the flash, the reflectors, the white background—and made this a whole production. There's no more voice chilling out in a lonely corner. All the attention has been shifted in her direction, and now she has to speak up.

I walk through the front door of our building and head toward my studio. It doesn't feel like home. How could it, when I've barely spent any time here?

Fortunately, there's beer in the fridge, and that's all I care about right now. I grab a can and sit down on my couch, pulling my legs into my chest. I don't know how to move forward, but I have a feeling life's going to come to me right now, whether I want it to or not.

Two hours later, it does.

There's a heavy knock on my door, and I don't have to pull it open to know who it is. The deadbolt is set, an automatic reflex after living around drunk college kids for several years. They may not want to steal your stuff, but that doesn't stop them from stumbling into your apartment because they forgot where they/ their boyfriend/their hook-up buddy lives. Lesson learned.

I shift the bolt to the left and turn the knob, pulling it back slowly. Baron has one hand up on the frame of the door. I'm struck by how much I want to kiss him right now. I never understood what people were talking about when they said someone knocked their socks off, and then I met Baron. His broad chest fills the space like he's a full-size picture standing in a frame. He looks almost like James Dean in his white t-shirt and jeans, but there's something so Midwestern about him, you know he's more kind soul than bad boy.

And that breaks me. I want to kiss this man, and I don't deserve to. He needs someone who's going to be there for him for all the parts of his life, not just the convenient ones.

"You haven't answered any of my texts or calls. What's going on?" Baron's eyes are full of concern.

I don't know how to have this conversation, but I know I need to have it.

I open the door up the whole way and wave him in. I watch the lines of his back as he walks over to the couch and sits down. I can't get over how he looks about two sizes too big for this place. I know I'm not that small, but I feel like I can stretch out my arms, twirl around, and still have room to breathe in here. Baron? He just doesn't fit.

We can't contort ourselves to fit in each other's lives. I hate admitting that, even though I've known it since the moment I figured out who he is.

"Monty?" he prods gently.

I walk over to him, grab my beer off the coffee table, and sit down on the floor. I don't trust myself to sit next to him—my logic falls to pieces the moment I get close enough to touch him.

"Rochelle told me today that you want kids."

His eyes pinch together. "Yeah?"

"So, I don't want kids." The truth feels like tiny blades running all the way up my vocal chords.

Baron leans forward, resting his forearms on his thighs. "Okay."

Okay? I feel like I need to repeat myself. Did he miss what I just said? "Baron," I plead. "We want different things."

He nods, and the simple gesture is infuriating. Doesn't he see how big of a deal this is?

"Seriously. I don't think I want a family. Doesn't that bother you?" I nervously pick at the rounded metal tab on my can of beer. I'm not ready for the answers to my questions…the real answers.

"I haven't really thought about it." His eyes are locked on me.

He's watching me like I'm a lion held back by a rickety metal cage. "This is kind of coming out of left field."

I shoot up to standing, unable to sit still for another second. I start to pace, beer in hand. My tab picking is starting to sound like a percussion line for my stress. "Well, you should think about it. It's a big deal."

Baron closes his eyes and sighs. "I know it's a big deal."

"Do you? I mean, what if we keep going like this? And ten years from now, I still don't want kids, what then?"

"I don't know." It's barely a whisper, but it stokes the fire that's raging inside of me. It's burning me alive, and I want to let it out, even though I know it'll burn him too.

"Well, I know what happens." I stop and stare at him. "You'll resent me, hate me even, and it will crush us both."

His eyes are heavy; I think I might be crushing him already. "What do you want me to say?"

I stop playing with the tab. I stop moving. What do I really want? "I want you to tell me I'm wrong."

"I can't do that." It's such a simple answer, but it burns straight through to the bone.

I drop to my knees. "Then what are we going to do?"

Baron walks over to me and kneels down, wrapping his arms around me and resting his chin lightly on the top of my head. It's meant to be comforting, but I feel like I'm suffocating. I can barely take a full breath. I hiccup unnaturally in and out until my tears finally break loose.

"It's okay, baby. We'll figure it out." He runs his hand over my hair in a gentle rhythm, and I let him.

I don't know if we'll figure it out, or if figuring it out will be the end of us.

This isn't a happy path forward. I'm in his arms right now, but the world will come for us eventually. When it does, there might be too much in between us for us to keep holding on.

I wake up, startled by my unfamiliar surroundings. It takes me a full ten seconds to realize I'm in my own bed. In my own apartment. By myself.

I roll over, grab my phone off my bedside table, and start to scroll through the alerts that have piled up while I slept—not that I actually did much sleeping. I rolled around for more than half the night.

And then I see it.

Inbox

Collins Aid United Recruiting

Dear Ms. Bell, We have an open contract we would like...

It's only a snippet. I can't swipe right fast enough. I fumble through my passcode. 0826. No. Crap. 0816. It's my own stupid birthday. Which is this weekend. I mean, *come on.*

I bolt upright and pace while I read the full email. They want to hire me for a contract at the end of this month as a trial run.

A trial run. In the field.

My heart is beating out of my chest, so I know it's busy pumping blood to all of my extremities, but everything is tingly and half numb.

My dream job called. They want me.

My subconscious tempers my excitement. It's only a temporary assignment, a three-week interview of sorts. It could go horribly wrong, and I could be both out of a job and back to square one.

Or I could work my way into a full-time gig at Collins Aid United.

Even my pre-coffee brain is tentatively optimistic for the latter option. I know I have the skills for this, and I know I'm not some crazy psycho who's going to break under jet lag and a lack of running water.

Hell, growing up backpacking with my dad—who is just a wee bit obsessed with being able to survive in the wild, because, SCIENCE—was enough training to prepare me for less than first-world living conditions.

And right now, I feel like I need to disconnect. My camera is still packed away. I haven't felt like myself, and even though I take pictures of everything else but me, it always feels like I'm baring my soul when I hear the shutter release.

Composition, speed, angle—they're rapid-fire decisions I make to try to capture things as I see them. What's more personal than that? I'm trying to show the world how I see it.

Frankly, I'm afraid of what I would see if I put a camera to my face. I'm living in a city I resent, submersed in a world I don't enjoy.

I love Baron, but out here, he's Bear. It's just not the same.

I knew the outside world would come knocking eventually; I just didn't know it would be this soon.

And now I have to decide what I need to hold on to, and what I need to let go.

Chapter 24

So far, my birthday has been a buzzkill. Aside from calls from my parents and Andie and the barrage of long-lost 'friends' writing *Happy Birthday* with the same ten million exclamation marks on my Facebook profile, today has been oddly silent.

Happy birthday to me.

Baron has had practice all day, and I haven't heard a word from Georgie…not that I really want to. Well, I wouldn't be opposed to a singing telegram telling me how sorry she is and that she has no idea what alien took over her body and made her agree with Rochelle.

But still. Judge me and my non-maternal instincts behind closed doors all you want, but don't agree with the mega-bitch to my face.

It's not that there isn't a part of me that agrees with her—there definitely is—but I don't want to stare at it in a mirror. That's like saying, *Here's a 10x mirror to check that massive pimple you have on the end of your nose.*

Nothing good comes from getting that up close and personal with your blemishes.

At least it's a proverbial pimple. I lean over the counter toward the real mirror in my bathroom and double-check my lipstick. Baron is taking me out to dinner tonight at Canlis, and I only had to spend two seconds looking at the menu to know this was a do-it-up-right sort of night. I spent half the day watching YouTube tutorials on hair curling and smoky eyes and contouring, though I gave up on the last bit after my first try turned out like a streaky nightmare.

As I look in the mirror at the final product, I'm pretty damn pleased. I've always told myself the story that I couldn't do my own hair and makeup, but given the right instruction, some new products, and plenty of time for try, rinse, and repeat…I changed the narrative.

It's not bad. I'm not going to win any makeup artist of the year awards, but I think I look like a fancy-dinner-date version of myself.

I walk out of the bathroom and grab my clutch just as there's a knock at the door. I open it up and Baron's jaw drops.

Mission accomplished.

We still haven't figured anything out. We haven't even acknowledged our conversation from the other day, but that isn't stopping me from being the most enticing version of myself possible.

And I haven't told anyone about my job offer. Not a single soul.

Real life is swirling around like a tornado on the edge of the horizon. I don't know whether I'm going to race out to meet it or run inside to shelter, so for the moment I'll just stand here watching the sky darken and listen as the earth becomes eerily still before the storm hit.

Two hours later, I'm slightly disappointed that fancy establishments like this don't list sweatpants as an option on their suggested dress code, because I think I ate enough to have a full-on food baby worthy of a stretchy waistband.

This skintight dress isn't doing me any favors right now.

The server brings out a birthday chocolate torte. It sounded simple, but the full latticework crisp sticking out next to a simple gold candle is anything but that. It's decadent. I'd take a cupcake with half its weight in frosting, but I'm not going to complain. These calories are not going to be wasted on my taste buds.

Baron sings a very off-tune but utterly endearing round of "Happy Birthday." I want to close my eyes and wish for something, but I don't know what I want. I guess that's a wish in itself.

Clarity. I squeeze my eyes shut and blow. *Clarity.*

When I open them, Baron has a gorgeous box sitting in the center of the table. It's wrapped in simple gold paper, but the silver and white bow on it is extraordinary. You could give me a Pinterest-worthy tutorial, a 3D rendering, and all the tools in the world, and I would never be able to recreate this.

I start to reach for my phone. I should take it out and capture this before I tear it apart—in a gentle and refined fashion of course, because, you know, fancy restaurant—but I don't.

"What is it?" I bite my lip, excited to see what's hidden underneath these layers.

Baron can't contain his smile. "Open it and find out."

Don't have to tell me twice. I grab the box, which feels surprisingly light for its size. I pull at the ribbon, and it slips soundlessly off the box. I dip my fingers into the folded edges of the paper and pull it open with a satisfying rip. I lift the lid off the box, and then I see it.

I feel as if I just chugged a glass of milk followed by a tablespoon of lemon juice. It curdles in my stomach, and part of me wants to hurl just so I can get rid of this feeling, but I know better. This isn't something you can boot and rally from.

He bought me the most beautiful vintage camera I've ever seen —a Rollei TLR. I should be launching myself over the table to thank him, but instead I want to curl up and cry.

"Do you like it?" His smile falters for a second.

I know I should say yes, but I can't wade through the bullshit field fast enough to find the reassurance he's looking for. He bought me something incredibly meaningful, but he still doesn't get it.

Me not taking photos isn't about missing the motivation or the right equipment. It's about missing me.

And that isn't something he can bring back.

His head dips low, and I am both disappointed in myself for not sucking it up and lying to him and oddly pleased that I have made him feel a quarter of what I feel right now.

Is that how relationships work? When you break, you can't help but cut them with your jagged edges? Because I didn't sign up for that. I signed up for the move-across-the-country-because-you're-crazy-about-each-other part. This part? This pain? It feels like rocks in my pockets pulling me down, and I'm dragging him down with me.

"I just thought—" Baron starts to explain.

I don't want to hear it. I don't want to go there. "It's beautiful, Baron, but it's not about the camera."

"So tell me what it's about then." His voice crackles with frustration.

I find myself matching it. "You don't get it. You're not around to get it. I hate it here. This isn't me. The football. The people. The job. None of it fits."

"Are you saying I don't fit?" The way he looks at me, his eyes are creased with pain, and I can't stop it.

I don't know what to say. I can't say yes, but I can't say no either. "I'm not really hungry anymore. Can we just get the check and…" I don't have enough energy to carry the thought through. Where are we going to go? If I climb into my bed on the first floor, I'm putting so much distance between us, I don't know if we'll be able to cross it. If I climb into his bed, I know I'll never forgive myself.

Baron wants me to be someone I'm not, and I can't pretend to not see that.

Not anymore.

He flags down the waiter, who smiles politely and offers to box up my cake. I didn't even take a single bite. The charred candle still sits in the center like a barren signal.

Clarity. I got what I asked for…whether it was what I really wanted or not.

I wake up the next morning in my own bed. My eyes are puffy from tears and last night's makeup. I know I would feel better if I walked my butt straight to the shower right now, but I don't have any desire to make my outside feel any better than my inside.

I grab my phone off my bedside table, pressing the home button and seeing a message from Andie.

Sooo…how it'd go last night?
Is birthday sex as good as the other 364 days of the year?

I choke back a laugh that sounds frighteningly similar to a sob —I would know; I have a very recently updated library of sounds to reference.

I twirl my phone between my palms, trying to decide what to say. He bought me one of the most thoughtful gifts anyone has ever given me, and I can't even look at it. It's a symbol of everything that's wrong here. How do I tell her that over text message?

I settle on a call. Andie answers on the second ring, and my heart starts to race. There's so much to say, and I'm not sure I want to hear myself say it all out loud yet. It becomes real when the words hit the air. They can tumble around in my brain with unrealized potential, but when I say them out loud, everything changes.

"Ohhh, perfect. I'm on the treadmill for my once-a-month, hey-I-worked-out session." I can hear the smile in her voice, and I close my eyes, trying to imagine her face. I wish I could be there in person. I miss my best friend.

Here it goes. "Um, you might want to step off for this."

"Why?"

"I don't want to be responsible for you flying across the room at high speed," I joke darkly. "Friends don't let friends treadmill irresponsibly."

"Well, if it's going to be good, I'll count the five minutes on the timer and call it done." I can hear the beeps of the machine, and the background music of the school fitness center dies down.

"I wouldn't go so far as to say it'll be good, but it'll be something."

I can hear a door open and shut on the other end of the call. "Okay, I'm hiding out in a racquetball court." Andie's voice echoes softly. "What's going on?"

I sigh. I'm not ready to let it all out yet, but I know I just have to suck it up and start.

It takes twenty minutes of nonstop power talking to tell her everything. My undecided ovaries. The job offer. The vintage it-shall-not-be-named. My stupid fucking clarity.

I would be disappointed in myself for only taking twenty minutes to explain it all, but I've learned to be efficient with Andie. Future doctors of America don't even have time to sign their names properly, let alone listen to longwinded ramblings that take forever to get to the point.

And I know what the point is.

"It sounds like you know what you want," Andie offers diplomatically.

I wish she would give me an out, an opinion on the right way to handle this whole situation, but who says I would listen? I didn't major in science like my parents wanted me to. I didn't avoid the football game when I was a sophomore in high school. I didn't stay in Michigan when I knew that the majority of rational human beings would tell me moving across the country for a boy was a bad idea.

I'm kind of stubborn, and I'm kind of proud of that. "I'm going to take the job."

"Good." I can hear Andie's nod of approval, even if I can't see it. "And what about Baron?"

I let out a long sigh. "I just feel like Bear Richards and Baron Richards are two different people." The thought comes from a dramatic place in my head where nothing will ever be fun again, but the minute I say it out loud, I hear the truth in it.

The person I met in Ann Arbor is a different person than the one I'm living forty floors below here in Seattle. I liked the carefree, easy-to-make-him-laugh version. This one is tired and stressed and disconnected. I can't blame him, but it doesn't mean I like it, and I'm also not a fan of being anywhere near the spotlight. My place is behind the camera, not in front of it.

I scrunch my shoulders up to my ears and pinch my face in as tight as it will go.

And then I let it go. "I'm going to move my stuff home and say goodbye."

I can barely think of what goodbye really means. I already feel like I broke the mirror. Each shattered piece is held in place by the sheer force of each tiny fragment pushing against the others.

"It's gonna be okay." Andie's tone is softer than I've ever heard it. She sees me holding these pieces together, and I know we're both hoping I can keep on holding them together until I get home.

"I know." I say it, even though I don't entirely believe it. I have to put my trust in Andie's words and then let them carry me for a while.

I'm going home.

Chapter 25

By the time I reach my hand up to knock on Baron's door, it's been six hours. Six long hours of researching how to rent a small moving truck, hiring people to help me load, and packing up my stuff. Considering that I never even finished unpacking, it was a frighteningly easy task.

I have a moving truck booked for the day after tomorrow. I know I'm taking a risk by not giving two weeks' notice at my job, but I have a mountain of prep work for this contract with Collins Aid United. It doesn't help that staying here feels like more time stuck in freezing water under a sheet of ice. I have to find my way to the surface, no matter the cost.

I pause to feel Baron's door beneath my knuckles. I've been giving myself pep talks all day. *This is what I need to do. It's the right thing to leave.*

I need to tell him I'm leaving for a job, but I know I'm really leaving for myself, and that is so much harder to swallow.

The door opens up underneath my still hovering knuckles, and I jump back in response.

"Monty, hi," Baron says, clearly surprised to see me outside his door. He has a bag of garbage in his hand, but he drops it off to the side and invites me in instead of completing his chore.

I don't think I've taken out the trash once since I moved here. It kind of startles me how easy life is here, and for a moment, I feel almost hesitant to let that go. *Am I making the right decision?*

Baron walks into the kitchen. "Can I get you something to drink?"

I know I'm most likely imagining it, but I feel like his tone has shifted along some imaginary line, as if he knows what's coming before I've even had a chance to say it.

I can't hold it in any longer. "I'm moving back."

Baron's back is turned to me. He's standing at the fridge, about to open the door, and I can see the thick muscles that carve their way down his back go soft and drop forward. If he had any idea that's what I came here to say, he didn't fully believe it.

It's real though. My Visa bill for next month will be a clear indication of how very real it is.

"I got a job offer, and it's going to require me to travel for a while."

He turns around and leans his hands against the counter. My immediate instinct is to climb into the space of his arms and comfort him, but I've shifted along the line too. This isn't the carefree romance it started out as, and there isn't anything I can say to make him feel better right now.

He looks up at me, his eyes pleading for something he knows I can't give.

"Can't you stay here and travel?"

I simply shake my head. Even if that wasn't financially stupid, we both know this is about more than a job.

"So you just made a decision to go. No conversation. Just a knock on my door and that's it?" I hear the control in his voice start to break.

It's a dick move on my part. The second I saw that email, I

should have taken the elevator up to talk to him, but I didn't. I don't know what to tell him.

"So you're just leaving?" His voice is hanging on by a thread.

"I can't stay." It comes out as barely a whisper. I've thought these words a million times, but saying them out loud is terrifying.

"I don't get it."

"Do you realize I haven't taken a single picture since I moved here?" I can barely say it. Every single word burns coming out.

Baron shakes his head. "No, I didn't know that."

I shrug. "You weren't around, so you missed the whole part where I realized Seattle isn't for me." It comes out harsher than I intend it to, but it's the truth.

I knew he would be busy, but I guess I never realized how the game out here would change him. This isn't just a job, it's a lifestyle, and it's sucked everything out of both of us.

Baron pinches his eyes closed, as if he knows he's losing the battle. "It's been a tough season. I didn't think it would be this hard."

"Me either."

"So what now? You move back to Michigan and then travel around. What about us?"

I hate this question. I've asked myself a thousand times what this means for us, and every time, I get the same answer. I know it's the right one, but it still hits my heart like a hammer, full force, every single time.

"I don't think we're going to work out."

It's a shitty way of saying it, but the shorter version is too brutal to say out loud. *We're over.* I don't want it to be true, but I need it to be.

I need to go back to honoring myself instead of trying to live in the shadow of someone else.

Baron closes his eyes. "You're not happy here?" It's as much of a statement as it is a question. He finally gets it.

"No." The answer is simple. It feels like it should be a long, run-on sentence of an explanation, when in reality it's just a period. That's it. I'm not happy. Period.

He wraps his hands around the back of his neck and pulls against them in frustration. "But you never told me that. You didn't even give me a chance to fix it."

"And what would you have done? Seriously? Tell me to not go to the football games? Pretend that part of you doesn't exist?"

Baron slams his hand against the counter. "I don't know. I would have done something." His eyes are shut, and I can tell he's directing the current of anger at himself.

I wish he would turn it on me. I'm the one who's leaving. This is my fault. It's the age-old adage. "It's not you, Baron. You couldn't have done anything."

"That's bullshit, and you know it."

I don't know what to tell him. How do you tell someone you love them but you don't fit in their life?

"I have to go do this."

He opens his eyes and looks straight at me. "And I have to let you go?"

His eyes open up my chest like a pickaxe headed straight for my heart. The air is somber between us, and I feel like our conversation has sucked all the oxygen straight out of the air. I walk over to him and rest my head on the curve of his upper arm, desperate to pull in what's left of the good air between us and let it trickle through my blood.

"Yes," I whisper.

He has to let me go, because as much as it's about him, it's about me too. I've lost myself in being here, and it's time to go back to find the woman I know I am and can be.

Baron turns his head and lightly kisses the top of my forehead. I close my eyes, trying to record the way his smooth lips imprint against my skin. I know I want to remember this forever, like a slip of paper you tuck away in your wallet and carry around always.

It hurts right now, but someday, the edges will wear down, and it will be bittersweet.

Baron showed me I could be brave, and I don't want to forget that.

I press my lips to the soft angle of his jaw, and then I untangle myself from him and turn toward the door.

I almost expect him to say something, but when I open it and step out of his condo, the air is still heavy with silence.

As much as I wanted him to fight, I know it's best for both of us if we just let go. After all, isn't that why I'm walking out the door? Because the threat of what happens if I stay is far greater than the pain of leaving while I still can.

The last thing on the to-do list before I need to pick up the truck tomorrow is to walk into Mr. Grant's loft one more time.

My nerves are rattling in their cages right now. My energy has nowhere to go until I walk in and hand over my resignation. I'm excited I'm never going to have to show up for one more crappy day of menial work here, but that doesn't stop my nerves.

Every single step makes this more real. I'm heading in a new direction, and even though I like where it's headed, it doesn't soothe my anxiety.

I walk up to the loft door and take a deep breath. I'm telling him I quit. What's the worst that can happen? He fires me first?

When I step into the building, I don't hear or see Mr. Grant. I call out his name, but I get nothing but my own echo in return. Hmm. He's not in the kitchenette or the equipment room. I check my phone, and it's 9AM. He should be here.

An hour and a half later, he finally shows up. Of *course* he can't even make quitting convenient for me.

"Oh, I thought I texted you I would be late this morning," he says as he throws his jacket on the table.

I start to pick it up, and then I realize that isn't my job anymore. "That's okay. I came in to tell you I'm quitting. I have another job offer, and I need to move back to Michigan."

He stops and stares at me, and I can't figure out if he's pissed or curious. "And where will you be working?" It's the first time he's looked me in the eye when he's asked a question.

"I'm taking a job with Collins Aid United to travel as a photographer with their teams." Okay, so I'm taking on a contract...one contract, for three weeks, and while it feels like a big deal to me, Mr. Grant would probably eat that contract as a snack before a five-course meal.

He continues to stare at me without so much as blinking until finally he laughs. It's an unnerving sound. "You'll never hack it out in the field."

His words slice my courage like paper cuts, but I'm not going to give him the satisfaction of letting him see me bleed.

"Maybe I won't, but I won't know until I try."

"I'm not going to give you this job back when you come crawling home." He sends more daggers my way, but these are too dull to cut me.

They only slice away my desire to leave this building without burning a bridge. Screw it, I'm not going to let this man bully me. "I wouldn't take it back if you begged me on your knees, Mr. Grant. This is a waste of my talent. I'd rather never make another cent from my photographs than step in here and stand on the sidelines of your life. You're a genius, but you're also a dick."

I see the flicker of surprise, as if my response physically slapped his face. I would love to pull out my phone right now and take a picture so I can remember it forever. Instead, I turn on my heels and walk back to the giant metal door.

I am worth so much more than this.

As I swing the door open, my hands practically slip off the handle. My body is in nervous overload right now, but I did what I came to do—and damn, it feels better than I could have ever imagined.

I wake up early, anxious to get moving. Everything is packed. I need to take the bus to the truck rental office twenty minutes up the I-5 and be back in three hours to meet the guys I hired to help me load.

And then there are the 2,326 miles between me and my destination. I'm pretty sure I'm going to binge eat French fries and McFlurries and listen to all the emo music I can, and I am totally okay with that.

It was so easy moving out here. First class ticket, apartment keys ready and waiting—all I had to do was show up.

Moving back home is exactly the opposite, and it feels like a penance I have to pay. I have to feel this, all the way down to my core, so I can embrace the mistake. If I gloss over the hard work, I might gloss over the lesson.

I walk out of the apartment building and something slams right into me. I struggle to keep my balance as I turn to see what just hit me.

I recognize the glossy jet-black hair immediately: Georgie. Her arms wrap around me, nearly cracking my ribs. I wouldn't put it past her to be able to bench as much weight as her football-playing husband. Georgie is a force, and while I still haven't forgiven her, I can't help but miss her a little too.

"Oh my gosh, Monty, please don't go," she pleads as she lets go of me. "Is there anything I can do to get you to stay?"

I shake my head. "No. This was an experiment, and I really wanted it to work out, but it wasn't for me." So, I need to shut down the lab and turn in my ID badge.

Georgie's shoulders shrug forward. "I'm so sorry. I screwed up at that game, and I've been distant ever since. I'm such a loser."

Her apology cracks the ice that had formed over our friendship. "You're not a loser, Georgie. You were so kind to me when I got here. I didn't know anyone."

"I didn't stick up for you. I stood there and let Rochelle get into your head. Even worse, I piled on, and because of my own stupid bullshit." Georgie sighs. "We can't have kids…or at least, we think we can't. We've been trying to get pregnant for years now. Even with IVF…it's just not in the cards for us."

"Oh, Georgie." It's my turn to wrap her in my arms. I squeeze her with everything I have. We spent all that time together, and I never knew. I wonder if Baron knows.

Why don't people talk about this? Why is our society so screwed up that women don't give each other space to talk about the dark side of fertility? We're all over here crowded together in the shadow of the motherhood arena, feeling like second-class citizens because we can't or won't play the game.

It makes me want to punch a wall, but that's not going to give Georgie a baby, and it certainly won't do anything to stop people from judging me for not wanting one.

I can feel a wet spot forming where Georgie's face is pressed against my shirt, and I pull her in even tighter. "It's going to be okay. You guys have the time and resources to figure this out. Hell, I'd lend you my uterus for nine months if I wasn't taking it with me."

Georgie pulls off of me with a devious smile. "Heeey, that could work. We could pay you if you want to stay." She lifts her eyebrows dramatically, as if she's trying to sell me a bright red sports car.

I'm pretty sure pregnancy is more like a minivan that hasn't had an oil change in ten years, but hey…

"I have to go, Georgie." I would put her in my pocket and take her with me, but that's not how this works. It sucks leaving friends, no matter how long they've been in your life. I may be going home to Andie, but I'm still going to miss Georgie.

She purses her lips together and blinks slowly, as if she's trying to come up with a last-minute game plan.

I cut off her scheming before it goes any further. "I need to do this. I need to travel the world and find myself."

"But you and Baron…"

My heart skips at his name, but instead of taking off into flight, it lands back down with a heavy thud. "It just didn't work."

Georgie shakes her head. "But you made him so happy. I've never seen him like that before." She looks at me, her eyes connecting with mine, and she sees it. Her face relaxes with understanding. She found the answer she was searching for. "But you weren't happy. This isn't your world."

"I need to go out and find mine," I say quietly, wary of the task at hand but optimistic it'll be worth it in the end.

"I don't like it, but I get it. I'll travel to meet you any time, anywhere—except maybe during a championship game."

I wrap my arms around Georgie one last time, grateful to have found her. I know she really will meet me anywhere, and someday, I'm going to have to take her up on it.

She lets go. "Do you need a lift to…"

I shake my head before she can finish. I'm heading toward my own adventure, and I have to use my own two feet to get me there.

Chapter 26

I make it home three days later with a pile of fast food wrappers at my feet and a whole lot of gas fill-ups on my credit card. I'm home, and that's worth the drain on my bank account.

I pull into the driveway, and I see my mom walk out of the side door just as I shift the truck into park. Damn, I'm going to be happy to be done driving this huge piece of unwieldy metal.

I hop out of the cab of the truck, and my feet land on the gravel with a crunch. My mom walks over and wraps me in a hug. Her hair is pulled back into a ponytail, and I can smell the floral scent she's sprayed on her neck for as long as I can remember.

She's wearing her ratty painting jeans and an old library t-shirt, but she still wears perfume. I know it's because my dad loves it. He leans in and kisses her neck all the damn time just to be close to her; the thought reminds me why I moved out to Seattle in the first place.

Because I would go to the ends of the planet for that kind of love.

I feel like I almost had it. I was holding the end of the rope, but it started to unravel before I could get my footing. I'm still in a free fall, but coming home means there's an inflatable crash pad waiting for me at the bottom.

"I love you, Mom." I squeeze her tight. "And I'm really sorry," I add as I pull away and head toward the back of the truck.

"Oh honey, don't be sorry. You're always welcome to come home."

I smile and shake my head. "No. I mean, I'm sorry about this part." I swing open the doors and point at the stacks of boxes we have to move from this truck into the house one by one over the next two hours. The truck is due back, with a $500 penalty for being late. This is why I'm not going to have kids, because this is what you do for them.

My mom puts her hands on her hips. "This? Pssh, boxes don't scare me. Your dad, on the other hand…"

"Yeah, where is he?"

"I took the day off to help you, but your dad said he had some big meetings he couldn't move. I just think he was being a pansy about lifting heavy boxes." She smiles when she teases him, and it makes me smile too.

My dad is one of the smartest people I know, but he's kind of a wimp when it comes to extreme physical activity. We love him all the more for it. You have to love people's crazy, otherwise it'll drive you insane.

"Let's do this." My mom rallies as she jumps up into the back of the truck and pulls down the ramp.

My mom's a badass, and I know if I have even one tenth of that in my blood, I'm going to take the world by storm.

After we get back from dropping off the truck—with fourteen minutes left on the clock—Mom suggests we have some iced tea out on the back deck. I know that's code for *Let's talk*. We spent the last three hours focusing on getting boxes from point A to point B with little room for chatting.

Now, we have all the time in the world. I follow her out the back door and slip into one of the white rocking chairs that sit in the shade on the dark wood of the deck. I run my hands along the arm rests and close my eyes. I remember crawling up into these chairs when I was little. I would carry a big stack of books outside and set them up on the side table one by one and read all afternoon.

It's always been one of my favorite places in the whole world. I find so much comfort in this chair, in this world that shaped who I am. I want to live here, my nose tucked in another book forever. But, I also want to see all the places words can never fully describe.

How can you want to leave home and stay forever all at the same time?

"So, my dear, are you running toward something or running away?"

Leave it to my mom to sum up the entire situation in one simple question. She has spent her whole life surrounded by words, and it shows.

I run my teeth along the curve of my lower lip while I sort through my thoughts like snapshots in my mind. Meeting Irene Collins at the beginning of this summer. Falling for Baron in the warm sunshine of a farmer's market. The isolating loneliness of sitting through football games in the overwhelming opulence of the owner's box. Seeing the Collins Aid United email glowing on my phone screen.

"Both," I finally answer.

My mom takes a sip of tea. "Sometimes you have to try a life on in order to understand if it fits you or not."

I can't help but laugh. "Yeah, football girlfriend does not fit."

"And Baron? Did he fit?"

My chest tightens at those two familiar syllables. "I don't know. Baron, the man, fit at first, but Bear, the football star, didn't. And we kind of figured out we don't want the same things in life." How can you love someone and be so different? We're puzzle pieces from two separate box sets. We snap together, but when you look at the colors of our pieces, we're parts of two pictures that clash when put side by side.

"Are they things that will change over time?"

"He wants a family." I sigh.

"And you don't?" It's a question, but it's asked without a single hint of disappointment. I know my mom would love to be a grandmother, but I also know my mom is a fierce advocate of women doing what is best for them. Have kids. Don't have kids. Stay at home. Work full time. Do what keeps you sane, and don't judge others for needing something different.

We've never had this conversation before. It's not exactly something a mom asks her twenty-three-year-old daughter. *Oh hey, do you want kids?* It hasn't even been on the radar.

"I don't know." I run my finger up and down my glass of tea, letting the tiny beads of condensation pool until they run down the glass and fall onto my leg. Just as much as I want home, I also want to see the world. I guess my thoughts about having kids are sort of the same. The picture of sitting on the porch with my own child makes me smile, but I also want to travel, free and unattached. I don't know how to want both things at the same time.

"It's okay to not know. I didn't have you until I had spent a lot of time getting good and ready. Both your father and I did."

"What if I never get ready though? I mean, I'm not exactly a maternal person to begin with." I let the fear slip out, and once it does, I realize how long it's sat in the closet of my mind like an indefinite monster. I knew it was there, but I didn't know exactly what it looked like.

"Oh honey, you don't need to fit some cookie-cutter definition of motherhood to be a good parent." She reaches over and grabs my hand, squeezing it like only a mom can. "I think you would make a fantastic mom, if and when the time is right, but if you don't ever find that slice of time when it appeals to you and where you are in life, know that you will lead a wildly full life regardless of your family status."

"Thanks Mom," I whisper. There's a swirl of gratitude mixing with the sadness. I know my mom is right, but it breaks me to think I can't hang on to Baron while I figure it out. It's not fair to him to not know if I want the same thing he does. He deserves someone who wants to be a mom, without question or hesitation.

It feels like someone punched my ovaries. Whether or not I want children isn't the problem; the problem is that I'm in love with a man who knows what he wants, and I might not be able to give it to him.

Chapter 27

I take my seat in first class and stretch out my legs. Collins Aid United has a policy of springing for the more expensive seats when the flight is longer than six hours, and I'm grateful. I don't know if I'm excited to have more room or terrified that I'm going to be flying over open water for the first time ever.

It doesn't help that all I can think about is the only other time I've flown first class. I try to push the thought out of my mind as soon as it enters, something I've been doing a lot over the past few weeks.

Not that it actually works.

I reach for my phone to turn it on airplane mode when a call flashes across the screen.

Baron.

I press accept and lift it to my ear, glad my coworker who's going to be sitting next to me on the flight ran into a friend in the airport and is going to board a bit later.

"Hi," I whisper. Maybe if I keep my voice quiet, it won't betray all the emotions I'm feeling right now.

"Hi. Georgie told me you were leaving today for your

assignment." God it feels good to hear his voice, but the good doesn't even come close to masking the ache.

"Yeah. I just boarded the plane, so I can't talk for very long."

"That's okay...I didn't know if I should call or not. I've been trying to give you space to figure things out."

And I've wanted him to call every single day, but I knew it wouldn't be easy walking away. I love the man even if I didn't love the situation.

I hear him sigh, and I know he's just as confused about this as I am. "I hope it goes well. I want you to know that. I want you to be happy, even if it's on the other side of the world."

"Thank you." My words feel tiny, but they're all I have.

"I'll let you, uh, get back to the safety instructions. Don't worry, the oxygen mask is working even if it doesn't inflate," he jokes halfheartedly.

I miss that. I miss him, but we both know I have to put the mask on myself before I can assist anyone else.

When I walk out of the arrival doors at the international airport in Addis Ababa, Ethiopia, I am greeted by a wall of rain, and it feels as if it's washing away all the uncertainty that's caked on my skin like a layer of thick dirt.

I said yes to this contract without asking many questions. I was satisfied with the when and how long. I just hoped when I got there, it would feel right and not like another big mistake.

After spending two weeks at home, trying to read every book in my TBR pile and then some, I was desperate to get across the world to a place where not every character or line would remind me of the man I was so desperately trying to forget.

I sat next to one of the field administrators, Evelyn, who was joining me on the trip, and she filled me in on the details. We had arrived in the land of coffee beans to deliver supplies and aid to a small medical clinic located in the middle of the countryside.

It's an important mission. For such a large country with an established history, there's little access to modern medicine for the population who live outside large cities.

As soon as we make it out of the hustle and bustle and into the rolling green mountains, my brain winds down. It's almost meditative, staring out the window at the scenery passing by me. I have my camera on my lap and I lift it up to my eye a few times, but I rarely press my finger down on the shutter release. There's so much beauty here, a picture taken through the gritty window of a dirty van won't do it justice.

So, I take it in and let my eyes capture and release every moment like embers that burn brightly for only a sweet second in time.

It takes hours to drive to the small clinic, the only one that serves an area of nearly a hundred mile radius. It's well past office hours, but there are still villagers milling around the building.

I step out of the van and immediately pull my camera to my face. The lighting is crap, but I hold my breath while I snap photos with a longer than usual exposure, praying I can capture something.

Evelyn notices my curiosity and turns to me after she grabs her duffel bag out of the back.

"Some of these villagers travel for a whole day to get here, and in monsoon season, it's even worse. We try to give the staff breaks, but it's hard to look into the faces of people who need your care and turn them away."

It's one thing to sit at home and read about the nonprofit's mission statement; it's another to see it in real life. If I can convey one tenth of the feeling that punches me in the gut when I see the people who would do anything to have access to simple medical care—and I'm sure there are thousands more in this country that don't even have that luxury—I'll have done my job.

I spend the first hour getting acquainted with the staff. Most speak English as well as some Amharic, the most common language used here. My brain is still processing the fact that I'm in a completely different country on a completely different continent. Every time someone speaks in a foreign language, it takes me a second to process it. I keep wanting to ask them to repeat themselves, as if I've simply misheard them.

But, I haven't misheard them. I am a stranger in a strange land, and instead of being overwhelming, it feels as if I just popped up for a breath of air after jumping off the high board. It's going to take a lot of energy to tread water, but I'm still damn proud of myself for taking the leap in the first place.

Every time I look around the large main room, I know I'm meant to be here. It isn't a feeling of home, but of timing, like if I had pressed the shutter just a moment too early or too late, I wouldn't have captured the image quite as clearly.

There's a closed door at the end of the hall I've seen nurses stepping in and out of. I've been so wrapped up in photographing and talking to the staff in the main section of the clinic, I haven't ventured to satisfy my curiosity. When a doctor walks up to the nurse I'm talking to and asks for her help, I follow them to the door.

When we step in, the three of us can barely fit in the room together. It's crowded with two bassinets, a couple pieces of equipment, and a rocking chair. It's barely the size of my bathroom back home. It takes me a moment but I finally see the baby resting in one of the bassinets. He's so tiny, like an old man shrunk down to a fraction of his normal size.

The doctor and nurse work on checking his vitals. When they finish, his eyes begin to flutter and his mouth opens in a wide O. It takes a second for the cry to develop, but when it does, it breaks the air of the room like a firework awakening a quiet, moonless sky.

The nurse picks him up and cradles his head on her shoulder, bouncing on her feet in a gentle rhythm. The newborn's eyes flutter once again, but his mouth closes and the cries stop.

"Shhh, Natneal," she whispers. "Shhh."

His cheeks are so smooth and full, I have the strong desire to reach out my finger and run it across his light brown skin, but I feel like I could break him just by breathing too heavily.

The doctor gives us a small smile. "I need to get back out to my other patients. I'll be back in an hour to check him again, but his vitals are doing exceptionally well." She exits the room, and the nurse and I are left to stare at this sweet little boy.

I can't take my eyes off him. He's so tiny, tinier than any baby I've seen, but his face is so round, it's looks like someone photoshopped one of the older baby's heads onto this skin-and-bones frame.

I wonder about his mother. Is she okay? I've already started to hear the horror stories of mothers lost in labor; it's part of the reason our work here is so important. Access to quality medical care and facilities is a serious regional issue, and the maternal and newborn mortality rate suffers because of it.

I lift the camera to my eye and focus the lens on this little boy. He's going to show the statistics who's boss, I just know it. I hear the satisfying release of the shutter, and I zoom out at just the right moment to capture the nurse pressing a kiss to the tiny threads of black hair pressed flat against his head.

She lifts her arm to glance at her watch. "I need to get back out too. You're welcome to stay here if you want. Natneal is a sucker for cuddles, and skin-to-skin time is one of the best things for him right now. We just don't have enough volunteers to spare."

I swallow slowly. "Are you sure?"

She laughs softly. "He may be tiny, but as long as you support his head, you'll be just fine. Sit down in the chair, pull the strap of your tank top down, and I'll put him right against the skin of your shoulder."

I bob my head in nervous acceptance and sit down as instructed. She places him onto my shoulder, and I'm shocked at how warm he is. He feels like a feather against my skin, but I can feel the rise and fall of his chest.

She smiles at us and turns to leave.

"Wait," I ask. "Is his mom…" I can't say the words; it hurts too much even to think them.

She smiles again, and the weight that temporarily fell on my heart lifts. "She's going to be okay. She walked ten miles in premature labor to get here. She's one of the lucky ones. She had some minor hemorrhaging, but we were able to stop it quickly. Neither of them would have survived if they hadn't made it here, but they did…that's why she named him Natneal. It means gift from God."

She walks back out the door, and Natneal and I are left alone with only the soft sound of rain falling outside. I've never been more grateful for a moment of peaceful silence in my life.

An hour later, I swear I've worn a line on the apple of Natneal's cheek from running my finger along its side the whole time. My arm is exhausted, but I can't stop. I feel as if I need to soak in every single precious second of this sweet baby boy.

My mind is anchored in the moment, but it slowly drifts from side to side with gentle waves of thought. Sitting here with Natneal hasn't awakened some dormant maternal part of my brain, but I can feel the fear of that indecision falling away.

I have to be willing to walk ten miles to proper medical care because it will keep both my baby and me alive. I know if I decide I'm ready for that level of dedication, I'll be just fine. Just because I didn't grow up playing with dolls and dreaming of the day when I could trade them for my own children, that doesn't mean I'm dysfunctional. It doesn't mean I don't care or that I'm not good enough. It just means I won't follow the same path as some other mothers do; being different doesn't make something wrong.

I'm still trying to hold myself back from veering toward thoughts of Baron. That water is still too salty, my wounds still too fresh—the sting isn't bearable yet. I have faith I will get there, just not today, and I'm okay with that. I have Natneal for right now, and that's all that matters.

I walk into our hut on the second to last night of the trip, and I'm greeted by the most perfect light filtering in through the window to the kitchen table where Evelyn and our translator are sitting with mugs of tea. The way the sun hits Evelyn's tan skin, it radiates pure warmth.

They're deep in conversation, and I press my camera up to my face and manually adjust the focus. As soon as the shutter hits, they'll look this way. I have one shot.

My breath fills my lungs, and I hold it. Click. They turn to me, exhaustion pulling at the edges of their smiles. I pull the camera out to look at the image in the viewfinder. *Oh, that's gonna be gold.*

Seattle zapped me of any creative ambition, but Ethiopia has filled it right back up. I find beauty in everything around me, and I want to capture every single ounce of it and share it with the world. That's why I fell in love with photography in the first place, and now I finally feel like I'm home.

Evelyn waves me over, and I walk to the table and sit down just as the translator excuses himself to head to bed early. We could all use an IV drip of caffeine. The hours are long here, and there's more to be done than we could ever hope to accomplish in the short amount of time we have. It's absolutely exhausting, but it's a pleasant exhaustion, one you welcome with open arms, because it means you are making a difference in people's lives. There's no greater task than one that benefits the community around you.

We're almost at the end, and as much as I want my big bed with my soft, comfy pillow, the thought of leaving kicks sand up into my eyes. I take pictures because we can never travel the same span of time ever again. Even if I come back to Ethiopia, it will be different: different people, different light, different feel. The pictures won't be the same, and neither will I.

And I love that.

Maybe someday I'll get to meet Natneal again. He and his mom left the clinic a little over a week ago, healthy and ready to go back home to real life. I understand the feeling.

"You survived," Evelyn says with an air of pride. "Not all first-timers do."

I run my fingers over the smooth circle of buttons on the back of my camera and smile; I did more than survive. "This has been a really good trip for me."

"Glad to hear it. Everyone at the clinic has nothing but good things to say about you. If your pictures are half as good as your attitude, the crew back home would be fools not to hire you. Hell, I'll hire you just to help out on trips, camera or not."

Heat rises to my cheeks from the compliment and I mumble a quick *thank you*. I haven't asked any questions about how this works after the contract is through, but the longer I've been here, the more I want to go on more of these trips. It's nice to know I'm not the only one who supports that idea.

"You're welcome," she says with a wink of a smile before she takes another drink of tea. "Have you given any thought to if you will? Come back, I mean?"

I don't hesitate for a second. "Definitely."

"And your family and friends are okay with it? This isn't an easy job, and it doesn't lend itself to having a normal life. Three weeks away, two weeks back is not exactly a normal schedule."

I think about normal schedules. I've never lived a normal nine-to-five life. I was in school for years, then I started working at the paper. Every week I went in for a few hours during normal business hours, but mostly, I ran off whenever an event was scheduled or news broke.

And then there's the past month. My life with Baron was the least normal it's ever been. Even though I was helping out at the photography studio, it felt like my life was in one of those funhouse mirrors, warped and outrageous.

Evelyn tips her head to the side as she studies my face. "Tough question?"

"I had a rocky few weeks before I got here. That's all."

"Relationship?"

That's all it takes for everything to come pouring out of me. Four measly syllables with a tip up at the end to show interest, and I turn into an inconsolable baby. A few tears turn into a river, which turns into a freaking moat on the table in front of me. Evelyn gets up and grabs a towel from the kitchen. I'm kind of embarrassed until I remember they don't exactly have tissues here. I grab the towel and wipe my eyes...and the puddle on the table.

Instead of sitting back down, Evelyn puts another pot of tea on, and minutes later, she sets a steaming mug in front of me with a simple instruction. "Let it out."

And I do, every single bit of it. By the time I'm done, the sun has set completely, and we light a candle in the center of the table.

When I finally finish, Evelyn sits for what feels like eternity. She purses her lips for a minute, and I'm nervous about what's coming next.

"Don't give up on him."

The nerves that had been wrapped so tightly around my heart release their grip. I didn't know I wanted to hear those words until they ran through my ear canals and had a dance party in my brain. I don't want to give up on him, but I don't know how to be me and still have him too.

"Bad timing doesn't mean it's not meant to be; it just means it's not meant to be right now." Evelyn reaches across and squeezes my hand. "Honey, I've been married twice, and let me tell you what I learned the second time around: when you find a good man, a truly kind and generous man who will be loyal to you, you do everything in your power to keep him. If he's as good a person as you say he is, he's not going to let you go. He might have let you fly off, but he's going to seek you out and make his case, because you're one hell of a woman."

I sit there, dumbstruck. She just smiles and stands up without another word, heading to the sleeping quarters...leaving me to ponder her words, this trip, and everything that has turned my life upside down these past few months.

Chapter 28

I swear I can smell the exhaust fumes of Detroit before we even touch down at the airport. After having spent the last three weeks in the countryside of Ethiopia, my nose isn't accustomed to the smell of the city. It would be gross if it didn't feel so oddly familiar.

I'm coming home with the same clothes and the same baggage, but everything feels radically different. I finally did what I said I was going to do, and at times it was terrifying and uncomfortable, but it was also deeply freeing.

Travel is intoxicating, and now I know I'm a strong enough person to handle the inevitable stomach virus and accompanying *can I please have my mom right now* blues. I'm strong enough to figure out my way through a village when I only know how to translate the words bathroom, water, and hospital. I also know I can take stunning pictures that are worthy of the magazines and galleries I admire, and I know damn well I'm going to do my best to get them there.

I did what I have always wanted to do, and instead of scaring me, it makes me want to keep walking in and out of airports for the foreseeable future.

The contract went well, and I'm hopeful I'll get another with Collins Aid United, maybe even a full-time offer. No matter what happens, I'm going to figure out a way to get back out on the road.

I have to.

When I get to baggage claim, I don't have to look for Andie. She comes running at me like a screeching bat, arms stretched out wide. She reaches me and traps me in the best hug I've had in weeks, and I decide this might be my favorite part.

Home is the best place in the entire world when you return to it.

"Ahhh, tell me everything. How was the flight? How was getting the first stamp in your passport? Were there any cute doctors over at the clinic?" She adds the last question with a dramatic bite of her lip and wide eyes.

It makes me smile. "Nope. Forty-five, married, and balding isn't really my jam."

There is so much to tell her anyway, even if there weren't any great romantic escapades. The Internet was hella slow at the medical center when it even worked—not that I had time to pen great long emails about my travels.

There are so many stories I know she's going to find endlessly fascinating. I mean, I was working in a medical clinic in an extraordinarily rural region. Doctors live for that kind of stuff. How do you MacGyver medicine when there isn't a judge and jury to come after you if it doesn't work out exactly as well as you'd hoped?

I didn't know it was going to be Andie picking me up until I touched down and turned my phone back on to about a million texts from her. Half of them were composed of emojis, and the other half were in all caps. I also had one text from my mom.

We're sending Andie. We'll get you all to ourselves tomorrow. Enjoy the night with your best friend. We couldn't be more proud of you.

I nearly choked up on the airplane, but my row was next in line to leave, and exiting an aircraft is no joke. I think the people behind me would have trampled me to get by if I had taken more than my unofficially allotted three seconds.

I get to spend the night catching up with my best friend. My parents are the absolute best.

"Okay, so where are we headed? I'm starving." Just ask the woman who sat next to me on the flight—it sounded like a pterodactyl hatched in my lower abdomen.

Andie looks at me with a sheepish grin. "I found a new place that has amazing wings."

She had me at wings, but I'm not going to let it go without some fanfare. "And how many TVs do they have?"

"Two or three," she says while she counts on her fingers, her eyes darting up to the corner of the ceiling in thought. She stops and looks straight at me. "Five tops."

I'm so hungry, I'm not even going to argue. "Done." The dinosaur in my stomach is taking no prisoners, and wings sound damn good.

What's a few TVs anyway?

A few TVs is enough to broadcast every major sporting event currently taking place on national television.

That includes the game between Seattle and Detroit, happening just thirty short minutes away from us, and of course, the hostess sits us down right in front of the giant screen that is blasting the game in its full high-definition glory.

Lovely.

I don't know what I did to the hostesses of the world, but I'm pretty sure I need to start bringing chocolate chip cookies with me or something to bribe them to seat me in the quietest, least sports-filled sections of their restaurants.

Is there something about me that screams sports fan? If so, someone should tell me. I'll tattoo right over that shit without a second thought.

There are only a few people in the whole place, so when the waiter walks over, I have no problem being honest.

"Can you change the channel, please?" I ask, sweetness dripping from each syllable. Just because I'm not ready to give up on Baron doesn't mean I want to stare at him on a gigantic television screen. Don't even get me started on keeping myself away from anything having to do with him on the Internet. I'm about two clicks away from taking my computer to the Apple store and begging one of those geniuses to figure out how to block me from drunk-searching him.

The waiter smiles like he doesn't give a shit. "What? You date the quarterback and he broke your heart or something?"

"No. It was the wide running end."

The waiter drops his head and slowly shakes it. "There's no such thing."

"Whatever," I say impatiently. "Can we just change it?"

"Honey, this is the biggest game on television right now. If you want me to change it, you're going to have to convince every single one of these fine people sitting here watching it."

A few heads turn around to look at me and scowl. Fine, I get it —I'm the only one who hates football. From now on, I'm going to have to double-check how many televisions a restaurant has before I walk in the door.

I turn back to Andie, and she has a massive smirk on her face.

"What?" I snap.

"Nothing." The way she coos when she says that word makes me feel like Hulk Smash.

"Ohmygod, just say it already. I know it's in there." I'm being harsh, but I can't seem to stop it from pouring out.

Her face turns serious and she's silent for a second, debating whether or not I want to hear what she has to say. "You still love him."

I press my face into the palms of my hands, letting my fingers snake up into my hair. "Yes." It comes out as a muffled whisper; that's all I can manage.

I kept myself as busy as I possibly could on my trip. I spent every waking hour taking photos or helping in the clinic. Life was easy when my hands were moving, but the minute they stopped, my mind swerved off directly into Baronland.

There wasn't a single moment I missed Seattle. I missed Ann Arbor and my old studio, I missed my parents' house, but I never missed a single thing about the city of Seattle.

Except for Baron.

The way it felt to have his arms wrapped around me. His half-asleep smile when we woke up in the morning and he kissed my forehead.

And then Evelyn waved oxygen toward the tiny little candle that was barely holding on in a windstorm, and my brain has been on a nonstop Baron trip for the last two days.

"Okay, what are we gonna do about it then? We can get drunk and try to forget about him. We can road trip to Detroit and make a giant sign that says I STILL LOVE YOU BARON. Whatever we need to do, I'm there, you just have to tell me which way to point the compass."

I shake my head. "It's not that simple."

Andie throws her hands up in the air, and for once I'm glad we're in a bar that's blasting sports—no one's paying any attention to us. "Come on, Monty! Yes, it is. You love him. So, we figure out how to get over it, or we figure out how to win him back."

"I love him, but I don't love his life. I was miserable out in Seattle, and he had no freaking clue. None. Isn't that a hallmark sign of a bad relationship? You can't even figure out when your girlfriend is ridiculously unhappy?"

"But did you ever tell him?" Andie asks softly as she leans forward.

Mic drop.

I scramble to come up with a response. "Shouldn't he have noticed?"

"He's a football player, not Miss Cleo. He doesn't get paid to read minds."

Our waiter walks up, oblivious to the conversation at hand, and asks for our orders. Suddenly the bar goes catatonic. Every single person—except for Andie and me—stands up with their hands on their heads and shouts at the television. I can't help but turn to see what's causing the commotion, even though I'm sure it's just a bad call or a fumble or something.

All I see are a bunch of people huddled into a circle on the field —what's weird about that?

A replay starts, and I almost look away, but I notice a familiar number: 43. I stared at that number enough this summer to know its significance.

Baron.

You couldn't pay me to look away now. I don't know what he has to do with the group of people huddled together, but my heart races while the replay scurries to connect the dots for me.

The bartender grabs the remote and turns up the volume.

"We don't know the extent of his injuries, but that couldn't have been good," one of the commentators explains.

"Okay, watch the upper right corner of the screen," a second voice instructs. "That's Arrant coming in at full speed and Davis coming up on his side."

I watch, unable to breathe. All three players collide, sending Baron in an upward arc. The replay slows the speed of the video down, and I watch each and every drawn out second until his head connects with the ground.

My hands fly to my mouth as I take my first sharp breath in. Oh god, he's hurt. How badly is he hurt?

The screen cuts back to Baron lying on the ground surrounded by at least a dozen people, half in football uniforms, half in polos and khakis. Then someone wheels a stretcher out onto the field.

I turn back around to the table and grab my phone, pulling up Georgie's contact info.

Can you find out what hospital they're taking him to?
I'm in MI. I need to be there with him.

I shove my phone back in my purse, and Andie hands me her keys before I even have a chance to ask.

"Go," she urges. "Don't worry about getting the car back to me. Just keep me posted."

She pulls me into a quick hug and I race out the door to her parked car.

I don't know where I'm driving yet, but I'll check every hospital in Metro Detroit if I have to. That's what you do when you're in love.

And I never stopped loving Baron, not for a single second. We may be two different people, but he has my heart. Forever and always.

I'm driving eighty-five miles per hour, and I still can't get to Detroit fast enough. I should slow down; this isn't my car, and if I get pulled over, it's just going to put more time between me and him.

He's hurt. I saw it on the screen, heard the sound of the crowd go silent when the other two players got up and he stayed down. I don't know how bad it is, but I have to be there. I should have been there when it happened. I should have been riding in that ambulance instead of standing in a bar arguing with the bartender about turning the TV off.

If I had gotten my way, I wouldn't have even seen it happen.

I could have gone my whole night without knowing the love of my life is in the emergency room right now.

I haven't seen Baron Richards in over a month. I walked out of his apartment five weeks ago, but I didn't know then what I know now.

When you find the love of your life, you have to fight to keep them. I gave up, and now I have no idea if I'm too late.

My phone dings, and I look down to see that Georgie texted me the hospital. I know exactly which one she's talking about; I took photos there once when the Michigan robotics team visited the children's wing to do an interactive demo.

I pull into the massive parking lot twenty minutes later, and I race to the front entrance. I remember there's a large circular desk near the entrance where the staff directs you on where to go, and I get there as fast as my flip-flops will take me. I think about ditching them for a hot second, and then I remember that I'm walking into a hospital. I don't know if I'd be bringing germs in or walking into them, but either way, my feet stay sandaled, even if it isn't exactly appropriate sprinting attire.

The desk is right in front of me, and I stop in front of the counter, nearly out of breath. I'm in great shape; it's not my lungs that can't keep up here. My heart is taxed out. Emotion is keeping it from running this race in a calm and orderly fashion.

The woman behind the counter looks up and seems unimpressed, or at least unaffected by the big eyes I'm trying to give her, the *please help me* eyes I've used on my parents and grade school teachers for years.

Okay, new strategy.

"Hi, my boyfriend, Baron Richards, is here. He was just injured, and I said I would meet them here." It's not exactly accurate, but I doubt Baron is angry enough to deny my exaggerated claims outright.

The woman nods without a single lick of an emotional response and starts clacking away on her keyboard. I worry for a second that maybe he's listed under a different name. I mean, I know celebrities do it at hotels—is that a thing in hospitals? A million and a half people know he's injured right now; what's stopping the crazed fan that thinks she's his girlfriend from showing up wanting to see him?

I mean, yes, I sort of just lied about currently being his girlfriend, but I *was* his girlfriend at one point, which is more than some stalker with posters of him on her wall can say.

Wait, can I get posters of him for my wall? *Ahhh, focus.*

The woman looks back up at me. "He's in the emergency wing right now. You can wait in the ICU waiting room until he gets transferred. Through that corridor over there and second hall on your left."

I offer her a hearty thanks and race toward the maze of hallways. I know I'm running to sit and wait, but I can't stop my body from acting out the urgency I feel coursing through every single inch of me.

When I get to the waiting room, I check in with the nurse at the reception desk and tell her I'm here to see Baron. She tells me she'll keep an eye out for when he gets transferred. I walk over to the 80s geometric print chairs and plop down. I quickly check my phone: the battery is at just above thirty percent. My charger is out in my duffel bag in the car, but I don't want to lift my butt out of this seat for a single second. I would rather stare at a blank white wall than miss the message that Baron is ready for visitors.

Fortunately, there's a stack of magazines on the table next to me. I may have to use a whole bottle of hand sanitizer after I flip through them, but this is a hospital—I'm pretty sure they've got the market cornered on disinfecting materials.

I start to thumb through my options when out of the corner of my eye, I see someone sit down next to me.

"Um, are you Monty?"

I look over and recognize those eyes immediately. I smile, already knowing who I'm talking to. "Yes. I am."

She sighs with relief. "Okay, good, 'cause I thought I recognized you from a picture Baron sent me, but I didn't know because, you know... Anyway, I'm Devon, his sister." She stretches out her hand. "He's going to be really glad you're here."

My heart skips at her assertion. I didn't know what to expect. I ran here on adrenaline without much thought to whether or not Baron would actually want to see me. I shake Devon's hand, grateful for the camaraderie. Who needs a magazine when you have a friend sitting next to you who is just as freaked out and trying just as hard to avoid freaking out?

We get lost in conversation about everything: Devon's time at school, my time in Ethiopia, what it was like growing up with three brothers compared to growing up as an only child.

Devon stops in the middle of telling a story about her brothers trying to make her football pads out of packing peanuts so she could play with them. She looks over at me and laughs. "I'm glad I finally have another girl around. I've put up with their tomboy-ing me for way too long."

Her words clasp around my heart and squeeze. I want to be around. I want to be the one Baron brings home for family dinners. It scares me that I might have screwed up my chance at that.

"I hope I can fix it," I whisper. It's scary to say the words out loud.

Devon wraps her arms around me. "You can. I know you can." She pulls away and wiggles her nose, as if she's trying to decide whether or not to continue. "He couldn't stop staring at you, you know? That night you two met. The whole time I sat with him at

Halftime, he kept looking over and smiling, like he was in on the joke you were telling."

I laugh, remembering it as perfectly as the beer haze I had that night will let me. "I was reading in the middle of a sports bar."

"Yeah, but it was more than that. You were being unabashedly you in that moment, and he couldn't take his eyes off you. He loves you—the real you—and I know things didn't work out in Seattle, but I know you two can fix it. When you love the heart of someone, you figure out how to make the rest of it work too."

I bite my lip. I really hope she's right.

I barely notice my name being called until the nurse at the counter practically whisper-shouts across the room. "Ms. Bell? Mr. Richards has been transferred, and he asked to see you."

I turn to Devon and give her an apologetic smile, which she returns with a smirk. "Go. I get his whiny ass all the time. Go tell him you love him, k?"

I pop up from my seat and walk over to the nurse. She gives me the room number, and I head through the swinging doors toward his room.

I have no idea what I'm walking into, but it's the man I love. I'd walk back into a football stadium if that was what it took for me to keep him.

Chapter 29

I walk into the room with my eyes partially closed. I have no idea what I'm going to see, and I'm not entirely sure I'm ready for it.

Any of it.

When I open them, Baron's eyes connect with mine. I know what I see. It's the man I love. The man I want to be with. It might have taken an injury to get me here, but I guess I never really stopped believing he's the one for me. It's been etched on my heart like a tiny little white tattoo. You have to squint to see it, and in some light, it disappears from sight completely, but it's always there, whether you see it or not.

"Monty." It's half moan, half sigh.

I step up to his hospital bed and take in the gown that's flung around his shoulders like a solid blue tablecloth that's a little too small to fit the long surface it's supposed to cover. They must have cut off his jersey, and his legs are covered with a thin pink blanket. I want to reach out and touch him, but I'm too scared I'll somehow hurt him. I have no idea what his injuries are or how severe they are.

He's talking though, and that's as much as I could have hoped for.

"How are you?" I want to know. I want to know all of it. How he's been. What happened today. What he ate for breakfast. How that coffee machine of his is. If it misses me.

"I'm okay. Better than expected, but kind of shaken up." He reaches out, grabs my hand, and moves his body over a bit, making space at the edge of the bed.

I take a seat, immediately grateful to feel the familiar warmth of his skin against mine. My mind is racing, but it's still calmer here with him than anywhere else. "What happened out there?"

"I don't really remember. I was running to catch the ball and then all of a sudden, I was flat on a gurney in an ambulance. One of the assistant coaches was with me, and he told me I got knocked up in the air by one player just as another knocked me to the side. It sent me into a half backflip and I landed on my head. The angle was just right that it knocked me out and herniated a disk in my neck. I couldn't feel my arms or legs when I woke up, which is one of the most terrifying experiences I've ever had. It's pinching a nerve. They treated it, and now I just feel a weird tingle up and down my arms."

"So, you're gonna be okay?"

"Yeah, I'm gonna be just fine." He stops for a second and squints at me dramatically. "But I might need some TLC to make sure I make a full recovery."

"You can have whatever the hell you want, Baron Richards." I want to add, *but you can't ever do that to me again*, but it feels like too much, too soon. How can I walk back into his life and make a declaration like that? Even if I am just being sarcastic.

Okay, mostly sarcastic.

Baron smiles at me and then pulls my hand up to his lips, pressing a sweet kiss against my knuckles. If I wasn't sitting down, I think my knees would buckle under all the swoon.

"I want you," he says as he pulls his lips away. Part of me never wants his mouth to leave that spot, but part of me wants him to keep talking. "I love you, Montgomery Bell, and I'll keep loving you until the day I die, whether we travel the world together just the two of us or if we settle down on a farm with a brood of kids."

"Yeah, I'm not signing up for the brood," I joke, but I feel the seriousness under my tone. I close my eyes and continue my train of thought. "You say that now though. What if you can't handle that decision in five years, or ten or twenty?"

"Monty." Baron grazes his finger along the side of my face, and I lean into the feeling.

He closes his eyes for a moment, and I can tell he shares my appreciation. He opens his eyes again and continues.

"Monty, there's no guarantee we could have kids in the first place. Look at Zane and Georgie. They've struggled for years, and they're finally getting to the point where they're starting to accept that it may never happen for them, but that doesn't mean they won't be happy together. They love each other, with or without a family. I would rather be with you and childless than have children with anyone else."

I'd never thought about it that way before, but he's right. We're never guaranteed fertility, and love isn't about perfect circumstances.

That thought hits a nerve, and I finally feel like I'm getting somewhere. It's as if the tunnel caved in on me five weeks ago, and I've been slowly trying to hack my way out with a pickaxe. I just broke through. It's not enough to crawl out completely, but I can see the light, and damn, it feels good on my skin.

"I'm sorry I left…that I didn't let you in." I don't know how to apologize for it all, but something is better than nothing.

Baron blinks slowly. "I didn't know what to do either. I felt you pulling away, and I let it happen. I gave you space, thinking I was being understanding, but I realized after you left, I was letting you go. I've kicked myself a million times since then because that's not what you do. You fight. You push. You let it get uncomfortable, and you figure out how to fix it."

He stops and shakes his head, as if he's beaten himself up about this for the past few weeks. "I didn't see it. I didn't want to see it. I tried to cram you into a box, and you are worth so much more than that."

I twist a piece of his hair between my fingers. I missed the feeling of him.

"And Georgie told me about Rochelle," he continues. "I can't believe what she put you through. If I had known—"

I cut him off. "But I didn't tell you. I didn't tell you any of it. I don't know why. I guess I just felt so isolated, and instead of reaching out for help, I curled into a tight ball and cradled that feeling like it was my precious."

I'm throwing that ring into the fire and letting it burn. I'm not alone in this, not anymore.

I can feel Baron's breath release the last bit of tension in his body. "We have to be honest with each other, starting right now. I'm being honest when I say I want you more than I want a big family. I think we should talk about if there are circumstances that would make you feel less *meh* about having kids, like getting help or you working and me staying home. Those are things we should talk about, but I want you. Full stop. And I'm not going to let you walk out of this hospital without me if you feel a fraction of the same way."

"I do feel the same way. No fraction. Just one big, whole, messy piece. I just didn't fit into the football world, and then when I realized you wanted kids…"

Baron pulls me in even tighter. "Well, my number one long-term goal is to hold on to you, so I think we're getting started off on the right foot there."

"I like the sound of that." I want to hold on to him too, with everything I have. I lean back against him, lowering my weight slowly down so my chest is curled against his side. I lay my hand over his heart, closing my eyes while I feel every healthy beat. It matches mine, like two drums playing to the same line.

We sit in the hospital for the next twenty-four hours. By the time they're ready to discharge him, I've seen a whole football team's worth of medical personnel, and survey says Baron is one lucky man.

He suffered a concussion, but he can still count the number of concussions he's had on one hand. More importantly, he has a herniated disk in his neck that is causing a compression on his spinal cord. The prognosis is good, and he needs to see a specialist to run through his options.

I'm still going to Nurse Monty the hell out of him, but I keep closing my eyes for a brief moment of gratitude every time I think about how much worse this could have been.

I need Baron in my life, and whatever differences we have can be figured out. Love is worth figuring it out. There's nothing more important in the world than that.

I'm ten feet down the hall from Baron's hospital room, on my way to grab some coffee while the nurse is working on filling out the discharge forms with him, when I see them.

I would recognize those curly spirals of evil anywhere.

Rochelle.

She's walking toward me with a gorgeous vase of flowers in her arms. "Well, well, well, if it isn't yesterday's news," Rochelle says with one of her perfectly shaped eyebrows raised about as high as her Botox will let her.

I take a deep breath. "Hi, Rochelle. Are you here to see Baron, or do you come to the hospital to suck the life out of people for fun?"

She gives me a tight smile. "I think the better question is, why are you here? Didn't you run out on Bear already? He makes the news and you come crawling back for a little attention."

"That's your game, not mine." I think she would walk around with a film crew 24/7 if she could.

She is such an evil—ugh. I can't believe I'm twenty-three years old and am still dealing with people like her. I'm done.

"If you'll excuse me," she says as she starts to step around me. "I'm going to go pay my respects."

I shift to the side to block her. "Don't bother. He doesn't need your bullshit any more than I do."

Her eyes go wide for a second, as if she expected me to back down and run away like a scared little kitten. Then, she puts her game face on. "Baron will always have room in his life for people like me. Football is family, something you fail to understand."

Her words are sharp, but they don't cut me like they used to. I finally realize she's protecting herself just as much as she is the world that got her to where she is. She loves football, but she loves where it's gotten her even more. At the end of the day, that's sad.

She's at the top of the pile, but she has to keep looking around to see if someone else is trying to climb up and steal her spot.

I almost feel sorry for her, except I know the pile she's on top of is full of all the carcasses of people she's walked her skinny little Manolos over.

"You don't deserve this life. You don't deserve Bear." She keeps trying to cut me, but my skin is rock solid.

"See, that's where you're wrong. I *deserve* love. I deserve every single ounce I can soak up. Everyone does—even you."

She snorts, but it comes out weak. "Don't worry about me, honey. I've got love in spades."

"I don't worry about you. Not anymore. I'm done letting people like you tell me who I can and cannot love. I'm done letting you shit all over me and tell me it smells like roses. I am in love with Baron Richards, the man, not Bear Richards, the football star—and for the record, that's a hell of an important distinction."

I turn around and start walking back to his room. I don't need a cup of coffee to perk me up anymore; Rochelle just shot adrenaline through my veins.

It feels good to finally stick up for myself. I'm not going to let some girl outside a field house or a hospital room be the one to call action or cut on my love life. That's my call. It always has been and it always will be, and I'm glad I finally realized that.

She calls out after me. "You're never going to be enough for him."

"Well, that's not your problem." I don't bother to turn around. "So don't let it keep you up at night."

I am enough for him.

I don't need to stand outside a football stadium and scream it from the top of my lungs. I just need to show up, and keep showing up.

And I plan on doing that. Every. Single. Day. From now until forever.

Baron and I head to Ann Arbor to drop off Andie's car and grab a rental as soon as we're discharged. Then we head to Ohio as fast as the turnpike will take us. As we're pulling up to Baron's family home, I can see the smile grow wide on his face.

Our car ride consists of relatively benign conversation, plus a nice soundtrack of my newest musical obsessions that my friends in Ethiopia introduced me to.

Just before we reach the house, Baron puts his hand on my leg and squeezes gently. "Before we go in and my whole family starts to fawn over you, I want you to know that I'm not going back."

"Back where?"

"To Seattle to play. I'm going to have to sit out the rest of the season, that's a given, but I'm not going to push to renew my contract with them or any other team. I'm done playing football."

I shift the car into park, my jaw practically dropping all the way down to the pedals.

Before he can say another word, a short woman with cropped hair just as dark as Baron's races out to the car. Baron pushes his door open and stands up with a small grunt. She wraps her arms around him, and I can tell she's trying to be gentle while still squeezing the hell out of him.

She pushes him away, her hands still connected to his arms. "Oh, it's so good to see you." Then she leans to the side and gives me an even bigger smile than she gave him. "You must be Monty."

We're ushered in quickly, and we run through the family introductions. Everyone is here minus Devon; she had to stay in Ann Arbor for school. Baron's brothers and their families live close by, and the house feels nearly as loud as a stadium. Children and hellos and questions about Baron, it all overlaps. The sound is pleasant, like the houses I dreamed of when I was little. Mine was always so quiet, like a library full of adventure tucked between pages. Baron's is one where the adventure swings wildly from the chandelier in the living room.

I can barely think past trying to make sure I remember everyone's names. I've got Alex and Marshall, his brothers, but my brain putters out after that.

Who am I kidding though? My brain is clearly back in the car where Baron just told me he wasn't going back to football. Part of me is having an all-out dance party, and the other part is sitting over in the corner rocking itself back and forth.

Is him leaving football really a good idea?

We walk into the dining room, where Baron's mom has a feast prepared. I sit down next to Baron, watching him completely relax into his surroundings. I've seen him like this before. This is Baron, the man I met in Ann Arbor, and it makes me wonder if maybe the part of him that wants to leave football has been there all along.

I still feel uneasy about it, but the idea is slowly gaining traction.

Dinner is full of family banter, and I happily sit back and enjoy the rhythm of a family that is so much bigger and louder than mine. Baron keeps one hand on my thigh through the whole meal. I love the feeling of him next to me; he's like a warm compress that relaxes every last muscle.

When everyone's plates are empty, I push away from the table and stand up, insisting that I clean up. Baron gets up to help, and I think everyone sees the look in his eyes that shows what kind of help he's talking about.

We walk into the kitchen and set down the plates, and then Baron reaches his hands around my waist and lifts me up onto the counter, pressing his head against my chest.

"This feels so good. I want you next to me." His voice is husky. "I've missed you next to me."

"Me too." I lean my chin against his head and play with the texture of his hair.

He lifts his head up and kisses me, and it feels like a sugar cube melting on my tongue...but it doesn't quite dissolve my fears.

"You can't leave football. It's your life," I whisper.

Baron shakes his head as he runs his fingers up and down my arms. My skin warms to his touch, and I know I never had any hope. "No, you're my life, and you heard what the doctors said: I'd have to have surgery if I wanted to go back. Do you know how many risks there are with that procedure? And what kind of risk I'd be taking every single time I went back out on the field? It's not worth it, Monty. You're worth it. My life is worth it."

274

"But you'll miss it."

"Not as much as you'd think. Playing in Detroit was great, but playing in Seattle didn't feel the same. Yeah, I'll miss it sometimes, but I'm so much more than just Mr. Sportsball."

I blush at my nickname for him, and he smiles.

"I heard you call me that one time when you were on the phone with Andie."

"Yeah, I kind of never knew what position you played," I admit.

He laughs with a shake of his head. "Wide receiver, but I'll answer to the position of Montgomery Bell's boyfriend now."

"Can we make jerseys?"

One of Baron's brothers walks in, laughing. "What color jerseys were you thinking? Maybe a nice neon hot pink?"

Baron just shrugs. "It's your team, your pick."

The man would wear a bedazzled hot pink jersey if I asked him to; I have to wield my power wisely.

I'm not really a football jersey type though. "What if we went with a nice soft baseball tee? Something that would feel nice and cozy while I lie in bed and read at night—that's my kind of sporting event."

Baron's mom walks in. "Damn, I am *so glad* Baron finally brought you home to us. I'll sit and read a book with you any day of the week. These boys can go tackle each other in the back yard."

I know what she means when she says it, but my chest squeezes happily at the word *home*. I've decided I don't have only one home in this world. It's such a small word with such a big meaning, too big to be attached to just one single place. No, my home is at my parents' house *and* in Ann Arbor *and* on the road, doing what I love.

And here. My home is here because this is where Baron is.

I am home where I am loved, and there's no place more true than in the arms of the one you love.

Epilogue

One Year Later

I open up my laptop back at our hut in Thailand and start to upload the photos from my session. I pushed my boundaries yet again with an underwater session off the coast with a few expats who surf and free dive here for fun. If the photos are half as magical as the underwater scene looked in real life, they're going to be gorgeous.

I've learned to lean into the discomfort, seeing it as a signal that I need to think about why I want to say no. Is it because I genuinely don't think I'll enjoy it, or is it just because I'm scared?

Seattle made me uncomfortable because I didn't like it, and I didn't fit. Because I got up close and personal with that feeling, I can pin the tail on the donkey when it comes to knowing the difference between temporary fear and true dislike.

I open my browser and type in the address for my email client, waiting an eternity for it to load. It took me at least half a year to stop biting my nails like a drug addict waiting for a fix every time

I'd travel someplace with crappy Internet—which, flash alert, is most places. Now, it just makes me smile, and I always appreciate my broadband when I get back home.

Well, back to the States. Home is more of a fluid concept these days.

Shortly after his injury, Baron moved back in with his mom, selling his condo in Seattle. We each live with our respective families, but we travel so often together, it feels more like a smart arrangement than anything else.

Work keeps me busy most of the time. I decided to forgo a full-time offer with Collins Aid United; instead they throw me contracts at least every couple months, and I intersperse other gigs in between for travel photography or just plain travel.

My Instagram feed is killer—doesn't hurt that I have a hunk of a boyfriend who makes frequent appearances.

I can tell he misses football sometimes, but he's really settling into his new life these days. When he doesn't ride shotgun with me, he's at home gradually building up a custom furniture business. It's slow, but he uses our travel for research. He finds inspiration everywhere, and the pieces he's dreaming up are incredible.

Plus, the man has honed his radar for expats that enjoy sports. He finds them in bars and coffee shops and hostels like ants to sugar water. He gets to talk shop; I get to read. Everyone wins.

Aha! My email finally loads, and I see Andie's name at the top of my inbox with the subject *Karma is a Bitch.*

I click to open the email and it takes forever to load the half dozen images, but I start to read the text of Andie's note at the top.

She couldn't hide under that fake smile forever. Glad to see she got what was coming to her...and then some. Hope you and Mr. Sportsball are loving Thailand. Go hug an elephant for me, k?

There's a long article below, detailing the scandal of a star quarterback and his philandering wife. Turns out, Rochelle was getting some quality time with a young star of a boy band while her husband was busy taking the team all the way to the playoffs. The paparazzi got a nice close-up of Rochelle sucking face with the pop star, and then looking very surprised to have gotten caught.

Part of me feels giddy. The other part remembers what it was like to have a reporter come after me, and for a second, I feel sorry for her—just for a second. Then I go right back to feeling justified.

You can't go around messing with other people's lives and expect them to stay out of yours.

I shut my laptop down just as Baron walks in, rubbing a towel through his hair after getting back from the beach. He plops down next to me on the couch and presses his nose into my neck. He's still damp from the water, and I can smell the salt on his skin. He nuzzles me, and it's like a puppy is sitting next to me. The feeling sends an image rushing across my brain like Paul Revere: Baron and me snuggled up on a couch we actually own with a puppy we adopted together. Puppies mean responsibility, which means staying in one place longer than two weeks.

The image doesn't send shivers of anxiety down my spine—quite the opposite. It sends shivers of anticipation. I know I'll get tired of traveling constantly. After being on the go for a year, I realize this is a phase of life more than it is a life. The frequency will wane eventually. It may not ever go away completely, and I kind of hope I always have a plane ticket booked to somewhere, but I won't say no to roots either. I can appreciate both, just as I can appreciate that we may want to let those roots grow a family…or not. It's something we'll decide when we get there.

Baron nuzzles me with a low hum that vibrates against my skin, and I lean into him, relishing the feeling.

"Want to go out for dinner tonight?" he asks nonchalantly.

"Sure, what were you thinking?"

"There's this place I noticed a while back…thought maybe we could try it."

Thirty minutes later, we walk up to a place called TJs, and I give

Baron the side eye. We're in the middle of Thailand, home of what might be one of my favorite types of cuisine in the whole entire world, and we're standing in front of a sports bar.

Baron just shrugs and opens the door for me. I debate whether or not to just turn around and walk the other way, but I love him too much to ditch him...and I do love Buffalo wings.

We're a little early for dinner, and no one's actually in the restaurant. As I look around, I notice all the TVs are off.

I turn to Baron. "Umm, are you sure they're open?"

Just as I see him nod, a man walks out from the back. "Ahhh, Mr. Richards. Just one moment." He turns around and disappears.

Baron shrugs again, and I wonder how the hell a guy in the middle of Thailand knows who my boyfriend is—and then I remember that *Bear Richards* played both pro and college football and was the spokesperson for at least a dozen ad campaigns. It's not like I walked into a bar and someone called me Ms. Bell. I'm not famous, he is.

The TVs flicker back on. At first it doesn't seem odd, and then I notice they're all playing the same thing, to the same soundtrack... and it has nothing to do with sports.

And wait a second—is that a picture of me when I was five?

I stand there shell-shocked as I watch images of Baron and me flash across the screens, first, as children and teenagers separately, and then finally as adults together. We've perfected the art of the SLR selfie, and all of our attempts—both cringe-worthy and swoon-worthy—flash across the screens.

When I look back at Baron, he's dropped to his knee. Everything stops. I can't breathe or think or feel anything except the mixture of shock and love swirling together in my body like two beads of dye dropped into a glass of clear water.

"I love you, Montgomery Bell. I love the woman you were. I love the woman you are, and I know I'm going to love the woman you become. Do me the honor of letting me be by your side for

279

every single day of it as your husband."

I drop down to the ground, unable to wait for him to stand up, and I press my hands to his cheeks, pressing my nose to his. "Yes. Every single day. Yes."

He wraps his arms around me and we kiss like today is the only day we have. When we pull back, I see a flicker of movement out of the corner of my eye. I pull away, heat rising to my cheeks at the thought of the poor man who works here wondering if we're about to get primal on his floor. Then I realize there's more than one body standing up by the bar.

I pull away and my eyes take a second to focus. I would know those faces anywhere. My mom, dad, Andie, and all of Baron's immediate family are standing just ten feet away. I'm so flabbergasted by their sudden and completely unexpected arrival that I have no idea what to say.

Andie gives me the widest eyes I've ever seen and asks, "Well, are you going to look at the ring yet?"

Everyone laughs, and I look back at Baron, who has a tiny blue velvet box in his hand. Inside there's a pearl set in a winding curve of diamonds that wrap around a delicate silver band.

"I got this on our first trip together after rehab. I went diving, found this pearl, and designed a ring"—Baron's explanation is interrupted by a throat clearing loudly—"with Andie's help, of course."

I look over at Andie, and she grins. "He didn't need too much help. The boy has good taste. I just helped add a little polish, and ring size."

I turn back to Baron. "You've had the ring all this time? That trip was nearly a year ago."

"I knew the minute I walked away from your table at Halftime that I was done for. You've always been the one for me."

"And you guys? How did you guys all get here?" My brain is running through the details of this equation, now that it's left the flabbergasted zone and moved into functional awe.

My mom beams. "Baron asked us all to be here, and we couldn't say no."

"And the whole Thailand bit didn't hurt, either," Baron's brother jokes.

"Georgie and Zane wanted to make it…" Baron offers an apologetic smile. *But they're going to have a baby*, I add in my head. Well, their surrogate is having a baby. I've been getting email updates from Georgie, and I'm so excited for them. Even if it wasn't exactly the circumstances they imagined, it's still the end result they've been dreaming of.

I look around and want to pinch myself. I can't get over it. Both of our families are here, and we're getting married. Then my stomach decides it has an opinion on the whole matter and growls like an alpha dog guarding its territory. "Wait, do they have good wings here?"

Andie nods her head emphatically. "Oh, hell yeah."

We push the tables together and sit down for a meal, the TVs still set to loop through all the photos of us.

I've never been more grateful for a sports bar in my life, and I really don't like sports bars.

Just goes to show, you never know what life is going to throw your way when you have no idea what the plays are or which direction you should be running.

I found my direction, and now I have the greatest teammate in the whole world running alongside me.

The End

Acknowledgements

The single greatest difference between writing my first book and my second was the amazing group of beta readers I had this time around. Beth, Tove, Mandy, Cassie, Ashley, Courtney, Sharron, Holly, Miranda, and Ashlei—I needed your fresh eyes to tell me that a pink football was just weird and work is boring. You were the first voices that championed this book, and I just want to reach across the Internet and hug every single one of you.

Becca, I can't quite piece together the right words to thank you. I was just this little newbie author over in my tiny corner of the Internet, and you not only said hello, but you brought a giant lantern with you. Your help has changed my writing, and I can't wait to turn around and rally behind you.

To my family, you all have given me the greatest gift in the whole world: your unconditional love and support. At the end of the day, it doesn't matter if I sell ten books or ten million books, and that gives me the freedom to do it my way. My way isn't always logical or easy or even right, but you love me anyway. Thanks for being my biggest fans.

To my POM author friends, thank you for kicking my butt in twenty-minute increments. I sit back and stare in awe at the beautiful words you write and how you take this community by storm. Thanks for letting me sit at your table. It's an honor and a privilege, and I just hope someday I can repay the favor.

Oh man, it is scary as hell to hand your baby off to another person (trust me, I suck at using babysitters). Caitlin at Editing by

C. Marie, I know my book is in good hands with you. You know that what reads well and what is grammatically correct aren't always the same, and it makes me trust you all the more. Thank you for being my wordsmith and an all-around awesome human being.

Judy at Write Techniques, thank you for being my sanity check and my *that* exterminator. Najla at Najla Qamber Designs, you make my project manager heart so happy, and Lindee at Lindee Robinson Photography, thank you for searching for my Monty and Baron. Wendy, thank you for being the final pair of eyes on this.

Matt, I couldn't do this without you. Even if I could, I wouldn't want to. You are a truly good, kind, and loyal man. The best parts of my leading men come from you. You're stuck with me, and somehow I think I got the long end of the stick on that one.

To my buddy who thinks the baseball mitt is a hat, I'll love you to the end of the universe and back whether or not you play sports, and I promise I'll try to learn the rules and pay attention if you do.

And last but not least, to my readers. Thank you for every single note, review, share, like, purchase, and page turn. There are trillions of words for you to choose from, and I am so incredibly honored you chose to spend time with mine.

Until next time…
XOXO,
K.P.

About K.P. Haigh

K.P. Haigh joined the adult world as a project manager. After spending years in spreadsheets, she put her love of blank notebooks to good use and started spinning words into love stories.

In a perfect world, K.P. would have a never-ending supply of coffee, carbs, and sticky notes. She corners the market on ridiculous facial expressions and is happiest when she's cooking for people or making them laugh.

She's always up for crispy French fries and can't wait for self-driving cars to take over the world so she can read on her way to everywhere.

K.P. lives in Seattle with the man who loves her crazy and their son, who inherited half of it.

Follow K.P. Haigh's addiction to caffeine, dairy-free baked goods, and the color green on Instagram.

Follow K.P. Haigh
Newsletter: kphaigh.com/newsletter
Instagram: instagram.com/kphaigh
Facebook: facebook.com/kphaigh
Website: kphaigh.com

Also by K.P. Haigh

Only Fools Jump

Only fools jump, and Zoey Porter is no fool—at least not anymore. One tiny mistake when she was eighteen led to two very real consequences—the kinds that keep you up all night and demand breakfast in the morning.

The only things Zoey has time for these days are dry shampoo, energy bars, and that magical photo filter that erases the circles under her eyes.

So when Elliott MacCallister knocks on the door like a #nofilternecessary god, Zoey knows she's in serious trouble.

With Elliott as the newly minted resident of her boss's pool house, keeping her distance is easier said than done.

Time to stock up on wine, cookies, and a portable fan—their summer just got complicated.

Only Fools Jump is like cotton candy for your soul—light and sweet. It's a full-length, standalone romantic comedy.